The RECLAMATION

BOOK 4 - THE MASON JAR SERIES

A NOVEL BY ELI POPE

© US COPYRIGHT 2020 – Steven G Bassett
All rights reserved.

No portion of this book may be reproduced, stored in a retrieval system, or transmitted in any form or means including electronic, mechanical, photocopied, recorded, scanned, or other, with the exception of brief quotations in reviews or articles, without prior written permission of author or publisher.
Scripture quotations are taken from the Holy Bible, NIV®, MSG®, KJV®
This novel is a work of fiction. All names, characters, places, and incidents are either from the imagination of the author or used fictitiously. All characters are fictional, and any similarity to people living or dead is coincidental.

Cover Design – Steven G Bassett
Interior Formatting – Sharon Kizziah-Holmes
Audiobook Narration – Paul McSorley
Audiobook Music Creation – Nikki McSorley – nmcmusiccreative.com

Published by 3dogsBarking Media LLC

ISBN: 978-1-7358159-3-0

DEDICATION

This book is dedicated to my mother. A better example for living life and loving others could not be possible. While she would rather the language and situations were not told in the way I tell, she knows that life in this world unfortunately has dark corners within and characters such as these fall into the traps of evil and harm to themselves and others. She also acknowledges that our Creator never gives up on his creations. The fact she still presses forward in reading these dark tales and wearing her pride for me boldly as not only the way the perfect mother would, but she is also proud of my writing abilities and accomplishments.

Thank you, Mom. You mean the world to me and will always be in my heart even when I am not fortunate enough to have you here with me on earth. I love you, to the moon.

Eli

ACKNOWLEDGMENTS

There are far too many thanks for me not to accidently leave someone out, but I will attempt to name the ones that have been irreplaceable.

My editor **Julie Luetschwager** has fixed my many mistakes and pointed out changes that make me appear to be a smarter author than I truly am. I say thank you, thank you, and thank you. You've helped keep me inspired to move forward and carry this story forward.

Sharon Kizziah-Holmes @ Paperback Press for her formatting. She makes the look!

My partner in the **Audible** side of this series, **Paul J McSorley**, whose professionalism and dedication to his craft helps catapult my written words to an entirely new level. What can I say Paul other than, right on, brother!

Paul's wonderful wife and music producer, **Nikki McSorley @ nmcmusiccreative.com**, for her work on my Audible books. Without your music talents, the entire setup mood for this thrilling tale would suffer tremendously. Thank you, Nikki! You rock!

All the beta readers that stay loyal to my writing, I appreciate you all very much.

My **Springfield Writers Guild fellow author friends** who share ideas, critiques and occasional beers. I respect each one of you!

Thomas Anderson @ Literary Titan Review for your reviews that truly show you understand my writing and its purpose. Thank you for the fine accolades and awards bestowed on each of these books of The Mason Jar Series. They inspire me to continue in this thing that never feels like work, but instead self-therapy.

Thank you,

Eli Pope

1

The room I was seated in appeared dingy and gave off a medical odor mixed with an overbearing scent of urine. This entire facility screamed of a much-needed deep-cleaning. Faint echoes of chains clinking broke the silence, which were followed by footsteps stumbling down the hallway. I attempted to tune my ears in a way to ignore all other sounds. The scuffle of boots became louder, and I knew people now stood just outside the closed room where I nervously sat waiting. Sensing it was him who likely stood just on the other side of the door immediately triggered my already tense muscles to tighten even more. The room's atmosphere instantly hung hot and heavy over me as if Grandmother tried to lovingly place a weighty wool blanket over my shoulders, not realizing the temperature already sat at 85 degrees with 90 percent humidity.

    I again glanced around the room, my thoughts instinctively gathered to the young age when I as a child of seven or maybe eight, formed detailed questions that I would then scribe onto the tablet I held. Of course, back then, the instruments of my trade were a rather large round yellow pencil and a Big Red Chief tablet in hand while I pretended to interview my grandmother from the living room sofa. She would smile, likely feigning to stumble on answers to each of my very pointed and difficult inquiries. After all, I worked at The Florida Gazette as their most dynamic journalist, and she the suspicious subject in question! "So, ma'am, did you know the pudding contained the poison?"

My short breaths became weighty. I sat nervous, my voice recorder and notebook lightly bouncing on my lap. *I can do this Lord, but please guide me.* Glancing around the room, my memories of being a child came flooding back once again. I'd wanted a moment like this as far back as one can remember the things a child craves. The importance such reflections bring us is something we commonly forget to appreciate after growing up. But now, here this moment sat—stirring reflections inside my mind. I sought refuge and comfort remembering this slice in time is what my early dreams were busy building. This is now the real thing and a dream being answered. A cop killer, a mentally twisted devil who'd been recently sentenced to Florida's electric chair was about to become my subject to interview. My legs, hidden beneath the mid-length skirt I'd chosen to cover them with, moved back and forth like nervous sea oats do along the beach at the onset of an oncoming storm. I'd conducted myriads of professional assignments since those days of merely playing the part, so why did this interview make me so damned nervous? *I'm strong like my grandfather taught me to be.* Words I repeated several times within my mind to shore up my confidence.

I attempted to calmly brush the wrinkles from my skirt as I stood up to formally meet the man who'd recently become the forgotten coast's most notorious cold-blooded murderer. He would be my latest point of interest and I came here to interview him for the paper who now employed me, The Orlando Beacon. But I'd spoken to co-workers of my hidden intent to write my first memoir. The overall topic would be how child abuse is instrumental in growing a man like Billy Jay Cader into an untamable monster. One whose probability of continuing the hate-filled torch to the next generation would be a difficult heritage to break away from without outside psychological help and the love of someone who truly cared.

There were clicks and chirps of magnetic switches and locks

before the door finally opened before me. I could immediately see a man with blackish-grey facial stubble and dressed in a bright orange jumpsuit standing behind several prison guards before he lowered his head.

Oh my God, this is happening! My heart raced as if to acknowledge my 28 years of age lacked the ripeness for the task. I took my deepest breath possible; then attempted to slowly let it ease out inconspicuously through my nose. I hoped no one else could hear the subtle wheeze singing through my nostrils to the hushed sounds of prison guard chatter because it seemed as loud as an out-of-tune French horn to me.

Mr. Cader glanced up at my face and I saw his dark grey and greenish eyes for the first time. I'd of course seen many pictures, mug shots and blurred photos from newspapers, which always seemed to focus on his dark inset orbs. Now standing within a few feet of him stirred a feeling I wasn't familiar with. Panic. I glanced into the dark pools of his pupils, briefly trying to imagine the awful sights they'd witnessed, the life draining out of the two officers as they lay bleeding to death. And of course, any other unknown atrocities he may have committed. There were many rumors floating throughout the area, and my plan is to eventually delve into those whispers of horrors, if the interview process grows to be congenial between us.

Needing to prepare myself for the character of the interviewer, I realized I at this moment couldn't even open my mouth to say his name. It made me suddenly feel like an amateur on my first assignment. I didn't know how I should address him, and I felt an immediate stabbing sensation in my stomach—*the guards certainly wouldn't leave me alone in this room with him, would they?*

I watched every movement made by everyone present with cautious observation; from Mr. Cader to each guard present. They sat him in a chair securely mounted to the floor in front of what I presumed would be my interview table. He leaned back and forth peering between the guard's bodies, never losing sight from every move I made as if he were a tiger maneuvering in for his prey. They continued to secure his cuffed wrists to the arms of the chair with chains that allowed him to bring his hands to his face. His legs were shackled to the floor immediately afterward. "Ma'am—uh, Miss Whitenhour?" One guard spoke when he walked up in front of me. "The inmate is secured and should not be of any threat to you. I will be standing just outside the door. You can call out if Billy makes any aggressive movements or uses any language you find offensive, ma'am. I assure you he cannot harm you in any way and I will be closely watching." The guard pulled a chair out for me to sit down and motioned to the other guards to follow. "Is there anything you need, ma'am, before we step out?"

I shook my head no, feeling the pinnacle of the moment upon me. Yes, I would be alone with Mr. Cader in this room. Help would be nearby, but the only people who would hear any conversation—would be the two of us.

I set my recorder and notebook down on the table noticing Mr. Caders' chains on his wrists would obviously not allow his hands to reach very far across the table. I took comfort seeing the table would not budge when I sat and pulled on it to help slide my chair up to the top where I rested my hands nervously cupped in my lap. I slowly spoke and broke the awkward silence between us. "Mr. Cader…I…I…would like to know if I should address you by any particular name such as Billy, or Jay—or of course, Mr. Cader. I'm fine with whichever you like. I just appreciate you considering my offer to hear your story from your perspective, to then write it in book form."

Clearing my throat, I tried to move my eyes away from looking down at my notepad and instead force them up to meet his. It took persistence on my part, but I overcame and met his intentional scrutiny. I attempted to let my nerves settle by mentally telling myself everything will be fine. *I know you're with me Grandfather.* I briefly felt my lips form an instinctive smile, sensing his presence beside me and the comfort of knowing in spirit, he was here.

Mr. Cader cleared his throat. "I reckon you can call me whatever you like, but people I considered friends in the past, just called me Jay. After livin' in here, I been called about everything possible, so you just pick somethin' and I reckon I'll answer to it."

I watched his blank and staunch expression, which I'd taken notice upon first meeting him; it slowly melted the edges of his dry cracked lips into somewhat of a smile. His wrinkled forehead and tightened cheeks seem to slip into a more at ease appearance. *Maybe he'd been as nervous about this meeting as I?*

"What should I call you, miss?" Jay asked.

"Amy Jo Whitenhour is my name but calling me Amy would be perfect." I attempted another smile and then picked up my notebook for no other reason than to busy my nervous hands.

"Well, Miss Amy, there's no reason for the two of us to continue this dance of awkwardness and prickly nerves—I reckon we'll be gittin' ta know each other—real well in no time." Jay scooted up closer to the table and placed his folded hands upon the top. I instantly caught his odor as he moved in closer. A manly scent, much like my grandfather's after coming inside from working outdoors in the heat.

With his arms stretched out, I could see the weathered ink up both arms from his wrists until the skin disappeared up under the short orange sleeves of his inmate uniform. He must have noticed my awareness of his tattoos because he moved his arms back down and to his sides.

"You needn't hide your arms, Billy Jay. I find them interesting. I'm hoping at some point you may even let me photograph you—artwork included."

"I never had nobody wanna take my picture, 'cept of course, the cops. Or for that matter, pay any attention to…uh…my artwork."

He smiled with more ease and his eyes lit up just a bit, erasing some of the bedevil they previously held. "Only person to pay close attention is my wife, Cat, and she's no longer able to do such a thing, but I 'magine you know that already." Jay's tone quieted a bit. "So, Amy, just what in hell made you decide to want to talk—or 'interview' me anyway? You gonna make me famous, are ya?" He let out a short guffaw.

"Why Mr. Cader, I believe you've already surpassed anything I could that you haven't already done on your own. I'm not going to lie, I do have a purpose for being here and I planned to ease into it, but if you'd like—we can lay our cards out on the table right now. I don't want to waste your time—or mine.

Jay sat silent for a moment before he chose to answer. "Well, little lady, I didn't mean to ruffle your feathers—least not yet anyways." He looked me in the eyes before he continued, "if—for no other reason, I'm ready to talk to you 'cause you're a helluva lot better thing to look at than what I'm locked up with back in there." He grinned, tilting his head behind him in the direction of general lock-up. "You give me somethin' to look forward to and that there says a lot, Miss Amy, 'cause I got nuthin' but time…well, until they hook me up…." He gave his entire body a quick shake as if he were being electrocuted. He smiled but his eyes dimmed to near empty.

I instinctively snapped back quickly, "First off, Mr. Cader, I'm not a better looking 'thing', I'm a female human being. Secondly, I will ask you very difficult and personal questions, questions that will more than likely make you look like anything but an upstanding citizen. I'll expect truthful answers and to be treated with respect even if you don't respect me, or women in general." I chose to ignore his attempt at humor by his body actions. After all, I'd become instantly steaming mad from his comment and I quickly slammed my hands down on the tabletop before I could think about it or catch myself. "Do you and I understand each other, Mr. Cader? Or would you rather me pack up my shit, and motion for the guards to escort you back? It's totally up to you." I popped my head to the side, toward the door behind him, where he'd gestured lock-up to be earlier. The spontaneous gesture caused my short dark curls in my hair to bounce and be liberated from behind my ears. "I'll just go back into the free world, and you can be escorted back into your personal hell." I pushed my hair behind both ears as I sat waiting for a response.

"Understood, ma'am." Jay dropped his head appearing he'd been out sported and put in his place.

"Well then, Billy Jay, let's get started now with all this cordialness over with." I sat back into my chair and skimmed through some notes in my notebook and then pushed the recorder button with my shaky finger to begin recording. "At what age do you first remember being punished by your father...?"

Jay paused and appeared to study me or perhaps his lengthy silence became his way to unnerve my assertive attempt to gain control of the situation. Before I could speak or begin to repeat the question, he began spilling a rather deep revealing answer, being his very first. I knew immediately he owned a story deep inside and he seemed ripe for me to pick it carefully from his vine.

"Miss Amy, I couldn't pin it to a single first memory when I got punished. 'Punishment,' which I would call 'beatings,' is all I can remember, from the beginning. Hell, after my momma died from the rotten lung, I left out on my own outta fear. Well, fear and knowin' there's nothin' for me with him but more of what I'd already been gettin'." The chains clinked together as Jay moved his hands up to his head and began rubbing his temples. It appeared obvious the subject immediately affected him. "After runnin' away—I'd occasionally go back to the fucker's house and peek through the windows to see him either drinkin' with some whore or passed out on the couch, bottle never far from his open hand. He's why I never took up drinkin' and I ain't heard nor seen the sombitch since I turned fourteen. My lasting real memory of him is a hammer bein' swung at me 'cause I bumped the carjack handle and damn near got him pinned under the truck. I'd prolly been 'bout eleven or twelve. I thought many a time after the beatin' I got for that..." Jay looked at me squarely, a tiny tear peeking from his eye. "...it woulda' been a far better grace for me if he had been pinned under that old truck and died a slow death, than recievin' the word 'grace' bein' shakin' from his gawd damned Mason jar." Jay stopped and let his gaze fall toward the table briefly before drawing his eyes back to mine. "I reckon if he'd died that day, mine and my beat down momma's world woulda' been a helluva lot different, don't ya reckon?"

I knew with his first answer, this interview would bring back my own memories and pain as a child. *The difference—I'd been gifted with grandparents who loved me dearly and kept me from my momma and daddy. Jay's answer made me want to kill his son-of-a bitch father myself.*

2

Walking out through the front door of Lake Correctional Institution, which opened in 1973 and still holds one of the highest use-of-force incidents in all of Florida's penal facilities, couldn't have come sooner. Once reaching the outside steps, I sucked in a big breath of fresh air and slowly let it escape. The shakiness of my tight nerves seemed to follow every breath as it exited from my lungs. I briefly paused to push my curls back behind my ears, certainly a nervous habit to give my hands something to do, but one that seemed to have followed me through the years. My grandfather teased me about the curls, it's probably why I always seemed to keep my hair short, from childhood on. I found myself looking at the blue sky and the horizon beyond the chain link fencing. *Breathe Amy, breathe.* Finally, I felt a calm enter my inner being. I couldn't imagine being locked up, not able to go outside and take in God's creation any time I needed to be reminded of the beautiful pallet of colors He created from. Another blessing I could count from being loved by my grandparents. I let my gaze fall back to earth from the beautiful sky.

The coiled razor-wire spirals, which appeared to be balancing atop the prison's boundary walls much like a gymnast on a balance beam, seemed such a contrast to the inviting freedom of the puffy white clouds that floated and collected in huge thick updrafts. Grandfather used to enjoy flying sailplanes and called them hot air thermals. I flew with him many times and as he would circle his plane, the updraft slowly causing us to lift higher and higher. He would then veer away and maneuver the craft chasing birds at such speeds and g-force my stomach would feel as if it were stuck in my throat. Sometimes I wanted to scream, but my stomach wouldn't let my lungs push it out. He would laugh and tell me that a maneuver like this would rip the wings off a typical engine-powered small plane, such as a Cessna 150. The ground would come rushing towards us until he'd pull back on the stick and level out, watching the little piece of yarn taped on the outside of the cockpit glass until it would indicate another thermal by flickering a certain way. He would then circle and let the plane slowly rise upward again and then repeat the thrilling rollercoaster ride through the air. I imagined we maneuvered through the sky thousands of feet above earth in a way close to how God traveled. I remember never feeling closer to Him, or my grandfather either.

With the thought of drifting through the outer edges of the thick white clouds, sitting in the front seat with him aboard his glider, a sound of relief sighed through my exhale followed by a warm smile. Picturing grandfather's precious wink he would always give me when he approved of how I'd handled myself in the cockpit or whatever else I did right in his view, was like icing on the cake of my memory. The recollection boosted my stride with self-pride in the walk back to my vehicle. He would be proud of how I handled myself today, the clouds and unsolicited thoughts of him surely were his way of letting me know so.

After passing through the final checkpoint, I reached for the radio dial turning up the volume of my favorite music station. Carly Simon's "You're So Vain" played. My eyes seemed to beg one more glance to the rear-view mirror's reflection of the hell I'd just escaped. I knew there would be many, many more visits to come. *Will I ever become accustomed to being inside such a desolate place? Lord, I hope not.*

First impression and thoughts of Billy Jay Cader muddled

through my head on the drive back to Orlando. Less than a forty-five-minute trip with no real scenery to appreciate, made it in fact, boring. The look I'd seen in Billy's eyes however, showed anything but bland. I couldn't seem to shake imagining the terror he must have felt at the punishment of his father's hands. His father's eyes of evil and hatred scorching through him were surely seared into his psyche forever, for as a child he most certainly would have begged him to stop. I'd gotten a tidbit of information, which suddenly re-entered my mind. Sgt. Tony Rawlings. Jay mentioned he'd also shot him when he killed the other detective, Sam Hayden. The change in Billy's eyes when he mentioned Sgt. Rawlings' name became cold and calculating. I wanted to delve deeper into their relationship but hadn't felt like the timing seemed appropriate yet. I will though, I never ignored the prickles on the back of my neck when researching a story. Those goosebumps always seem to lead me to something deeper under the surface. A substance others usually missed.

The newspaper pictures and television stories of Sgt. Tony Rawlings intrigued me even before my attempts to tell the story of Billy Jay Cader from a different angle. Tony, a family man turned divorced, didn't have the appearance of what I perceived a Florida State detective would look like. He wasn't small nor muscular; his hair appeared thin, but no baldness seemed to show. He wore those thick, black-framed glasses too. He seemed more suitable as a banker than a cop.

The way Billy Jay's entire facial demeanor changed when he spoke his name—this image is now the one of Jay I concentrated my thoughts on. And his hollow eyes. *Humanity seemed absent many times throughout our interview.* Tony may not look like a cop to me, but Billy Jay most certainly carried the appearance of a killer. A cop killer. Now a man with no future and more than likely no regular visitors to the hell he now called home. *I'll be his one spotlight in his week, if he's telling me his story and not raping me with his eyes.*

Thoughts bounced back to a personal comment Billy Jay made, almost immediately after we'd met. It sent a quick chill throughout my body, and now suddenly I remembered how I shivered for a brief second. It felt like when the cold air hit your body in an opening between your clothing—straight to bare skin. Goosebumps. He'd looked at my upper body from the table to the top of my head slowly, calculatingly, then tilted his head to the side where he could see my skirt and bare leg before bringing his eyes back up to meet mine. "You look a lot like Gina. Short dark hair—beautiful hazel eyes. I'd bet money those jewels hold an interestin' backstory. Your lips are a bit thicker than hers, but yeah, you remind me a lot of Ms. Gina. Almost her twin." And then his smile widened toward his cheeks before he quickly changed the direction of his observation like he didn't want to share his reaction with me.

Ignoring it after the chill left, I'd put the quick event out of mind. Now driving down the flat straight highway back home, the eerie moment crept back into thought. *Who is this, Gina? Is it a good or bad thing I remind him of her?* Suddenly as if the same cold chill swept back through my open window and blew through the gap in my blouse, a briskness returned. *Brr.* It of course is a balmy upper eighties afternoon with high humidity; no reason to have a chill other than the thoughts of Billy Jay and his uncanny and hair-raising demeanor about him. *There's more to his story than meets the eye. There, but for the grace of God, go I.*

3

Sgt. Rawlings began getting frustrated. It seemed he held most all the pieces to the puzzle, but he couldn't make them fit in any order to see the picture clear enough to solve the problem. He slid his glasses up and onto his forehead and firmly massaged his temples. "Jay, you son-of-a-bitch—where would you dispose of the girl's bodies? You were all over several states, but in a big rig..." Tony spoke aloud to only himself. "...did you bring them back home with you and put them somewhere closer?" Tony's fingers suddenly stopped rubbing his head. *The bastard lived on a farm outside of town. He could have brought them back in his trailer and unloaded them at home!*

Tony picked up his phone and dialed Hank's extension. "Hello, Hank..." Tony barely gave his new partner, but old friend, time to answer. "It just came to me...outta nowhere. We need to get permission to search Vertis and...let me see..." Tony quickly rifled through some folders spread across his desk. "...awe, here it is, Vertis and Judy Bullinger. We need to get their permission to search the property out there..." Tony paused to listen to Hank's response. "Yeah, their place is an old farmhouse with some property. It's Jay's old house before he ran."

Hank Robbins was only twenty-nine and the youngest and newest addition to the Florida State Homicide Division. The "kid" had just recently become Tony's partner. Tony recommended him to be moved up just after Sam passed and he himself healed and returned to work. Hank had been a good friend of Sam's and his family.

Tony wasn't great at being patient and did not like the down time between an idea's formation and the proper flow to implementation. He knew this about himself, yet knowing the problem seldom helped in squelching his being antsy.

***

Ben saw Darrell in the store and hesitated at first. Almost out of reflex he began to dodge down a different aisle. *This is ridiculous. Why am I hiding from Darrell?*

Darrell grabbed the can from the shelf and caught Ben in the corner of his eye. He quickly turned, "Hey Mr. Dane. How are you?"

"I'm doing good, and please, call me Ben. Small town, no need to be formal!" Ben snickered and flashed his friendly smile.

"Yeah, really small after all the hub-bub and especially when your last name is Cader." Darrell smiled. "Seems everyone knows who I am. They usually avoid me too." He grinned again.

"How's the wife and baby?"

Gina came around the corner holding a couple of things she'd grabbed. "Darrell! It's great to see you! How's the sweet baby I've been hearing about and Mitzi?"

"They're here in the store somewhere, we split up so we can divide and conquer here with the groceries." Answered Darrell. "…and Katie is doing great! Mitzi too."

"Where are you living these days?" Gina asked.

"We moved to the apartment down below Mitzi and her mom's old place. Kyle lives in the other downstairs apartment with Violet."

"I'm so sorry about Kyle." Gina replied, "And your momma, Cat, how's she doing? I really miss talking to her."

"You know, she's coming along. She seems to start refreshing her memories and then they disappear again. She enjoys seein' Katie though. Katie always puts the gleam back in her eyes."

About when the conversation began to wane, Mitzi came around the aisle pushing the stroller and holding an armload of groceries. "Hey there, you two! Haven't seen y'all in a while."

Gina quickly knelt to get a good look at Katie. "She's beautiful!" Gina glanced up toward Mitzi and before she could say another word, Mitzi spoke.

"Of course, you should go ahead and pick her up, Gina!" Mitzi smiled.

Gina reached in and slid her hands under Katie and carefully lifted her out of the stroller, never hesitating. She pulled Katie close and snuggled. Gina looked over at Ben and then back to Mitzi, "We've got one on the way too!"

"What?" Mitzi questioned. "I mean, I thought I noticed a pudge, but thought maybe it could just be the restaurant biz!" She laughed.

"No, although I am eating like a horse lately! You sure have bounced back to your thin beautiful pre-baby body!"

The two girls began a conversation, one that pushed the guys out and into a brief silence. Ben leaned over to Darrell. "I don't suppose you would be interested in coming to work for me, would you? I could certainly use the help."

Darrell tried to hide his look of shock. "You would really be interested in hiring me, sir?"

"I'd like to find someone who I could train to do a lot of the things I oversee, kind of like a manager of sorts. I have a feeling Gina will be needing more of me around as time draws nearer." Ben looked to the ladies briefly. "This opportunity I'm talking about, could branch into something that could hopefully become somewhat of a career to work in to. I'm wanting to look at other ways to invest into this town, do my part to put it on the map. If things go like I plan, I'll need someone I can trust and count on.

Oversee different businesses as we launch them." He winked at Darrell and smiled. "I think you could be the puzzle piece to fit the role."

"I'd need to talk to Mitz, but I personally would love to come work for you. I'm not my father...well..." Darrell stuttered a moment and paused to collect himself. "...I mean, I reckon you know Jay ain't my father anyway—but you know what I'm saying...."

"Darrell." Ben interrupted. "I don't hold anything of what you are thinking against you in any way." Ben reached over and patted Darrell's shoulder. "You're a fine young man supporting your family and I'm a restaurant owner needing good help. That's all there is to it. I know Gina would approve or I wouldn't be asking." Ben squeezed slightly on Darrell's shoulder. "You think about it, talk it over with Mitzi and get back to me." Ben winked and moved his hand away and motioned Darrell back to their wives.

Gina handed Katie back to her mother and they all said goodbyes and parted ways. Gina whispered in Ben's ear, "So, are you ready? I think I am. I hope I can do this right and be a mother our baby will love and count on."

Ben leaned over and kissed her. "You will, baby, you will."

Gina couldn't help but instantly flash back to a memory of a deserted gravel road ending at a river. She looked down to her tummy and slightly shuddered. Bringing her hand up and lightly rubbing the bump protruding out from under her blouse, she glanced back up to her husband to see if he'd caught wind of her mood change.

Ben noticed but chose to say nothing and instead put his arm around her shoulder and drew her close in, giving her a kiss on the top of her head. "I'm ready, Gina. And you will be a perfect mother, I've no doubt whatsoever." Ben briefly looked upward as if he quickly spoke a prayer to the One who'd kept him on the straight and narrow since the night he'd been saved. *Truly saved.*

4

Joyce held a lingering question from the day or so after Ethan returned from Springfield, Missouri. Where in hell did Ethan's watch disappeared to? He wasn't ever without it. He slept with it on, he made love to her with it on, it seemed a piece of jewelry he'd worn with pride from the first time she'd met him at her interview. The few times she tried to inquire its whereabouts, Ethan quickly blew it off and changed the subject. The truth is, Ethan is not the same person he was before he left. Joyce hated the fact she now began to doubt and be suspicious of his actions, but the thought he may have someone else in his life, had crossed her mind. He'd been so perfect in the beginning. *Were all men like this? Actors who played the part until they grew tired of the production.*

Ethan exited the master bath, his white long sleeve shirt untucked, and the cuffs rolled back a single fold—enough to see that he wore no wristwatch. He smiled and asked, "Are you about ready, sweetheart? I've got court today, so we need to head out soon."

"Yes, Ethan. I'm ready, I must slip on my heels. Do you have all the files you need for the Ketner case?"

"I believe they're in the car's backseat." Ethan answered.

"What time does the judge hear the case?" Joyce asked.

Ethan looked down at his left wrist as he turned out of habit to check his watch. Hesitantly, he looked back up and to Joyce.

"9:45am and not a minute later. Judge Rowe does not appreciate tardiness. He goes by your rule—ten minutes early is twenty minutes late, or something like that...."

"You better wear a watch like you used to—then...." Joyce said with an innocence she knew Ethan would see through. He looked over but said nothing in response. She knew he felt her jab and today, she didn't care. She'd watched her happy world begin to dissolve and it felt the familiarity of nineteen years earlier. Déjà vu. Way back then, Roy Burks had begun pulling away right after he'd found out she was pregnant with Mitzi. *What could Ethan's reason be unless it was another woman?* "Ethan?" Joyce almost wished for a brief second, she hadn't chosen this moment to question, but it was too late now.

"Yes, sweetheart?"

She paused long enough, Ethan turned after picking up his car keys and stared with question in his eyes. Joyce looked down for a moment before lifting her eyes up to meet his. "Ethan, are you sure this is what you truly want?"

Ethan's eyes squinted, as if in hesitation to answer her.

"Because—I can move back out if it would be better—I mean..." Joyce paused and briefly reflected her thoughts. "...I mean, I don't want—us—to come between my work. I don't want to lose my job or opportunity because I've mixed personal pleasure with business..." Her shoulders slumped. "...unless—it's already too late? I can move back upstairs above Mitzi if I can keep my job..." Joyce cleared her dry throat as Ethan stood with a look of not knowing how to answer. "...or if that's not possible, I can stay for a while with Darrell and Mitzi...."

Ethan put his keys back down on the table and slowly moved toward Joyce. "Sweetheart, where is this coming from? I don't love you any less today than I have since we first met. You are everything to me." He held his arms open to Joyce with a short enough distance to force her to make the move to walk into them.

Joyce stood firm. "I shouldn't have said anything this morning. I know Judge Rowe detests council being late to his bench." She took a step back, not sure if it happened to be just a shift of weight from one leg to the other, or a subconscious move to show defiance in his weak offering of an olive branch. "I'm going to let you go ahead and drive yourself, so you're not late and I'll drive to the office after I settle my nerves a moment or two. We'll talk about all this later this evening. Okay?" Joyce forced a smile to convince Ethan she'd be okay, and everything would work out.

Ethan took a step back and reached again to pick up his keys. He turned toward the door, taking the steps to the hallway table where his briefcase lay. His hand curled around the handle, and he quickly lifted it up as he turned back. "I don't understand what this is about, but you are correct, Judge Rowe does not accept apologies from defense attorneys who show up late." He turned to twist the handle to the front door and then returned his gaze to Joyce. "I've never been married, or for that matter even shared close living conditions with a woman." He took pause. "... in my entire life. I don't know the standard rules or how to acquire the knowledge of cohabitating, so I do pray you will show a little consideration for my lack of understanding what my role should be at this moment. I thought, I guess in my feeble male mind, life between us is progressing toward the next relatively usual step." Ethan squeezed the handles of his bag with a tautness causing his knuckles to whiten a bit as he continued. "Apparently, I'm foolishly blind and mistaken." The door opened as Ethan stepped across the jam. He turned and tried to smile. "Of course, you are still employed. You will remain so unless you make a choice to the contrary. I also have not made any changes in the way I feel about you. Again, a choice I will set at your feet. I'll not attempt to force anything. I only ask humbly..." He looked into her eyes briefly. "...that you do not make any hasty decisions without letting us sort all of this out." He pulled the door closed, both slowly and softly showing no anger in any way. It wasn't two minutes until she heard the tires of his car slightly chirp as it took off up the drive.

She knew it wasn't entirely in her head alone. If it was a test to see if Ethan would lose his temper, he passed very easily with flying colors. She noticed subtle hints of anger from what she had dropped on him, but the responses he'd given were lacking anything she would fear. Not from the tiniest of curtness in his voice, the white knuckles in the grip of his bag she'd noticed or finally, the squeal of his tires as he left. There were no physical reactions like with Roy. She'd sported a swollen cheek from him more than once. He'd sworn after each time his temper took over that it would be his last, but it stung and made a memory for her. And more than one. Nothing similar seemed to show with Ethan. *I'll call Mitzi. I need to see my girl and my grandbaby anyway. I almost know what her advice will be, though....*

5

The phone rang four times before Mitzi answered. "Hello?" She answered out of breath.

"Hey, baby-girl. How are you and our little Miss Katie?"

"Mom! It's great to hear your voice." Mitzi answered, drawing a deep breath. "How's life on the beach of the famous and wealthy?" She laughed, expecting either a reciprocating giggle or something like, 'Oh, Mitzi, stop! He's not rich and famous, he's just comfortable.' But only silence filled the connection. No defensive response or laughter came from her phone's receiver. "Mom? Are you okay?"

"I'd like to talk to you sometime soon if I could? I need..." Her response halted and she cleared her voice a couple of times. "...I need your ears and advice, that's all."

"He didn't hurt you, did he? Is he there?" Mitzi questioned.

"No, no. It's nothing like that, never mind. It's just—it's just things seemed to have changed between us suddenly. I don't want to talk on the phone, though. Can we meet for lunch or something? You can of course, bring my sweet granddaughter! I always feel better when I hold her and see your smiles watching me."

"Oh, mom. If I'd known I could be your medicinal comfort by smiling with my daughter—I would have gotten pregnant years ago!" She giggled and brought an obvious chuckle from her mother. "Of course, we'll meet you for lunch. Coffee Caper?"

"No, no, too close to work and Ethan. I'll swing by and pick you two up around noon and we'll find a place."

"We'll be ready, and don't worry, we'll cheer you up and help fix things. Love you!"

"Love you too, baby-girl." Joyce placed the receiver in the cradle. She thought about asking if she could stay a couple of days with them, but suddenly she realized no urgent danger existed and she didn't want to act too hastily on just her hunches. Her quick plans to pack and be gone by tonight were now changed. Advice is what she needed. *Advice from a nineteen-year-old mother! And her daughter to boot, how funny.*

***

Joyce pulled up the drive to her daughter's apartment and as she parked, she looked up to the second floor where she and Mitzi began their Apalachicola experience. Memory flashes of CJ or Crazy Jay as Mitzi named him just after their meeting. Mitzi came from the womb filled with her crazy sarcastic humor and Joyce quickly fell in love watching her grow into her quirky character. There could never be another who could replace her. Joyce stared up at the deck surrounding the top of the quad-plex, memories reflecting of the good but also scary times with Jay as a neighbor. Life was different for her now, living with Ethan. The man who came rushing into her life filling her heart and soul with love and attention like she'd never seen before, seemed to be disappearing quickly into something uncomfortable and suspicious.

Joyce's car door swung open and her long slender legs slipped from the seat as her feet hit the ground. Her hair blew across her face in strands from the Florida breeze blowing in from across the bay. She stepped out and adjusted her skirt, catching it with her hand from lifting in the light gust. She gazed toward her daughter's front window and saw Mitzi holding sweet Katie in one arm and waving to her with the other.

They are the picture of happiness making life worth living. Joyce sighed.

6

Jay walked down the hallway between the separate cells. Some empty and others held fellow inmates. Friends and foe. Jay enjoyed being somewhat of a hero of sorts, because of single-handedly taking out two law enforcement officers and wounding another. His story quickly became talk amongst the facilities population long before his stay began. The fact two were Florida State detectives and one of the other fatalities, a sheriff—gave Jay the respect to walk taller than most new inmates were allowed. Jay would tell the stories over and over to the inmates who asked. Those stories and actions were Jay's badge of honor, and he wore it with pride. He needed to for survival.

This stint of incarceration felt much different than his first taste of being locked up as a young wet behind the ears boy. This sentence would likely end up with him doing the seated death-dance in the electric chair. The punishment as the Florida State judge and twelve seated jurors plus two alternates handed down to him. Jay knew he'd never see freedom again, of course he never savored much of a taste of it anyway. The days dragged by, he began to talk about his form of judgment, sentencing, and punishment that his daddy passed down to him. The Mason jar with its little tiles of retribution for those who were deemed worthy. The entire process drew interest from his few fellow "friends" within the 'glass house.'

"Jay, I like it. I fuckin' like it a lot." Lyle responded after hearing about such an idea. "I got several in here I'd like to invoke 'the Mason jar judgment' on." Lyle laughed with a grave undertone in his voice.

Lyle Lee Ruby, every bit of six-foot-three and towering over most others on the death row cell block. His body muscular and his square-jawed face housed dark black, beady rat-eyes. Most inmates gave him a wide berth when coming close in hallways or the cafeteria. Lyle's brother Lloyd, another man of large stature, was housed at the same prison, but they were not housed together. Warden Wilkerson didn't allow it. The two brothers were caught after breaking into a Capitol City Savings and Loan in Tallahassee, Florida. Both brothers entered the bank before closing time and were successful hiding in a utility closet until the bank closed for the night. They thought they could break into the vault while the employees were gone and leave before the facility re-opened. After many failed attempts at cracking the vault door, they lay in waiting until the employees re-opened. The police were quickly made aware, and Lyle and Lloyd took hostages. The entire ordeal lasted a day and a half and Lyle ended up raping and killing one of the young bank tellers he'd held. The two brothers were arrested after police concurrently stormed all entrances. Lloyd now served his twenty to life stint, while Lyle received the death penalty. Lyle and Jay hooked up almost instantaneously, with Lyle quickly taking Jay under his group's protection.

Between the two, Jay and his new large friend, they formed a group of seven trusted inmates, of which six held a small wooden tile with a letter carved into it. There would be only four different punishments and two tiles containing forgiveness or grace. B stood for beating, S stood for stab or shank, H stood for hang, C for choke, and G for grace. One tile for each punishment, but two of the grace tiles. This being a concession they all agreed to, because inmates already convicted for their aggressions should have a second chance since they'd already suffered once. Six of the

Trusted Seven, their new group name, would hold the tile in their possession, with the seventh holding the 'vessel.' Once a week they would exchange them between each other so no sucker would have to hold onto a tile reading grace for more than a week or two at a time. Grace, considered a necessary part of the equation, was completely against what each member truly believed in. After all, none of them ever enjoyed the gift of grace in their own lives. The silent seventh member would be there to break the tie if it should ever happen that the six carrying the tiles split the vote three to three to carry out the sentence. Being incarcerated of course, kept them from owning a glass Mason jar. A red handkerchief would be used, and it would be carried to the conclave each week by the silent seventh member, who held no tile. The Trusted Seven, or T-7, were now officially formed. Jay, even though his innovation became instrumental in bringing the group together, would hold no powers above any other member's stature within the group. The Silent Seventh, or now known in code as the SS, would be the floating member in charge for the week they carried the 'vessel,' the handkerchief. All the newly founded group of cons agreed it to be a superb arrangement of judicial distribution within a boundary where they otherwise held no other control.

 A first trial hearing amongst the group about a fellow inmate worked without conflict between them. After their official formation, they in agreement, sentenced this first defendant within four months of Jay's entrance into his new world of confinement. The christening defendant, James William (Jimmie) Tuttle, one of Florida's sickest child molesters to date, was found guilty in a Florida courthouse of over twelve child kidnappings and rapes. This included both male and female, their lives each ended in assorted torturous murders. Jimmie had already appeared a target for abuse among the inmates because most held no love or use of prisoners caged for violent or sexual crimes against children. Many times, crimes against women were also highly frowned upon.

The tile, which the SS blindly pulled from the bundled red handkerchief and tossed into the circle of members, held the scribed letter 'H' on its face. "Hang the son-of-a-bitch." They each nodded in agreement one by one, with none of the six tile holders raising objection to the punishment the Mason vessel revealed. Verdict and sentence now served on a cold early evening before lock-up, a mere two days later. Jimmie's hanging body was found five minutes after inmate count was completed and he was deemed missing. Guards found his half-naked body hanging by a bed sheet dangling over a pipe above the linen table in the laundry hall.

Written into the facilities log as a suicide, Jay and Lyle now both committed their first retribution murder within the walls of the glass house they were incarcerated in. They'd successfully carried it out in just under four months using their revised version of the Mason jar punishment, and they'd made it look like suicide.

Warden Wilkerson lined up all death row inmates the day after Jimmie's body was found and he gave his usual speech. "Men, we are held accountable for the actions we take in this world. We can only assume upon leaving this world and entering the next—that we will continue to be charged and eternally punished for our actions committed here in this life on earth. May God have mercy upon James William Tuttle's soul," but he added, "may he hang a hundred more times in hell for what he's done with his hands here on earth." And no more words were spoken.

After an overnight of hushed rumblings amongst the inmates, the members of T-7 were careful about congregating together and chose to use their setup protocol of passing messages only between three gathered members, no more.

Jay wasn't sure if the warden and the penal system bought the suicide story, or if they just didn't care enough about the life lost to investigate. There is, of course, one more theory; a theory each of the T-7 chose to believe. Maybe Warden Gerald William Wilkerson-aka Warden Willy, silently appreciated us inmates coming up with a tidy system of bringing revenge upon the sick and sadistic vermin of the world. It didn't matter to Jay the reason, all he cared about was having the ability to carry out his form of justice, even though he now shared control with six other fellow prisoners. Now Lyle Lee Ruby held prison respect for him, which is a commodity he appreciated. Other stone-cold killers amongst the population seemed to keep their distance, giving him the time to relax in the new world he lived. The world that had also brought a purdy "thing" to look forward to once a week.

Amy Jo Whitenhour. Hmmm, she reminds me so much of sweet, delicious Gina.

Jay now sat back against the concrete wall, perched on his worn-out cot, nestled in his sparse, caged cubicle. His eyes closed, appearing to be asleep as other inmates passed by. Heads would turn, but not a word or action ever taken. No one ever dicked with Jay or Lyle. No one.

7

There he is again. In the corner of my mind, peeking out and drawing my attention once more. Not being able to imagine why, but I found myself mulling my interview over and over ever since last week on my way home from Lake Correctional…my thought went blank for a moment.

I shook my head as if I could rattle those invasions loose from my brain and then shake them to the floor. Why couldn't I get Billy Jay—out of my head? I'd never been so invaded by anyone before. Especially not a man. For the most part I've never trusted one enough to let my guard down. I knew it to be partially my daddy's fault. But not only a man, but a calculating cold-blooded killer. What's wrong with me? An inquiry I now wished to have the capability to ask my grandfather. He always knew the answers to my questions. Never once did he fail to provide me the knowledge to solve a problem I'd stumbled across. But this question, I would have to answer on my own and it truly stumped me.

My grandfather, to me, is the greatest man to ever live. He'd become my mentor, my hero, and my salvation from the hell that began early in my life. Jay and I had grown up with somewhat differing lives, but we held common parts to them. I don't know, but Jay is in my head today and I find myself wishing the weekend away so I can go back and start where we left off. He's an enigma I feel drawn to solve. His eyes have stories within them. The dark tales show the most, but there must be some happy moments trapped behind the blackness. I want the entire narrative.

I'd been afraid at first to meet the monster eye-to-eye that I'd read about, watched news clips on, and listened to local gossip speak of. I've faced my Goliath though, never needing to launch my stone from its sling. I felt driven to dive into deeper waters, into the caverns and tight turns of what drove him to become a killer.

A smile gently washed across my face as my memories of Grandfather mixed with the imaginary battle of wits I imagined about Jay. The two were not alike in any way, but I shared some of the same feelings now for both. Not the love like with Grandfather, but a curiousness of how each of their characters would have met on a parallel between them. They both held mystery in their eyes. The two were strong in the physical and I believe they shared strength in some of the mental aspects also. They both held and shared a rescue between them. My grandfather on the rescuing side of the equation and Jay more on the need of being rescued like I was. What difference would it have brought had he been able to be saved in my place?

Shaking my head at the question in thought, I redirected my original daydream back to the story of when Grandfather and I were out on his sailboat once. We'd ignored the advice of Grandmother's forecast of the oncoming weather as we packed our daypacks. "Oh, Myrtle, we'll be back before the squall, we're just headed outside Pierce inlet to do some shallow reef diving. No worries, honey." My grandfather told her.

Early morning air on Grandfather's sailboat always invigorated me. The breeze, the salt, Grandfather at the helm—life at its best. When I picture his smile, it still gives me goosebumps as if he were still beside me. The warmth he exuded just by his presence always overwhelmed me. I knew I felt safe no matter what. His smile assured it.

I overheard my grandmother's concern about the weather but shook it off once we got down to the boat slip holding 'The Other Woman' still nestled safely with her ropes. Grandfather loved answering people at the café as he paid for his coffee at the register, when they would ask him a question like, "Where you headed Jake? Grandfather would immediately answer in a boisterous tone along with a look of lust, "I'm going out with "The Other Woman" of course. It's too nice a day not to ease her out of her slip. A great morning to let some breeze blow between our sheets, feel the up and down of the ride, you know, get our sea legs wet!" Their eyes would quickly become balls of white that encircled their pupils left wide open in shock before I'd cut in, "Oh Grandfather, tell them it's your sailboat's name for cryin' out loud!" Their eyes would shrink back down to normal, and a calm breath would exit their open mouths as laughter would certainly fill the room.

I could feel the laugh churning in my gut now, but back then as a young girl I would blush from embarrassment, wanting to crawl under the table and hide.

The dive began perfect with no hitches. Grandfather trained me after I turned twelve and this if I remember correctly, was my tenth dive with him. We were going in and out of reef tunnels and Grandfather held his speargun at the ready. The reef tunnels were a new experience for me, but I knew I would be safe. I'd never been let down by either my grandmother or grandfather since being rescued by them from my momma and daddy around age eight.

Grandfather must have seen a fish because he kicked his fins quickly and disappeared around the edge of the reef and he disappeared from my sight. He'd never left me before and I remember feeling both fear and anger that he would do such a thing. I kicked my legs wider and faster, but they quickly began aching and cramping from the strain of slicing through the water. I would scold him when we returned to the surface. I rounded the jagged edge of the reef and quickly realized why he'd kicked away so fast. A very large hammerhead shark circled my grandfather while he tried to keep him at bay with the tip of his speargun. Several times the shark would look as if it were turning away but instead would turn back without warning and attack. That shark came very close to grandfather's body before he could maneuver his speargun point and fight back, poking and jabbing at it. I saw him punch him in his face several times. I didn't know what to do. I'd always been able to ask him but being under water made it impossible. Finally, my grandfather reached down to his leg and pulled his dive knife from its sheath and stabbed at the shark. A small stream of blood trailed off as the hammerhead quickly conceded and turned, swimming away until he disappeared into the bluish blur.

Grandfather looked back to see if I was okay and when he saw me, he looked at his dive watch. He hand-motioned me to come toward him and I kicked as hard as my legs allowed until I nestled into his arms. He led the way up until we were almost to the surface, and he motioned to stay. I remember him watching the perimeter around us, I presumed in case the great hammerhead returned, which thank God, he never.

We continued our safety stop, bleeding off the gases in our bodies from breathing the compressed air. After several minutes I followed him off at about a forty-five-degree angle back towards the anchored boat so we wouldn't have to top-water kick too far on the surface. I remembered my grandfather telling me once how sharks like to swim close to the bottom, looking up for animals in distress and then attack from underneath, their victims rarely seeing them come.

My heartbeat pumped hard, and I didn't realize just how deeply and quickly I'd started sucking my air from my tank. In the last several feet I reached for my grandfather's buddy-breathing regulator, because I'd sucked my air tank dry. Later I found out I also emptied his too, leaving him with one last breath to get him to the top.

When we finally climbed aboard the boat, I fell to the deck in exhaustion. I believe my grandfather was surely more depleted of energy than me, but he never let it show. The surface became much choppier than when we'd submerged, and the clouds, which had been sparse, were now collecting tightly together and darkening as the boat wobbled roughly back and forth in the troughs. This wasn't the proper time to scold him. Fear began to set in once more. I felt the boat's action become more rutted as my fear returned. Catching a glimpse of my grandfather's eyes as he looked at me, I immediately began cranking the anchor up as he unfurled the storm jib and maneuvered the bow into the wind. The sheet had never roared as loud rippling in the wind before, but he knew exactly what to do and I somehow managed the necessary actions needed as a crewman would at the proper time.

Our boat rose the troughs and then dove into the hole, repeatedly, as the drops of rain began to fall. My captain never retreated. This is how I remember my grandfather. Strong and decisive and acting without fear. He the rescuer. I picture Jay being the shark, attacking out of protecting his space, becoming fiercer as he is attacked, defending what he'd fought to obtain. Both strong, with resolve in their actions, and both with self-validating reasons. I believe Jay more than likely grew into becoming predatorial from the lack of love and guidance. I can't immediately hate him for that. I just need to understand him. My grandfather grew up in a loving home. He learned love because he'd been taught and shown love as was my grandmother. They in turn rescued me from a life lacking both love and faith; both options Jay never knew, so he learned to survive by any means he could.

I think I knew his story from the moment I saw him, but I needed the details to prove my thesis. Tomorrow would bring our second meeting and, replacing the fear I held the first time, I would now go with compassion for someone who'd never seemed to be afforded a chance from his start.

8

The sun tried its best to peek between the darkened billows. Those attempts were held at bay by a few large, deep gray clouds still hanging low. My vehicle rolled down the highway splashing the puddles left from the morning showers. In my mindless trek down the interstate, I concentrated on the possible scenarios today could play out. Could he still be sleeping? Maybe Jay is mulling through second thoughts of meeting me or possibly the opposite and collecting his memories to have them close at hand upon facing my questions.

Again, I performed the early conceived habit of giving my head a quick shake as if to jar the thoughts from clinging to my brain. It was a silly habit I'd formed as a child but one I seemed unable to store on the shelf out of reach. Leaning forward to adjust the volume knob, I twisted it to the right until I could decipher the tune that played. "Back in Black" by AC/DC. The driving beat pushed me to twist the dial further to increase the volume. "Back in black, I hit the sack..." The windows were rolled down on my grandfather's blue 1972 chevy truck he'd left me. It remained his baby, his pride and joy throughout all those many hours we shared together driving in it. Of course, I now sat where he used to sit. He would have loved this raucous tune, grandmother, not so much. Grandfather would have been stomping his left foot to the beat as his right foot mashed down on the accelerator while he moved his shoulders with the rhythm. We were the perfect match, my grandfather and me. I'm suddenly reminded he no longer lives on this earth, but with Jesus in his world and I instantly miss him again. My mind seems to always operate this way. My grandmother always said I possessed a vivid imagination and I supposed she'd been correct. My active brain always jumped from one thought to another when I sat alone, unable to remain focused unless I held a pencil in my hand or worked at my computer in my office.

The smell in the air blowing through the window caught my attention. Its cooler freshness made me instantly know the truck is on the south side of Lake Apopka, even though I couldn't see it for the trees, let alone the fact the land elevation sat above me, the road in a bit of a trough. The cooler air seemed to always find this one area to escape the water's surface and carry down the small decline of the hill, finding its way blowing across the turnpike. Maybe my grandfather's way of letting me know the ride is two-thirds through my days travel to Clermont, home of Lake Correctional Institution. My heart began to pound inside my chest a little harder. This time, the anticipation came from digging deeper into Jay's past world instead of from fear of the unknown like last week's visit.

***

Waiting alone in my interview room wasn't nearly as daunting the second time. I knew the regiment that would follow once the door opened. I still found myself trying to filter the peripheral noise on the other side of the door; trying to listen intently for the rattle of chains and low thump of footsteps down the hallway. I couldn't refrain from fidgeting with my recorder and notepad, twirling my pencil between my index and middle finger. Sniffing the air as I'd walked in, I noticed the familiar odors from last week. The place still needed a thorough scrubbing and maybe a color change of paint to enhance the depressing ambiance it reflected. Maybe the current color was derived from the intentional purpose of spreading gloom over any who sat here. The exterior held its own misery within the curtains of the metal chain-link fencing and razor-wire coils that reminded the animals held within that they are no more than caged, rabid, and dangerous vermin who were removed from a world of rules they chose to turn away from.

I thought of how society and humanity wrestled each other constantly, and the fact this subject used my internal thinking as the arena of battle between each. Occasionally I can almost hear the bell denoting the end between rounds. Before the match could ever have the chance to end, I already knew which side of my thinking would be the winner. It wouldn't even be by concession or an accounting of points by way of knockdowns, blocks, uppercuts, or round-houses. The champ would hold the winner's belt by way of a knock-out or ten-count. I tried, as a journalist, to hold back my personal beliefs to present the facts from an outside point-of-view. Sometimes though, this rule becomes too ambiguous to truly hold to the fire of reality. I did, however, remind myself to attempt such a standard.

The door eventually swung open, and the guards led Jay to the table to be cuffed and shackled as before. I was in such deep thought I never heard his arrival I'd strained to perceive in advance.

Jay appeared differently today, his eyes less dimmed, mouth not as taut, which allowed the beginnings of a smile to form. "Good morning, Billy Jay."

Jay's lack of immediate response led to a silence loud enough to resound above the clatter of the chains and shackles being attached. It brought instant wonder to my attention. Was I correct in my scenarios and maybe he indeed is having second thoughts of participating? I certainly hoped it wasn't the case.

The same guard walked around the table and faced me once

again. "Ms. Whitenhour—Billy is secured, and I will be standing outside the door if you need any assistance. Are you okay, ma'am?"

"Yes officer..." I squinted as I strained my eyesight to read his last name sewn on his uniform. "...Officer Valens. I appreciate all you are doing, and I should be fine, sir." We shared quiet smiles and nods of gratitude and once again, he and his fellow guards left the room and closed the door.

"Good morning, ma'am." Jay finally answered. "I figured it'd be easier to reciprocate the greetings after they left." He smiled slightly before he continued, "I also hoped we were friendly enough for you to call me Jay again, like I told you my friends do."

Straightening my stance in the chair—as I scooted towards the table, I quickly pondered his question before answering. "I...um...am...slightly concerned how our relationship should be defined. It's maybe too early to call ourselves more than acquaintances at this point..." I cleared my throat. "...I don't believe it would be healthy to bounce back and forth between the two until we get to know each other better and better establish how deep our 'friendship' will become. A fair answer for you at this point?" I looked with question; my brow raised waiting for a response.

Jay straightened his body as he scooted upward in his chair; the chains clinked together with his movements. "I thought by the end of our last visit—we'd established boundaries within our new 'friendship'. I'll admit my respect for most women up to last week, weren't always the highest level, but you showed strength when you set me in my place—and brought a respect I never felt before. First time I've humbled myself to a woman, I'm afraid to say, except for my momma, of course."

I studied his response as closely as I could in an ongoing dialogue. There seemed to be buried within, both a bit of concession mixed amongst some carefully disguised aggression. I wished I'd taken those psychology classes while in school to help me decipher his response closer. I wanted our relationship to build into one of trust so I could truly understand what made him what he'd become. I knew he owned an intellect beyond his southern-backwoods dialect, and I did not want him to use his street-smart education to play me like a fiddle he'd kept hidden in the closet; never publicly exposing his ability to perform.

Me balancing on a tightrope above a crevasse, he my audience, who closely watched how I would respond to the breeze blowing against me. I didn't want to show my fear of falling, nor did I want to lose his attention of watching my talents. We continued for a short time in this odd dance of rebuttals as if we were performing some sort of vocal rumba together. I finally tired and reached for my recorder, flipping the switch on as a segue into journalistic mode. He stopped his unrehearsed choreography of words and rested his arms on the table in obvious surrender, aborting the dance between us.

His intent seemed obvious to me. He'd been doing an exploratory button search, pushing to see which ones he could get away with and which either shut me down or roused an aggressive response. He'd obviously honed his intuitiveness of others to gain control of a situation. I imagined him an excellent actor in any circumstance from years of necessity to survive. I admired his ability, but at the same time would remain very aware it existed. I'm up for the challenge as I'm sure he also enjoyed the underlying sparring between us. I got the feeling if I didn't spar at all, he would refuse to open his past and expose his inner demons, which I wanted to unbury and write about so much. There seemed a match between us, much like the match I'd felt with my grandfather. The difference being the spectrum of the match we shared. We were opposites sides fitting together in the middle as one sized gear meshes into its counterpart.

"Billy Jay..." I started yet hesitated. Then upon drawing a

measured breath, my brain told me I felt ready to move into the deeper waters now, away from the shallows. I'd treaded long enough. Time to stop kicking to keep afloat above the surface, and face downward to dive into the dark clouded waters of Jay's hidden unknown, deep into his abyss where the dangerous sharks could be cruising. "…Billy Jay, we've talked in depth about the lack of love along with the outright torturous traits that your father used on you. Are you ready to tell me more about your mother and where your feelings are about her?" I looked into his eyes to see if I could determine if truth or an act would be presented. "Did you have good feelings about her?"

Jay's eyes immediately dropped to his hands, which were now nestled into his lap. He quickly steered them back to meet mine, his lips pursed. "I wanted to care about her. She'd shown at one time she loved me. At least it felt like what I'd heard love is." He looked away and to the tiny window high on the room's wall and letting light enter from the outside. "She felt the same fear I'm sure as I did. Not knowing which action would bring out my daddy's anger. What word spoken he would hear and get set off from it." He turned back and continued, "It didn't ever make sense to what drew a slap across the face from nowhere. Sometimes I believe he hit just to get a reaction that would make him feel important in the world. Not just the control of us, but to see the pain and fear he could bring on, so he could feel something himself. I know my momma lived under the same umbrella of caution, not knowing what could flip the switch in his head and poke the tiger within."

I followed up quickly. "Did your mother ever stand up to your father in your defense?"

Jay let out a short guffaw. "Pff, my momma did stand up for me one time I remember. I's probably under the age of ten. She paid a hell of a price for it too, as well did I. I don't ever remember a second time. I would catch her look at me with a glimpse as if it could say words…" Jay sniffed and lifted his right hand to rub his eye. "...those words would be—Billy boy, you know better, son. It'll be over quick." Both eyes began to shed tears. Billy acted quickly to attempt wiping them away without notice, but he knew the task to be impossible.

"What happened to her, Billy...when she stood up for you the one time?" I asked.

"First he blackened her eye with a quick fist. He turned to me and said, "boy...you get your ass in here and watch what you caused. He grabbed a handful of her hair and drug her into their bedroom. He turned and yelled again. 'I said—git your ass in here and watch!' I ran quick as I could with fear of what was gonna happen." Jay's hands now both sat on the table-top, gripped together so tightly his fingers became bright white mixed with ruby redness.

Jay asked me a question, which sent instant chills up my spine making me dread a possible dagger into my heart.

"You sure you wanna hear the outcome, Ms. Amy? It ain't pretty and it left a horrible scar for me, one that ain't never come to heal." His eyes darkened, any sparkle existing moments ago, were now vanquished.

I hesitated but felt this to be a moment we needed to share. "Yes, Billy Jay, I believe I probably need to hear it as much as you need to speak it. It'll be good for you in the long haul." I said it hoping quietly I meant it, instead of just selfishly needing to hear for my manuscript.

Jay laughed. "Long haul, that's funny. My long haul draws shorter with each minute! I can almost feel the 'lectricity surging through my veins. But I'll tell you, long as you don't hold it against me and remember—you said yes." His eyes widened and then shrank.

"I won't blame you, Billy Jay, the story needs to be your story—uncensored, your words from your mouth. I won't throw a punch from out of nowhere, I promise."

Jay looked at the ceiling tiles and nervously looked side to side as if what he began to say, should not be heard by anyone else.

After a full minute of silence, his words began to spill from his lips. Sometimes in a quiver, sometimes with hate and harshness, but he didn't pause, and he didn't hesitate. I felt his story too ugly to be false. I'd heard the saying about truth being stranger than fiction and what he began to tell me is hard to hear and painful to visualize.

"After draggin' my momma to the bedroom and yellin' for me to move my ass quick—the moment I stepped into the doorway, he hit my momma's face so hard—it threw her body across the bed. He turned again to me and told me to get the fuck on the other side of the bed so I could see my momma's face. I moved quick as a rock skippin' 'cross the pond, full of fear and tears. My momma's face already swelled like a grapefruit, her eye barely more than a open slit on one side of her face. The son-of-a-bitch flipped her over onto her stomach like she's nothin' more than a sack a potato's. Before she had time to know what was happenin', he pulled his pocketknife from his jeans. He slid the blade underneath her pants, blade up, and cut through all the way up from the inside of her leg 'til her bottom was exposed. I thought he's gonna give her a whippin' on her bare ass like he did me—but I's wrong. He finished pulling her pants off until they were in his hands. He looked at me and tossed 'em to the side of the bed 'fore he proceeded to cut her underwear off. As he tossed 'em to the floor he said, 'boy, this is what women and mommas is good for, and not much else.' He unzipped his pants and I saw somethin' I'd never seen before. He grabbed her from each side of her waist and hoisted her upward. He pushed his 'somethin'' real close to her naked backside and momma screamed, but I stood frozen not knowin' what to do. He hollered every time I tried to look away, 'you keep watchin' this boy.' He slid his hands up her back until he grabbed her around her neck and began squeezin' 'til momma started chokin'. He turned and looked at me again and said, 'you get the hell on outta here now Billy, and don't you forget what you saw, you little waste of a good time. I don't reckon I even knew what he meant by it, but I think I prolly knew it wasn't no good."

The room fell silent. Billy Jay's eyes were vacant. His hands shook, making the chains jingle a tune I never wanted to hear again. His quiet sobs blended with the metallic tune, and I fought the urge of my entire body to heave in emotion. I felt the pain for Jay, picturing this event as retold it straight from his mouth. How could he ever have lived through this and not been broken forever? I suddenly fought the urge to vomit. My stomach wrenched, but I refused to let any bile escape my mouth.

I'd collected questions to follow up on, but I knew my voice would never allow the words to exit my mouth in an intelligible form today after hearing his horrific life experience as a ten-year-old child. I reached to the recorder and flipped the switch off. Every move I made, felt like agony drug through quicksand in slow motion. The low rumble of chatter and footsteps from the other side of the closed door seemed louder in the silence-filled room we sat in. Nothing felt appropriate except to sit and let the atmosphere settle from the aftermath of the bomb Jay's experience just dropped. I wanted to get up and run around to his side of the table and hug all the comfort into him I could, but I couldn't. I also wasn't sure how he would embrace my condolences.

How would I know how to continue from here? I would have never imagined asking about his mother would bring such a horrible story. I realized in this moment—there would be no safe path laid out to avoid the landmines lying in wait that might be detonated in any given moment from any question asked. As a journalist, the realization of interviewing someone with such a disturbing history, held the capability to devastate the relationship one builds between each other. It could happen instantly without warning. Was our relationship destroyed while we sat blankly staring at each other in the aftermath? This story is surely real and not just a test to see how I'd react. I presumed Jay to be full of deceit, but could he be this devious as to make such an ugly tale as this up?

I needed to leave. I felt the urge suddenly. How would I form my exit strategy to be able to return?

"Jay…" I spoke in quiet hesitation. "…I think it's best we end early and let today gel. I don't feel like we will be able to let go of this moment and continue today. Are you in agreement?"

Jay closed his eyes a moment before re-opening them. He almost appeared like he now washed the moment away from thought. "Ms. Amy, I'm okay either way. I know my story must be horrible for someone who's not lived in my shoes." He cleared his throat. "I did warn you and asked if you were sure if you wanted me to finish…."

Time now moved into a form I wasn't familiar with. Each second clicked loud enough for me to hear from the clock on the wall nearly fifteen feet away. Each small jolt from the second hand's movement from one line to the next brought a booming click. I felt my pulse thunder in my wrist and chest with each heartbeat closely following in tempo with the sound of time slowly slipping. My internal thoughts slowly bounced into each other as if gravity ceased inside my brain. It ungrounded those individual ponderings to float without restraint or will. I wasn't sure how to respond, *am I about to pass ou*t? I attempted to steady myself as I moved my hands to grip the edge of the table. Not sure if my expression ever changed or showed any sign of what began happening to me on the inside, I attempted to form a sentence to speak. "I…I…realize Jay, you indeed…um…."

Damn it, Amy, be strong. I heard the words inside my head spoken loudly. My grandfather's voice. I knew immediately he resided inside my soul.

"Pussycats and wolverines." Jay said in a monotone voice. A

string of words that made no connection or sense to me in the form delivered.

"What? I don't...did...I...what did you say?" I tripped over each word as I spoke it, trying to translate what I'd heard Jay say against how his words could possibly pertain to the situation.

"In this world, Ms. Amy, there are two variations of people—least ways with men." He paused but barely an instant. "There's pussycats—like me in my beginnings, 'specially with the cruelty of my daddy, and later during my prison stint at the work farm." Jay's eyes regained some of the sparkle as if a fog lifted from around them. "Then there's wolverines. Men who don't take no shit from no one or no situation. Again, like my daddy. He'd be what I would call a rabid wolverine. So much hate inside him, he didn't know or recognize anything human. He's a rabid wolverine with his paw caught in a trap of what society is. Lashing out at anything he saw as a threat that could lead to weakening him."

All I could muster from my mouth is, "An interesting analogy, Jay. It speaks volumes. What work farm are you talking about?"

"After my momma died from cancer and I ran away, I met an old woman who caught me diggin' for food from a dumpster back behind a burger joint. I reckon she'd never seen a boy of fourteen findin' food on his own. She pitied me. Took me into her keep and gave me a room and food. I was a frightened pussycat, and she took me in like a stray and tried her best to tame me into something normal." Jay smiled with a lightened expression across his face. Watching him seemed to settle my nerves back down. "Ms. Pasternack, her full name, Lila Pasternack. She was a nurturing old pussycat. Tried to teach me the correct ways of life and even tried a couple a times to take me to church so I could know Jesus."

I reached up and pushed the recorder button to re-start it and sat back into my chair to let Jay talk until he ran out of steam.

"Her kindness showed me that the world wasn't all meanness and full of wolverines. But she ended up mistaken. 'Bout two years later, I came home after workin' with some ditch-diggers only to find the wolverines, in fact, had broken into her home and killed her. I found her naked on her bed with blood everywhere. Made me sick. I threw up all over the bathroom. She smelled like spoiled meat and piss. That's when I realized kindness gets you ravaged and eaten by the animals of this world, ain't no grace for pussycats, so you best avoid 'em all."

Jay sat back and looked at me. A minute or two passed and I felt like he would sit silent until I responded.

"What happened when your mother got cancer?"

"My momma smoked cigarettes ever sense I remember. She always broke into coughing fits. Daddy smoked too. Always coffee cans and dinner plates filled to the top with crinkled up butts. Damn, they stunk. Probably why I never started smokin' either. The smell and momma coughin' up blood and all. I just remember her and my daddy sayin' they were goin' to the doctor to see why momma been coughin' up blood real regular." Jay glanced toward the window again and then turned back. "You smoke, Ms. Amy?"

"No Jay, I never have."

"Mighty smart of ya." Jay paused, then continued. "Daddy and momma come home later in the afternoon and my momma's face held a real sad look to it. Daddy looked different too, but I can't say I remember it bein' pitiful like my mommas was. We celebrated my birthday a couple weeks after, nothin' but a chocolate Twinkie with a candle from the year before poked in it. Momma died in her bed two days later. Daddy made a call and 'bout 'n hour or two later a black car with a couple a guys in suits picked up momma's body. I could tell right away life would get nothin' but rougher for me—so I left a night later. Never saw the son-of-a-bitch again, 'cept through the window every once in a while, when I missed my momma and wanted to remember her." Jay shuffled in his chair making his chains and shackles rustle and clink. "I reckon I'm 'bout tired a talkin' for the day. Can we just sit here a bit before you call the guards in? I'd like a minute just to sit quiet amongst a friend 'fore I head back into the other wolverines. And Ms. Amy…I reckon you already know this, but I ain't no gawd damn pussycat no more. You can't be one of those in prison. Pussycats get treated like my daddy did my momma that time. Ain't nobody ever doin' that to me again—never." Jay's eyes blinked, showing a moment of ferociousness within them. "I'm a rabid wolverine like my daddy. I 'spect to be put down one these days real soon. Ain't gonna fight it. I just ain't gettin' fucked by no man ever again like at the work farm. Back when I's just a scared as hell pussycat."

I reached up and turned the recorder off, and we sat quietly for about a half an hour. No more words were spoken, we just shared occasional glances between us. I wasn't certain what thoughts were jingling around inside his head, but the ones in mine were disturbing at best.

The guards eventually came through the door and unshackled Jay, leading him towards the hallway and back to general lock-up. He turned once he stood at the door's threshold. "See ya next week, Ms. Amy."

I turned, my arms full of the recorder and note pad. I smiled and nodded in agreement, I couldn't muster the words yes or good-bye.

Once I got out to my truck, I slowly climbed in, numb from my interview experience Jay shared. My stomach hurt when I lifted my leg up into the cab, crawling in by pulling on the steering wheel like it were the saddle-horn on a tall stallion helping me up on the mount. After situating myself in the seat, I drew in a large breath and slowly let it exit along with some tension in my shoulders. My mind kept trying to wrap around the horrid experience of Jay being forced not only to watch but be accused of being the reason. Devastating to a young boy already beaten down. The thought of his son-of-a-bitch sperm donor daddy using sex in such a vial and violent way to punish them both brought both feelings of rage and pain in my heart on their behalf.

I choked. The bile almost came up before I could choke it back. I pushed my door open once more just in case and sure enough I instantly leaned out and vomited everything that was once held inside. I quickly looked around to make sure no one saw me.

Damn Jay's father to hell—if he isn't dead and buried already. My thoughts, as a journalist, spurred into wondering if he happened to be alive and could possibly be found. I shook my head no right away, knowing the urge to kill him would be much too strong in myself. Besides, I don't want to put a face on a devil. He's only one in a bazillion demons on this earth at any given time anyway. They're thick like a cloud of skeeters on the Okefenokee Swamp after a gentle rain. Poor Jay. Sex could never contain the meaning God created it for after watching his mom suffer and get choked the way she did.

I inserted the worn and tarnished Chevy key into the ignition and with my foot on the clutch I gave it a twist. She fired right up, and I thought of my grandfather's sailboat's name and laughed. I should call his truck, "The Hunk of Love." Yep, I christen you The Blue Hunk O' Love. I mashed the pedal down after passing the guard booth and smiled again, fighting the urge to dwell on Jay the entire drive home. Out of habit, I reached and twisted the dial of the magic radio, which seemed to always play the song I needed to hear at the time I wanted it most. Like rolling the craps dice, I pushed my luck to hear what song was playing. "When you're down and troubled and need a helping hand…" I shook my head not believing it could possibly be just my luck. I instinctively looked out my window and upward to the puffy white clouds gathered and rising. I think I instinctively expected to see his sailplane circling overhead. I knew it must have been him who dropped the dime in Heaven's jukebox to play this James Taylor's song, "You've Got a Friend" at this specific moment. I'd never really believed in coincidence. It just never seemed in my vocabulary. It's God. Small, unexpected miracles just when you need them most, even if you weren't cognizant of how much of a gift it really was at the time.

9

Joyce and Mitzi decided to head over to the little dive in Port St. Joe, Poppy's Net and Pasture, the hide-away Ethan introduced them to. When they pulled into the parking lot, Mitzi noticed the waitress they'd had last time getting out of the passenger seat of a old gray sedan. "Hey Mom, look over there. Look familiar?"

"Looks like our waitress last time."

"Yeah, the one who remembered Ethan, right down to what he drank, from like twenty years ago." Mitzi said. She grabbed her mom's arm before she started to swing her door open and climb out. "Hang on a second. Let's just watch and see what's goin' on."

Joyce slid back and turned her head to match the direction of her daughter's. "What, are you a detective now too?" She snorted.

"I got strange vibes from her and Ethan. Something is there between them. I just don't know if it's a jewel or a turd, but there's something they were both avoiding, yet poking."

"Mitzi! Where do you come up with these little vernaculars? Lord, I feel like I'm sittin' here with Granny or Elli Mae of the Beverly Hillbillies."

"Did you see that?" Mitzi asked.

"See what?"

"The guy just handed her a stack of bills. Is she a prostitute?"

"Oh Mitzi, for cryin' out loud! I'm done playing Cagney and Lacey with you. I'm going into order; I have to be back at work. Remember? I work for the waitresses next john! Are you coming?"

Joyce began to turn and reach for the door handle.

Before Mitzi could grab her mom's arm, the door opened, and she stepped half-way out. Mitzi turned and pulled the handle on her side, trying to scoot out in unison. "Um, Mom..." Mitzi mumbled at the same time she rushed around the front of the car to get next to her. "She's coming up behind us...."

Joyce turned first to her daughter and put her hand up to her mouth. "Oh no, what shall we do?" She then turned to peer behind her when her hand pulled on the front door to enter. "Oh, hello again...um...I'm sorry, your name is on the tip of my tongue...."

"It's okay, it's Cali, Cali Lea Jenkins. I remember you and...."

"Mitzi, she's, my daughter. Hey Mitzi, this is Cali." Joyce turned back and raised her eyebrow slightly. "Is it okay if I call you Cali?"

"Of course, Joyce, isn't it?"

"Yes, it is. My you do have a good memory!" Joyce answered.

"Comes from being a waitress, one of the personality traits a waitress needs to keep up with—helps pay the bills." Cali smiled and winked.

Joyce looked over at Mitzi and gave her an "aw-ha" look, to which Mitzi rolled her eyes. "It's all about tips, right?" Mitzi said with a bit of snarky sarcasm.

"I can go ahead and seat you two if you like. Is Ethan meeting you today?"

"No, not today. We girls are on our own this time." Joyce smiled.

"I'll put you two out by a large window where you can see the best view of the beach. It's kind of in the back, out of the way, but I'm not hiding you...just taking extra good care of you! Okay?"

"It's fine Cali, we appreciate the best beach view." Joyce smiled and began following her. She glanced back again at Mitzi and gave her a knowingly "see how wrong you are" look. Mitzi responded by sticking out her tongue.

Cali placed menus on the table but leaned in after they got seated. "The red-snapper tacos are the best today. Caught fresh yesterday and have been cleaned and soaking in Poppy's special marinade. Delicious!" She winked. "Can I get you drinks and then a minute to think over your meal choice?"

"I'll take the tacos and a sweet-tea, please." Mitzi spoke up.

"You know, the same sounds perfect for me too." Joyce echoed.

The minute Cali left, Mitzi leaned in close to her mother, "That bitch is guilty of something…"

"Mitzi B! You can have questions, but I didn't raise you to make unsubstantiated accusations, nor use the language like a drunken sailor does. Shame on you!"

"Oh, here we go with the lawyer, slash, Mother Theresa. Guess what Momma? I got a sixth sense about her and I'm sticking to it. There's something, it's practically written on her forehead, and I'm just the one to dig until I find it." She rolled her eyes at her mom. "But I'll keep my opinions quiet until I uncover some 'facts' showing you just how right I am…" Mitzi sat straight up in her seat. "…and I hate to tell you, but your sweet boyfriend Ethan, is involved with her up to his eyeballs. He's just too suave to let it show."

"I wanted to talk to you about Ethan and I, but I'm not sure it's a good time or place now. It sounds like you've already convicted him along with this barely known suspect you've cuffed and night-sticked…" Joyce's eyes welled up a bit. "…I…I'm just lost baby girl. I thought this was my chance to be happy…and…" Joyce picked up her purse and fumbled through it until she found a tissue. "I just don't know what happened…ever since…ever since he came back from the Federal Medical Center in Springfield. Things changed—and not for the better. I have suspicions too. I'm just not wearing them on my sleeve like you, but I do have them. In fact, I have a bag packed and am hoping to stay with you and Darrell and Katie for a day or two while I figure this thing out."

Her eyes dried a bit and she continued, "Could I...maybe stay a day or ...."

"Of course, Mom. I'm sorry. You know me, though, I open my mouth and my opinion doesn't just fall out but bursts out like a cannon ball. Of course, you can stay. Long as you need. It'll be the couch, but it's comfortable and yours as long as it takes."

Joyce smiled and wiped her eyes once more showing some relief. "He's a good man. He's been so giving to me. Something must have happened there. Something he's just not ready to talk about. He carries so much pressure with his work. He takes it very seriously and is upset because he overslept and missed a meeting with CJ—I mean, Jay. He was going to defend him, but since he missed, another attorney took over. I think it's one he personally has problems with." She looked up and saw Cali bringing a tray with their drinks. "It's gotta be what the problem is...."

Cali leaned over and placed their drinks and smiled. "The food will be right out, ladies."

"Thank you." Joyce answered. She continued after the waitress turned toward the kitchen. "It's the strangest thing, and I know it's probably nothing, but Ethan always wore this watch. It looked very expensive and before this trip he wore it constantly, and I mean always. It contained sharp edges and once when we were in bed..." She blushed. "...it...it bumped my breast and scratched it. I thought he'd take it off right away, but he didn't."

"Where are you going with this, Mom? He likes his watch—it's expensive and he doesn't want to lose it...."

"He hasn't worn it since he got back. And—when I ask him about it—he avoids the question completely. Believe me, I've asked several times and it's as if the question is taboo."

"Have you looked for it?"

"Everywhere. I feel guilty about digging through his desk and things, but...."

"Sounds like he's lost it. Or left it somewhere he shouldn't have."

Joyce's eyes suddenly appeared hollow and empty. "Exactly what I'm afraid of. Not only may I lose a man I quickly fell in love with, but I'll lose my home and job also. I've never been a fighter before, and I have no idea what I'm up against or if the battle has already been lost."

The waitress walked up behind Joyce with two plates of steaming red snapper tacos. "Here you go ladies, I just know you are going to love these!"

As she set the plates down, Mitzi in her usual no holds barred fashion, blurted out, "So Cali—just how well and what do you know about Ethan? I'm asking for a friend...." Joyce's eyes widened in shock and disbelief. Cali didn't even appear shocked by the question. *The look she wore almost foretold her knowledge of something being off today with us,* Mitzi thought silently.

Cali leaned in close and scanned the room over her left shoulder, then her right. "You ladies really wanna know what I think of Ethan William Kendrick?" She watched Mitzi immediately nodding up and down in agreement. Joyce just sat looking dumbfounded. "I won't say unless you both agree." Joyce looked over to her daughter seeing, of course, she was nodding yes. Mitzi cocked her head sideways and spoke to her mom in a silent language with her eyes—she squinted and tipped her nose towards Cali. Joyce's dreadful look turned to Cali again and she nodded a begrudging yes.

"For starters, as far as Ethan's concerned..." Cali's voice lowered to a whisper. "He's fucking dangerous, pardon my French. He scares the piss outta me, and I personally would rather eat crumbs with bums, than steaks with snakes, if you know what I mean?" She pulled back and straightened her apron. "I know it sounds shocking and hateful, but that's just a hint of what I think. We do have a past. One I wished never happened..." She paused checking their expressions. "...but I'd be glad to talk to you deeper about the subject..." She looked around the room once more. "...when I ain't swimmin' at a pond he regularly fishes in, if you catch my drift."

Mitzi immediately looked over to her mom with an "I told you so" look in her eyes.

Joyce's head dropped slowly towards the table. Her face becoming flush with a look of devastation. She felt her world of happiness collapse around her.

Cali walked back toward the kitchen, disappearing around the corner.

"Why in hell would she be so willing, out of nowhere, to fill us in on her thoughts of Ethan? Especially knowing he and I are a thing. Mitzi? What's your take on it baby-doll? Why wouldn't she think I'd run right to Ethan and report what she's saying?"

Mitzi eyed her momma and then in her usual pre-law class mentality asked the question. "What feeling do you have right now about Ethan. What resoundin' emotions swallowed you up overnight?"

Joyce looked into her daughter's eyes and answered almost immediately without thought. "Desperation. I feel scared and desperate."

Mitzi stared and nodded in agreement. "I'll bet that's what she'd say right now too. She sure 'nuff held the look in her eyes when I asked her about him. Her attitude changed to it like a fucking light switch being flicked every way but where the light shines." Mitzi looked down and then back up. "Sorry 'bout the ugly word, it slipped. Happens every time I find out my momma may be gettin' played by a rich, shifty snake wearing a James Bond tuxedo."

Cali returned to their table a couple of minutes later and asked how they liked their fish tacos. After they answered, she slid a piece of paper on top of the bill and smiled. "Hope to see you real soon, ladies. Enjoy your afternoon."

10

Jay stepped through the opening of his cell out into the hallway the minute he saw Wendell Comb saunter by his crib. "Psst, Wendy!" Wendell stopped and turned around and flashed five open fingers on his left-hand next to his right-hand flashing two. The code he just flashed, held a name of a defendant for their judgment. Jay caught up and walked with him.

Wendell turned and faced Jay. "Got one to pass on. Name is Kenny. Kenny Humphrey. He got popped for a bank job where civilians were dropped. He ratted on his partner to get outta the chair or becomin' a lifer. He ended up gettin' a ten-spot. He's just now comin' through the fish tank. Supposed to be here next week. I personally don't think he ought to see his second week here. You?"

"I wanna hear more 'fore I cast a ballot, but I don't take kind to snitches. How many civilians got dropped? Any kids or women?"

Wendell paused in his tracks. "A mom and her two kids. Story is, it wasn't Kenny that did the triggers. He'd been the vault guy, but snitches are bitches. Shouldn't be no questions on this one. You turn—you burn."

Jay began walking again, leaning in closer when they walked by occupied cells. "Well, run it through and see if we need the SS to break the tie." The two bumped the tops of their wrists together in agreement and Wendell continued down the line.

Jay turned back around and returned to his crib. It was about time for Lyle to do the nightly meet before lock-up. Jay stepped back into his cell and sat on his cot. It's Friday and he'd been ready for his weekly meet with Amy Jo, who was his one bright spot who took him away from the rigid routine of living in this damned glass house. Thoughts of her gave him time to steal away from the daily grind of prison life.

"Hey, Jay..." Lyle stepped in quietly, instead of his typical waltz. "...word is you might be goin' soft. We can't have the man who came up with the game goin' all spongy with pity on defendants. Is the pretty little reporter bitch gettin' into your head?"

"Kiss my ass, Lyle. We gotta pick and choose our defendants. We can't kill 'em all. The dogs are only gonna look the other way so many times. You think they haven't figured us out yet?" Jay guffawed. "We can't go rookie, or it's done. Fuckin' Wendell is just grabbin' and stabbin' and that shit won't keep flushin'. We gotta' be smart." Jay pointed to his noggin. "Rome was killed in only half a century, even though it took a thousand years to build! You get my point?"

"I don't need schooling about Rome, it ain't got nothin' to do with the Mason jar. I'm worried about you. That's all I'm sayin'. We made this machine our skill. This machine needs to keep poundin' away."

Jay stretched his body and then slid back on the cot and leaned against the cement wall. "Wendy is callin' out cons who haven't even made it through the fish tank. What the hell's up with that? There's plenty of rotten fish right here already landin' outta water."

Lyle walked over and leaned in close to Jay. "I'm just sayin' I hope you don't let the reporter bitch make you a soft sponge. We don't need it." Lyle pulled back and stood straight.

"You threatenin' me now? Don't forget you'd still be a tall tadpole outta water, splunkin' basketball with the blackies if I hadn't introduced you to the game. Don't fuckin' tell me how to run it. That's all I'm sayin'."

"Ain't no one single one of us king here, Jay."

"That's right—nobody, the same shit flows all way's around." Jay's temple veins were beginning to thicken and pulsate.

Lyle surely noticed Jay's blood stewing before he turned and headed out through the opening. "Catch ya later, Jay." He waltzed out much shorter than he crawled in.

Jay relaxed a minute and thought again about his meetings with Amy Jo. *Is Lyle right about my turning soft since I've been meeting with her? And if I am, what business is it of his. Maybe I'm growing tired of the whole "judgment game."*

LIGHTS OUT IN TEN sounded over the speakers.

The bosses came through soon. Jay stripped down and slid under the sheet. The quicker he fell asleep, the sooner tomorrow would come. It seemed like less than ten before the doors squeaked and clanked as they slid into to the closed and locked position. The end of another day in paradise.

11

The drive between my grandparent's farm and Lake Correctional afforded me both a wind-up period on my way to Clermont, as well as the unwinding time on the return trip. I never knew how either would play out until I sat in the seat rolling down the road. I liked to think both were times of reflection that would help me in the writing process. Time to fertilize my creativity in planting the thoughts that were needed to grow the words. Once the field is fertilized and planted, watering the garden, or the interview process with Billy Jay, is a necessary nurturing of my work to eventually harvest the crop, my book about Jay. My bounty when harvested would hopefully feed hungry minds wanting to fill their curiosity of what abuse can create. I didn't know if every author pictured their profession in the same way I do, a farmer of sorts, but I needed to take such abstract thoughts and mold the process into something I knew. My grandparents were farmers, so my experience kind of made me think like one. I came from the farm after being rescued from a life of abuse. Nowadays, my seeds are words and I plant them in rows or sentences, my acreage, paragraphs. My grandfather tilled his land and nurtured his gardens meticulously. I inherently do the same in what I cultivate. Grandmother always helped him in every way possible within her capabilities. The two of them weren't just farmers, they were the farm; I'm not just an author, my life is writing.

It's just me living in the home they built together so long ago, it seems like a lifetime since they've been gone. The fields and equipment now rented out to others who want to become part of the land as they were, but don't have the funds to own it. I searched long and found a family who seemed to fit well with my grandparent's point of views and lifestyle. I'm not sure if I chose them, or they chose me, but the deed is done. I rent it out for far less than I could if I were to accept the highest bid. My grandparents would never want me to pick dollars over compassion for the land or people. The two of them showed me over and over, by example, how Jesus expects us to live. I strive to continue the family tradition that they instilled; and one day maybe I'll find someone to carry this heritage on along-side me with children of our own. But for now, my writing is the crop I tend, and this specific piece of work I till nightly, is my true farm. I want it to produce the best yield possible, so I drive, and I reflect both to and from Clermont once every week and then come home to plant Billy Jay's and my discussions, or seeds, into thoughts on paper that eventually grow into chapters. My grandfather's truck I drive is my tractor, his memory my strength, Jay's story my produce. *Thank you, Lord for those who work in your name, for without those, there go I as Jay has travelled, a broken road leading nowhere but hell on earth and in the afterlife.*

***

"Good morning, Jay." I now understood the entire process of checking in and waiting for Jay to be brought down to our room from lock-up to be shackled and cuffed before we begin. Now instead of a formality, it seemed an almost unnecessary process. How in the world could someone ever break out of a prison like this? I realize after thinking about it, there have been recent incidents of escape from prisons throughout the country. News stories periodically run alerts on such events, but after seeing the razor wired fencing, guard towers with guns ready at the draw, electronically locked metal doors, cameras, and such—make it seem impossible. But yet it does still happen. Jay, however, seems resolved he will never see the outside of these walls, even content with the fact. I've heard though, most inmates incarcerated have only one true thought and job. That passion is to escape. Is Jay any different than most of the men he is tightly packaged together with?

"Been lookin' forward to seein' you Ms. Amy. The weeks seem to get longer each time." Jay smiled and while he seemed to be in a satisfactory mood, his demeanor felt more reserved than usual.

"You seem a little down today. Anything you want to share?" I asked almost knowing ahead of the question he would indeed begin sharing stories I could never imagine myself. I turned on the recorder because in the past, I'd missed the important conversations before we officially began.

"Seems some of the boys inside think I'm lettin' you make me soft."

"What do you think about the idea? Do you think it's true?" I asked.

Jay flashed me his devilish smile, which clued me in something unexpected would certainly be coming "down the pipes." A term he often used referring to his rebuttals. His way of warning me ahead of time.

"I think they're just jealous 'bout my time away. 'Course I tell 'em we sit and sip Coca Colas and eat bon bons while we chat." He grinned for a second. "I'd like to tell 'em you flash me shots of your lady parts while we talk—but I know better than to do that after callin' you 'somethin' purdy to look at.'" He grinned and let out a guffaw.

"You know I don't like the disrespectful talk, right? I suggest we move on to a conversation that doesn't show such a thing."

"I'm just funnin' Amy. Hell, give a con a break upon occasion."

He tilted his head as if humbling himself before he glanced back up at me. "I do respect you, Amy. You got grit and fire. I wouldn't want nobody else tellin' my story 'cept you. Serious though, Lyle Ruby give me a subtle threat yesterday about my going 'spongy' these days. A man surely ain't expected to stay hard forever. Even a cold-blooded killer like me gets tired just sittin' idle."

"I hate to break right into the interview stuff, but…" I reached over and positioned the recorder a little, "…I have a couple of questions I need your outlook on."

"I suppose you can just fire away when ready."

"I'm curious if there is anything you wish you would have done differently? You know, any serious regrets? We all certainly have at least a couple. I know I do."

"Well now, seems you've just opened up an opportunity for me to suggest I will tell you one of mine, and then you can reciplicate. I mean, uh, reciperacate. Well, hell…I reckon you know what I mean…I tell you; you tell me…." He wore frustration across his face for a moment.

"Reciprocate is the proper word, and I wasn't planning on doing that, but I imagine I would be game for it at least once." My answer elicited a smile on my face. I could feel it and noticed Jay did also.

Jay grinned like he'd won a hand in poker where the pot held handfuls of cash. "Well now, do I have regret…" He reached up and rubbed his chin while looking to the ceiling appearing as if he were thinking deep about the question. "…it's hard to just think of one 'Johnny on the spot' like this. When I think about what's been done to me through my life, makes it hard to feel remorse 'bout passin' it on. Makes me wonder if my daddy has regret for takin' all his frustrations out on my ass, if he's even alive." Jay smiled all the sudden, looking like the cat who ate the canary. Did he just think of a regret he thought I never would suspect to hear?

"I reckon I regret the day I was taken by surprise by those damn cops—you know, the one I killed and the other one who's still got it in for me..." Jay looked into my eyes. "I regret not grabbin' my good book of Ms. Cela's that sat on the table. I reckon it'd be good for me to be readin' 'bout Jesus again. Yep, not havin' my Bible. That'd be my first regret come to mind. Your turn, Ms. Amy."

"I didn't have any idea, Jay. This wasn't really my thought about regret, but I'm glad you wish you still had it. Do you want me to check and see about trying to find what happened to it and get it to you?"

"I sure do miss it. I was readin' regular in it before. That'd be real nice of you, Ms. Amy." Jay smiled. "Now, back to your regret...."

"Hmmm, I have a big regret. I imagine if I tell you, you'd never have seen it coming."

"What do you mean '*if*' you tell me? I told you—you tell me. Your turn. That's how this 'reciperication' works." He smiled as if he knew he'd mis-pronounced the word again.

"Okay, Jay. The regret that immediately pops into my head concerns my father..." I felt my heart pounding as I searched for the right way or words. "...I regret the first time I remember my dad abusing me, um, sexually..." This is more uncomfortable than I imagined. "I...uh...I wish I would have...have had the guts...to...to tell him it was...it was...wrong...what he was do...doing to me." My eyes were wet instantly. My face and ears red-hot. It's like I could picture my daddy right this minute—sitting right where Jay sat. "...or at least I...wish...I'd have kicked him where I now know it would drop him like a log in the mud and leave him squirming like a pig."

Jay's face looked still and frozen. Almost looking like he was dead. I couldn't imagine how someone so used to the ice residing in his heart, could suddenly look cold with sadness or compassion. Surely not from my words, I thought. Certainly, he wasn't feeling compassion for me.

"Ms. Amy, I'd kill that son-of-a-bitch for you if I could. A young child don't deserve harm from their father or nobody else." He sat and looked at me without moving even an eyelid blinking. "I believe your dad to be a rabid wolverine too."

Silence settled in between us for several seconds. To buy time, I moved my head around scanning the room noticing the dust clinging to the walls and the dirty wax built up where the walls met the floors. I thought to myself...*what a filthy place when you look at it closely. Our world replicates this room to a "t."* I looked up at Jay and the question popped inside my head and exited through my lips before I took the brief seconds to ponder its outcome. "Jay— you stated a couple of weeks ago you were a rabid wolverine like your father. Is a wolverine one who thrives on abusing others? Is this the kind of wolverine you are too?" I paused, feeling the physical and mental pain I endured from my daddy more than once or twice. It'd been a lifetime since I'd even laid eyes on him, but it felt like yesterday in this moment today. I struggled to ask the question, but I felt inside I was being forced and had no choice in the matter. I must, so I struggled and spit it out, fearing I already knew deep down what his answer would be. "Have you ever raped little girls like my daddy raped me?"

Jay sat cold, deathly still...like a hunter waiting in the blind for his target to step clear from the trees for a clear shot. I watch his facial expressions and eyes closely. I see he feels my questioning stare upon him, yet calmness seems to encircle his demeanor. I always wonder when I'll cross the invisible line of "friendship" we share and enter the territory from pussycat to wolverine in his view. I know, of course, he would never see me as a viable opponent, but still, what statement or question will I ask that takes me from one side and adds me to the opposite? If he and I were just two friends sitting across from each other at a table in a park somewhere, how would our interactions differ? Would it change dramatically without large uniformed and trained prison personnel merely steps away to safeguard me? Awe, there lies the rub. It hit me like a freight train. All these weeks with Jay I sat listening to the horrible circumstances he'd dealt with his entire life up to now. And now, now I'd been easily sucked in. My compassion for humanity evolved into pity and sympathy. I'd befriended him, yet I couldn't really call him a friend. But did he do the same with me? Or am I either a play toy or sounding board where he could hear himself talk about his past? Relive it in some selfish act involving me. Is he really my friend in his own eyes? Or would he turn on me on a dime if I questioned his motives from across a table in the park instead of sitting placidly staring at me? Would he let his anger free and become the rabid wolverine, knowing there wouldn't be a knight in shining armor to come to my rescue? The silence inside this room was a crack of thunder in its own right, and then the storm broke wide open....

"Ms. Amy, gawd dammit, where'd that come from?" His words sliced through not only the silence, but like a razor-sharp blade into my thoughts. I shook my head back and forth quickly, again attempting to rattle the thoughts free from my brain, but they continued to boldly cling to the sides in the background, screaming bloody murder in voices only I could hear.

"Yes...yes...Jay?" The cloud lifting slowly from my internal reflections. I was certain I appeared rattled or shocked by his intrusion. "I'm still waiting for an answer, Jay. We've touched a nerve of mine and I need you to answer me honestly. I don't want games or lies..." I forced a sternness across my brow. "Have you done dark unthinkable things to young girls?"

"Ma'am—you're writing a book about a man who will never see the light of day outside these walls—ever again. Do you think I give a potter's damn about playin' games with you now? I murdered two cops and wounded another—I ain't ever gettin' outta here and I'm damned fine with it." Jay answered in a much less elevated tone and demeanor than I'd expected.

"You still haven't answered the question."

"Damnit, Missy, I'm gettin' to it. I'm layin' foundation here; you don't build a gawd damn house without a foundation and you don't admit to rapin' and murderin' young women without layin' a foundation of explanation."

My head dropped instantly. I knew today's session of interviewing would either be a lengthy one—meaning to strike while the iron is hot is best; or a short trip because my body and mind suddenly begged to cut and run. I felt one more realization in this moment. Jay *had* done dark, horrible things to young girls—and I now, more than likely, knew something no one else was cognizant of. I also momentarily displaced the similarity I'd once seen between him and my grandfather. A feeling burned inside like a friend stabbing me from behind, into my heart unknowingly—unexpectedly. A pain too sharp not to drop me to the ground fast, like a lightening flash.

Jay's head tremored slightly. His pupils seemed to dilate and his lips minutely quivered. He held a look of savvy—he knew I now suspected deeper secrets owned, but not yet ready for me to unearth. My body and mind felt disconnected from me. I felt disassociated to this entire moment. My head spun and my breathing felt rapid. I fought hard to keep my eyes from rolling up inside my head, but they refused my command and the movement proceeded against my will.

"Guards! Guards!" Jay pounded on the table-top and the sounds of metal clinking together were the last thing I remembered. The room became darker than any shade of black I've ever seen.

BANG.

12

The television screen went black for just a second before the "Breaking News" logo "popped" in bright red lettering, all caps. It just pissed Mary off when this happened. Her show Remington Steele went black smack dab in the middle of solving a crime. "Damnit!" She spoke loudly when Tom Willard began with his blah, blah, blah update. "Damn little town trying to play bigtime like Kansas City or St. Louis...."

"Tom Willard with Breaking News from Channel 10 News, Springfield, Missouri with a report. Police have discovered two women's bodies found on the property of a downtown area warehouse early this morning. Springfield police are asking anyone who may have seen something or has any information on these photographs of the two young women, found deceased, to please come forward." The first photo is of Sarah Marie Gaynor, daughter of Eldrich James and Elizabeth Anne Gaynor, Springfield's well-known, and recently deceased, founders and major shareholders of Gaynor Pharmaceuticals. The second picture is of Jaime Lynn Smith. Both young women were employed at The Alibi Room Cigar Bar, a recently opened business found to be owned under a shell company by none other than Sarah Gaynor. Further details will be released as this story evolves.

***

"Deaths of both women are listed suspicious. Elizabeth Anne Gaynor passed away five years ago remember? Unexpectedly from an overdose. Gaynor Pharmaceuticals has been under a cloud of controversy since the time of Elizabeth's death." Tom said to his producer, John Allen, about the breaking story. "Eldrich Gaynor died under suspicious circumstances eight months after the passing of his wife, a case that still remains unsolved. There's something different about this, John. I have a gut feeling. I saw one of the bags of evidence being handed over to a detective…" He looked down at his notebook. "…Detective Ray Gallum. It looked like a damned expensive wristwatch. I don't know, but I want to follow this closely."

John held his hands out in a manner of putting the brakes on. "We gotta wait, Tom. Get your horses lined up in the stall before you open the gates for the race. I know you're excited and so far, we have the jump on this story—but since the Gaynor family is involved—we need to take time. I can't let the studio be opened up for slander lawsuits or have the gawd damned police chief all up in my ass for letting evidence slip out, which could damage their investigation." He leaned in and reached to grab Tom's arm. "Slow and steady, work with the chief on this one."

"From the chatter I heard, John, the scene inside, along with the sidewalk next to the warehouse, appeared grizzly. The one who fell or whatever off the roof…the blood trail flowing from under the blue tarp said it all. It was a big friggin' tarp. Sarah's body was supposedly found naked in a 1936 Ford sedan."

"Stay on it, Tom, take the time you need to develop the story— the right way—not the tabloid way." John patted Tom's shoulder as he headed back into his office. "Oh, and good work, Tom."

13

"Son-of-a-bitch! You've got to be kidding me? Of course, we announced we were law enforcement! Sam was no rookie, and neither am I. Tony's neck began to glow red. "Clemency? Really? A guy can kill two police officers and wound another—get proven guilty by twelve jurors after sitting through all the bullshit the prosecutor presented..." Tony slammed his hand on his desk. "...then get sentenced to the fuckin' hot-seat to fry..." He pulled his badge from his waistband, slamming it into the waste can beside his desk. "...I quit, Chief...."

"Now, Tony—cool the hell down, this shit happens when big name defense attorneys go digging." Replied Randy Fennigan, or Chief Fenny, as he was known.

"No! Not gonna do it anymore. If that fuckin' governor grants clemency for that worthless piece-of-shit sociopath..." Tony stood up. "...then I'm gonna walk. It was a good shoot for us and criminal felony murder one for him, times two! Our only fault was me missing center mass with a finishing headshot! He heard us and knew who we were, hell, he was sittin' ready and fuckin' ambushed us. He'd just executed that damned sheriff hours before and he didn't think we'd come to question him? Bullshit, Fenny!" Tony stood, his chest puffed out and veins bulging from his temples. "I lost my partner and best friend to that SOB, and Sam's family lost a father and husband. And he's gonna escape frying? Twelve damned jurors spent over two weeks listening to his lawyer's BS. It's over, he was found guilty, Fenny. Done. I'm just waiting to see his ears smoke and eyeballs explode for what he did to Sam and his family…" Tony fell back into his chair. "I…I shoulda' been at that front door…not…not…Sam…I got no kids to support."

Chief Fenny bent over the desk and leaned into Tony's space, face to face, eye to eye. "This is where we dig the hell in, Tony. We search for more, we lift every gawd damned stone, and we knock at every frickin' door in this damn town…" Fenny put his hand on Tony's shoulder and squeezed. "We find another way, a guy like this piece of shit, has more to hide somewhere, you were already on some trails…" Fenny let go and bent over grabbing Tony's badge from the trash. He buffed it against his shirt removing the dust and restoring some shine back into the front before carefully laying it on the desk under Tony's face. "I can't let you give this back—the job ain't done yet, it's just a glitch in the path getting' there. I trust you'll get back on track." He reached back over and patted his shoulder a couple of times. "Trish and Clint are counting on it. Sam wouldn't want you to give up and quit. His boy deserves a dad who died a hero with no question. You can give that to him." He gave Tony two more quick pats on the shoulder and then turned to head back into his office across the room.

Tony shook his head back and forth in disbelief of being caught not knowing for certain if they did announce who they were. "Damnit!" He hit the table again and then reached for his badge, staring at it, still shaking his head. "Sam, I'm not gonna let him get away buddy, if it's the last thing I ever do, I'll watch that fuckin' devil burn, and I won't sleep 'til I smell the stink of rotten bacon in the air…" He got up and tucked his badge back into his waistband. "…I promise, Sam."

14

It'd been months since he'd gotten talked back into staying on and reworking the Cader case. Several times he'd felt close to new evidence on the missing girls only to have things fall through. The phone rang and Tony picked up his extension, immediately reacting to the conversation heard on the other end. "Hank, get in here, buddy, we need to head out to the Bullinger's farm. ASAP!"

"What's up?" Hank asked.

Vertis found something this morning he says we've got to see. He said his wife will never be the same. She's been in the bathroom getting sick and bawling her head off ever since."

"What the hell does that mean?" Hank questioned.

"Vertis wasn't specific, but he said we'd definitely want to see what he's stumbled onto. He said to be prepared with some Vic's vapor rub, because we'd need it…" Tony glanced up to his partner. "…sounds to me like we may have gotten our break, but too late. Gonna be some sad relatives if I'm correct."

"That's probably the news, I bet, but sounds like it's no time to stop for breakfast on the way out either."

"Hank, do you always think of your stomach first?"

"Yep." Hank chuckled as he holstered his weapon and tucked his leather badge wallet into his waistband. "Let's roll, partner."

"You may wanna hit Micky Dee's before we leave Panama City, not much to eat on the hour and a half between. I need coffee anyway, something to wake me up other than this nasty crap."

Tony laughed while he shoved the coffee pot containing a thick black liquid back on the hot pad. "The only thing makes it coffee is the fact it's in this coffee pot, but the consistency is more like well-used engine oil containing grit collecting at the bottom. Sometimes I wonder if vehicle maintenance doesn't leave their old oil here to warm it up enough to pour it back into our squad cars!"

Without even a snicker to answer Tony's assertation of the coffee dilemma, Hank shot back, "I'm not buying a breakfast I'm just gonna lose before lunch. No point in it. I'm too damn practical for it!"

"Practical, huh? Sounds like the new nice way of stating you're a tight ass. If it's your way of sayin' buy me breakfast—it ain't gonna work. Don't forget your damned wallet in your top drawer this time either. We may want lunch before we head back."

"I have a feeling I won't be eating breakfast, lunch, or dinner tonight. My stomach is already queasy since I heard 'bring the Vic's.' Pretty much ruined my appetite for the day." Hank let out a guffaw.

An hour and a half later they found themselves pulling up a long gravel drive to a small white farmhouse sitting just beyond an old shop building to the right. There sat an older gentleman now standing up off the front porch rocker. He looked weathered in appearance while he began to make the short walk to Tony's unmarked Buick. One strap of his overalls unhooked and dangling, it flopped with each step. The stained t-shirt he wore looked like it hadn't been any shade close to white for years.

"Y'all must be the ole boys from the state po-lice?" Vertis asked after he pushed the brim of his straw work hat up, which previously covered his face. He dug a hanky from his pocket and wiped it across his forehead while he stood and faced them. "'Leven in the mornin' and it's already got that sultry heat a cookin'. My pits is already smellin' like an old onion. I thought this damned summer be 'bout passed." He shook his head and tucked his sweat drenched hanky back in his pocket, then held out his hand to shake theirs.

"Hello Vertis. I'm Sgt. Tony Rawlings, this is my partner, Detective Hank Robbins..." Tony reached out and firmly shook Vertis' hand. "...so, I understand you made a discovery of sorts?"

"Yes sir, been quite a unexpected morning. I got up early and went out to my shop—there's a wood deck out behind it where I got me a cleanin' table for dressin' meat and such. Shot me a gall damned feral hog yesterday early evenin'. Damned pig been tearin' the shit outta my garden and I thought I'd cut him up into bacon and steaks 'fore it got too hot this mornin'. I had me a damned of a time pushin' the shop door out to get through it. Fuckin' door began to piss me the hell off! Bottom of the damn thing be catchin' on somethin' just past the door jam, so I kicked it like hell 'til I got her passed." Vertis motioned for them to walk with him to the shop. "Well, sure 'nuff once I got her open, I be damned if the deck boards weren't all pushed up like they's warped or somethin'. A couple of 'em popped up and it looked like cement slab or somethin' underneath. Musta' happened just a day or two at most. I swear that damned deck sat flatter than cow shit just the other mornin'! Looked like a gall damned cement tank of some kind. Musta' just floated up through the deck. Been here 'bout three years and never knew it existed. Scratched my head just wonderin' what the fuck it be for? Any fool knows in this Florida swamp land, ain't nothin' buried stays in the damned ground long." Vertis reached into the side of his unbuttoned and gaping overalls and stuck the hand Tony just shook earlier down in, scratched himself, then pulled it out and rubbed the sweat off his brow with his finger. "Got me a pry bar, an old axel from a '36 dodge truck, and I pried them damned boards up. You'll never guess what I found." They were about halfway to the shop, Vertis continued with his story.

"My ole lady brought me my cup a mornin' Joe and she said it looked like her daddy's old water cistern she grew up with.

Catchin' rainwater before indoor plumbin' I 'spose." Vertis stopped walking and leaned into Tony and Hank as if he held a secret he wanted to share. "Judy grew up white-trash. Outhouse out back, no 'lectricity, no runnin' water…" Vertis smiled and started toward the shop again. "…but she was purdier than a princess wantin' to fuck any farmer willin' to get her outta dodge. I snatched her up while the gettin' be good! She never washed real regular, cause no runnin' water and what not, but I learned to love the scent of a salty woman, you know what I mean? Hell, ifn' her smell got too stout, I'd just bury my nose in the pillow real deep 'til I got done what needed gettin' done…" Vertis punched Hank's arm and smiled again larger than before. Sure enough, he only owned six or seven teeth between his upper and lower jaw. Vertis continued his talking, "…well, while the misses still stood there on the back deck and all, I slid the metal lid open on the top the tank, and shit, the smell 'bout knocked me back off my damned feet, but I poked my head down in for a second and saw what looked to be blue plastic barrels inside. Pert near filled the bottom of the tank. Seven of 'em, nestled tight together. Old wood ladder standing up in 'bout the only open spot between."

Tony looked at Hank after hearing Vertis tell them the number of barrels. Hank nodded back and mouthed the number—seven.

Vertis led them around to the side door and opened it up to the sight of a feral hog hoisted upside down from a rope. The rope ran through a pulley, which was hung off a ceiling rafter. He'd been gutted, a bucket of blood underneath him, some splattered and spilled around. A second bucket sat near the first, but full of organs and intestines. Flies buzzed around it, landing, and then taking back off in a frenzy with the multitude of others, back and forth between those two barrels and the opening in the carcass. They paused at the door sitting partially open. Vertis held his hand on the door and continued his story. "I asked Judy to go fetch me some Vic's VapoRub—you know, from "Hill Street Blues," I remembered cops pokin' it into their noses to help kill the smell a death." Vertis grabbed the blue container of it from the shelf, opening it and then applying a finger full under his nose, again with the same finger he'd scratched himself with, before he passed it to Tony. "Anyway, after she came back, she watched me climb down into that tank and I unsnapped a retainer latch on one of them barrels and popped it open. The smell instantly filled that tiny area I stood in, and I puked. My guts dang near wouldn't stop retchin'. I took a gander inside between times of pukin' and well— I'll just let you see what my wife and I saw, then we'll do some talkin' bout it. I guarantee you won't stay in there long." He forced the door past the tall part of the decking and looked back at the two officers. "Better smear that there VapoRub cream on thick. If'n ya don't, you'll be wishin' you hadda'. That there smell pert near knock a damn buzzard off the fuckin' gut wagon, real quick like."

<u>15</u>

Tony wore a thick clump of clear Vic's, partially poked up inside each nostril. Hank smeared some also poking it deep into his nasal canals as he hovered above the cistern opening. Hank pointed his flashlight into the darkness while Tony worked his way down each wooden rung on the unsteady ladder. He stepped over on the top of one of the barrels and retrieved his flashlight from his back pocket. Flipping it on, he shined it around the large, dank room, which held the seven containers. He led the beam of light over to the open barrel beside him before turning and leading the light-beam to its contents. "Oh, my Lord...."

    Standing above and peering in, Hank saw Tony retching and the sound echoed throughout the enclosure before rising upward and exiting through the opening. Hank pointed his light into the barrel opening while Tony bent over and began violently tossing cookies. Inside the blue barrel bore a sight he instantly knew he would never be able to unsee, along with the probability the other six barrels more than likely contained variations of the same thing. Twisted and broken bones with gooey skin dripping down until it reached the pool of God knows what liquid it contained in the mixture. He couldn't imagine how horrible it would have been to live through what these girls lived through before being broken and bent into the shape they were forced to fit inside. Although Hank hadn't practiced his normal routine of eating breakfast, He knew his system well enough to know exactly what was about to happen.

He quickly stood up and ran to the edge of the deck where the grass grew tall against it. After uncovering his mouth, he heaved and let what little bile rushed up, shoot from his mouth and into the tall grass. It wasn't but seconds later Tony stood leaning over the deck edge himself, doing the same thing. Vertis stood at the doorway with a look of familiarity of their experience.

Tony wiped the liquid splatter from his mouth and turned to Hank. "That sick son-of-a-bitch. Words will never explain the hate I feel inside me and the wrath I want to lavish on the demonic piece of shit."

Hank continued to hang over the ledge spitting what bile remained in his mouth. "Don't make me go back over there…" He wiped his arm across his mouth and then spit one more time. "I can't imagine what those poor girls went through. Nobody deserves to end up like this. How does anyone even do it?"

"A gall damned monster does that shit. Ain't no human does it, be for dang sure. Monster such as him needs his damn head blown off." Vertis called out from the doorway. "I'd be damned proud to hang his balls above my front door. Is the sombitch still loose? Cause I'll help ya hunt him down and deal some swamp justice! I know how ta keep my mouth shut too."

Tony turned and lifted himself off his knees. He looked at Vertis. "He's locked up tighter-n-a fish's ass, Vertis. Damn good thing too, sounds like." He turned and slapped Hank on his back as he looked back at Vertis, still leaning on the door, a cane now clutched in his hand. "Let's go see how your misses is doing."

"Ever what ya want, Sarge, she be a tough ole bird, but seein' and smellin' that barrel a stew—I reckon she be feedin' me suppers of the garden variety quite a while now." He looked up and winked at Tony. "You know, no meat and all. Kinda' stole the thunder a finishin' up that hog."

Tony glanced away to avoid continuing the conversation and then back at Hank. He hollered out before heading through the shop door. "Call in the forensics team—sure as shit ain't enough Vic's to get me to dig those barrels up and look 'em over."

Vertis and Tony began to walk away with Vertis pointing with his cane at different things that blended into the scenery. Hank watched a moment wondering when Vertis pulled the walking cane out and why. He obviously didn't need it to assist his mobility. He laughed briefly to himself and then Hank hollered out of nowhere, "We got him. Fucker's gonna dance the electric waltz now for sure—right?"

16

A clinical odor overwhelmed me. I wasn't cognizant of where I was, but it felt like a hospital room. *Why would I be in a hospital?* Blurs of starkness between black and white moved around me mixing. The images caused me to strain my focus on the movements. Why did my head hurt so much? *Was I involved in a wreck?* My forehead pounded as I tried to lift my hand from my side to rub my temples. My vision blurred, and I felt the pulse of my heart throughout my entire body. My fingers throbbed. All I could think was—*why was I overthinking every movement I tried to make?* The blackness other than the white blurry shapes moving about in front of me were all I could contemplate. I held no idea where I just came from. Not a clue of what happened even twenty seconds ago when my thoughts came up with—this notion. My words tangled together inside my thoughts and the idea I may be crazy entered into the jumble. *What was I supposed to do now?*

A sudden warmth enveloped me like the family wool blanket my grandmother used to cover me up with when I was young and scared. All cozy underneath. Only the top of my head from my nose up was exposed while my frown always became a smile underneath where no one could see it. And all of this with the mere sight of her warm glowing eyes. Grandmother's eyes sparkled. They always did. My grandmother's smile was mesmerizing, and I always felt the love inside of her before I ever saw her face. Her love entered and filled any room she walked into before one could physically see her. *I always assumed it was magic, at least it's the way she always made me feel.* This unexplainable wizardry was all I could now understand or make heads or tails from. *I know I'm trying to explain it, but there are no words, and the foggy haze makes it difficult to keep track of my thoughts....*

***

"Dr. Kaye, I have a pulse but it's very weak."

"Nurse—she's suffered a syncope episode...." Dr. Kaye stated as he moved his stethoscope to different areas of my chest and sides.

"She'll be okay. She's fortunate she was seated when she fainted, and her head only fell to the tabletop. She'll probably have a small hematoma at the anterior wall of the neurocranium."

I hear sounds but they fade in and out. Concern is a feeling I'm suddenly aware of. It feels as if I'm straining to decipher the sounds creeping into my mind. I can't seem to find a switch to turn off these flashes of thought...*My breathing feels as if with every breath I inhale, my altitude rises. I feel...I...see...I...I...I see Grandfather...He's ...he's...the clouds are so thick...my stomach is floating, Grandfather...I'm okay though...I'm trying to fight it.*

"Amy, breathe, baby-doll...Grandfather's right here, you're not alone baby-doll...you're never alone...sweet-heart. Grandmother and I are always watching over you...."

I suddenly felt warm. My body surged. I saw silhouettes above me moving around in slow motion. *My focus...dammit...why couldn't I see through the foggy shadows?*

Waves of...of...of life surged throughout my being. Everything in this moment...changed everything. I suddenly felt aware again. *Where was I just seconds ago?*

Like a trampling herd of buffalo causing the earth to rumble...my consciousness was instantly reborn. A bright light shined upon me. So, blinding, I wanted it shielded. My eyes ached. "Where's Jay? Jay!" I screamed at the top of my lungs. I wasn't sure exactly why I felt the surge inside me so powerful and overtaking, but I felt as if I were failing a mission and lost my charge. "Jay." I called out again without realizing why. "Jay! Billy Jay!"

***

"Amy Jo. That's right…look over here. Focus on me, come on…that's right…." The nurse looked to the doctor and replied, "Doctor…she's regaining cognizance." The nurse held the flashlight to my eyes and then pulled it back away. *I jerked. I know I did.*

"Ms. Whitenhour, you're okay, honey. Doctor Kaye is here and I'm Nurse Stratton, you're gonna be fine."

"Where…I…what hap…happened? I…I…Jay? Where is…Jay…?"

"Mr. Cader is back in lockup ma'am. You blacked out, but you're in our clinic here inside Lake Correctional and you're gonna be fine, honey."

"I was…interviewing…um…interviewing Jay…."

"Yes, Ms. Whitenhour, you must have either been under some stress or maybe sleep deprivation? Anyway, your head dropped onto the tabletop when you fainted, so you're gonna have a headache and we'll want to keep you here for observation. You're gonna be fine though."

"Can I continue to interview…um…."

"I'm sorry Ms. Whitenhour, but Mr. Cader has been returned to his housing unit and once Warden Wilkerson reviews this incident, he'll decide when your interviews can continue."

"When they can continue? Jay didn't do anything to cause me to…you know…to…pass out…or…or whatever you're saying…happened."

"Don't worry about any of that now. Don't put the plow before the mule." Nurse Stratton smiled and touched her hand. "They know how important this is to you, I'm sure."

***

The drive home was totally different than all the others I'd endured. It was late when I was finally allowed to leave. I was afraid I would be kept overnight. I told the doctor and nurse I was fine and would take it slow. Sitting and watching the white dashes roll underneath me felt almost hypnotizing. I fought the temptation to watch them by moving my head constantly, not focusing too long on one thing as I tried to replay what Jay said before I apparently blacked out. I glanced at the recorder lying on the passenger seat. I reached over and hit rewind for several seconds and then hit play, so I could hear from Jay's mouth what words he'd said moments before.

"Seems some of the boys inside think I'm lettin' you make me soft."

"What do you think about the idea? Do you think it's true?"

"I think they're just jealous 'bout my time away. 'Course I tell 'em we sit and sip Coca Colas and eat bon bons while we chat. I'd like to tell 'em you flash me shots of your lady parts while we talk—but I know better than to do that after callin' you 'somethin' purdy to look at.'"

"You know I don't like disrespectful talk, right? I suggest we move on to a conversation that doesn't show such a thing."

"I'm just funnin' Amy. Hell, give a con a break upon occassion."

This didn't make sense to me. This is starting from the beginning of the conversation, just after I hit record. The tape should have been just seconds before the last thing said or what happened after I fainted? "Someone's messed with my recorder while I was out!" I said aloud as I pounded the steering wheel on the truck. "Warden Wilkerson, you son-of-a..." I choked my sentence down before I finished the expletive. It was almost as if my grandmother's hand reached across the table quickly covered my mouth. A smile crept across my lips for a moment before the nurse's words popped back into my thoughts. "Warden Wilkerson will review the incident and then let you know when the interviews can resume...." I spoke her words aloud as if I were telling my grandfather what transpired this day. My grip tightened the wheel of the truck so tightly, my fingers began to cramp. Anger filled my thoughts as well as invasion of my privacy, my property. "You'll not shut me down or censor my work, Warden Wilkerson!" *I may need an attorney if they try to keep me away.* I reached for the radio and turned the volume knob slowly to the right until I heard .38 Special's hit, "Hold on Loosely." I couldn't help but sing the chorus at the top of my lungs as I steered Grandfather's truck down the interstate, windows open, sun dropping towards the horizon. I always loved this time of evening when the sun was about to extinguish itself into the ocean's waters. "...if you cling too tightly, you're gonna lose control..." Grandfather would have been singing along with me, and for just one crazy moment, I swore I heard his deep voice loud enough in my ear, it caused me to glance over to see if he was sitting there twisting his shoulders to the beat and stomping his foot. Again, I realized just how fortunate my life was and the reason why. I felt the tear carrying the sorrow, which instantly welled up in my heart from missing him; it gently rolled down my cheek and found comfort somewhere on my shirt collar. My smile returned across my face as if he gently patted my shoulder, giving me strength when I felt weak. Like he always did. *I love you, Grandfather. Thank you for all you gave up putting me first in your life. You're still my rock.* The sparkle of my grandmother's eyes gave me goosebumps of loving joy and suddenly, the rest of the drive home felt right.

17

Georgie stood looking out toward the front gate from inside her screen-door. I noticed her the minute the truck headlights shone across the home of the family who now farmed Grandfather's land. She was the daughter of Juan and Marcia Rovaria, the wonderful couple I'd found to rent the fields out to be planted and managed almost six months ago. It was their farmland now and they were strong and persistent in working it.

Georgie Anne Rovaria was beautiful and wore deep, dark hair she kept short like mine. Many who saw us together swore we could be sisters. We practically were, being about the same age and other than her skin tone slightly a deeper coffee color, I suppose we did look a lot alike. I was perfectly happy with it, because she was gorgeous to me. And so warm. Such a smile she always wore; it was contagious and could turn anyone's rough day upside down and into a warm, happy finish. She'd turned my mood many times, especially lately. I shared about every thought I owned with her. Billy Jay included. She now knew him almost as well as I, even though she'd never seen anything but pictures on the newspapers or television. I remember the first day when I told her I was going to interview a killer and what followed in her voice. She'd said to me, "Oh, Amy Jo, why would you put yourself in such an awful place? From everything people say—and those scary eyes—please don't put yourself through that...."

I, of course, didn't listen and as I shared different conversations he told me, her compassionate side awakened also. Her feelings of course, more hesitant. Georgie would wait by the door just like tonight, to hear more of his story. And I loved her for it. She now waited almost every week on bated breath for me to talk about my and Billy Jay's conversations and what he'd revealed. I knew from the first time Georgie, and I talked, God put the decision for me to rent our farmland to her family for this reason. I needed a true friend like Georgie, to share my thoughts and wants in this world. I'd been completely alone too long since my grandparents passed. Georgie was my gift I didn't even know I wanted or needed. *Thank you, Lord, for those serendipitous miracles you provide* us, *even without the asking.* I slowly pulled the truck up to the carport and opened the door.

"Amy Jo! Where have you been?" Georgie was standing beside the truck before I even pulled to a stop. "I've been worried about you."

She hugged me so unexpectedly and tight, I nearly dropped my tape recorder and notebook, yet my grin remained wide and loving. "I'm fine, Georgie, really. It was just a long day and if you like—you're welcome to follow me in, and we'll talk—maybe even have some wine.

"I wouldn't take anything else but! Seriously, you are hours past your normal time of getting back. I was about to call the police and put out a search...."

"At least twenty-four hours missing, Georgie. That is what the police would need to call it a missing-persons case, and I'm nowhere near that; but thank you for caring about me, just no need to worry so easily. I'm a big girl!"

The entryway shined brightly because I always left the porchlights burning. Day and night. It's the way my grandparents left the place. "Gotta' leave the lights on, so a visitor or someone in need can easily find the door..." Both grandparents would repeat almost word for word when I'd accidently turn them off.

They always whispered to me before bed. *Jesus is the light, always walk toward the light little Miss Amy Jo.*

"Why are you so late tonight?" Georgie asked.

I tried not to give her my look of worry, but she being such a close friend, spotted the frazzled look in my eyes immediately. I still replied, "Oh, nothing," just to attempt calming her enough and possibly keeping her satisfied as not to dive in immediately on the events of the day. "I need to pour a full glass of wine first, Georgie; then I'll tell you all about it."

Reaching for the refrigerator, I opened the door and leaned in so I could see the brightly lit interior. The bright bulb exposed nothing but two bottles of wine, an outdated package of turkey, and an assortment of condiments and such. I scooted a half empty bottle of pickles, and slid relishes, and a very old looking jar of mayo from my way and grabbed the closest bottle of Moscato. I slowly closed the door after snatching it firmly in my grasp. Life's blood, I thought to myself tonight. Again, my thirst to be relaxed overtook my hunger for food and nourishment.

"You should come eat with us; you know Momma is worried about you. You eat like a bird, your refrigerator tells on you, Amy Jo."

I rolled my eyes and caught myself in a smile. Grandmother always accused me of the eyeroll when I didn't like what I heard but knew it to be true. I handed Georgie her favorite wine glass from the cabinet. The base of the glass was wrapped with a small flip-flop and Georgie's eyes gleamed as I continued, "You gonna preach at me about my lack of good meal choices—or enjoy drinking my dinner with me tonight?" Georgie quickly made her choice by taking the glass. I imagined she was just indulging me so I would continue to fill her in on my day.

"This time, Amy Jo, you win the battle, but I'm not quitting the war of trying to keep you healthy." She giggled and in this instant the light caught her eyes reflecting her beautiful brown iris' making them glisten. Warmth flooded my insides as if I'd swallowed the finest, smoothest, mellowed whiskey, warm all the way down into my belly.

"You know you're gorgeous, Georgie, why do you waste your beauty here on the farm trying to save me instead of chasing surfer boys on Cocoa Beach?"

Georgie paused as she held her glass up to be filled with the bubbly blueberry white liquid. "Because you need saving, Amy Jo." After her glass was filled, she waited until mine reached the top with the fragrant fruit-filled drink and lightly bumped her glass into the one I held up to meet. Georgie spoke her toast in her wonderful accent I'd grown to love hearing. "Here's to saving the best 'til last and the last until gone."

TING.

Music to my ears, both the sound of crystal bumping together in unison and the way her words rolled smoothly off her tongue. *I suppose if she were a man, I'd have fallen in love six months ago when I saw her silhouette dressed in her straw hat and blue-jean shorts as she directed the moving company where to put the furniture from their truck. But at least I gained a confidant and life-long friend. After all, girls are supposed to fall in love with boys.*

18

Gina woke up feeling odd. She'd been waking up sick and then sometimes craving things she normally would never want. She also woke up with a dark question each morning, which needed attending. She needed an excuse though. She didn't want it to worry Ben and she certainly didn't want him to go with her. She suddenly remembered Ben asked to have Jay's Bible. The one Ms. Cela gave him. His concern being Jay would eventually want it and the officer just couldn't turn Ben's somber look away. "What could a Bible hurt, right Mr. Dane?" Questioned the young officer when he handed it to him. *Where could he have put it though? If I can find it, I'm just doing the "right" thing.* The next thing Gina would need to think about, if she found it, was how would she get away with being gone? She remembered Clermont being about five or six hours away. *I could be honest and offer to take the Bible and see how Jay is doing. Hmmm, or could I say I needed shopping time. Think Gina*, she said to herself, knowing no matter what, she couldn't afford to hurt Ben another time. She looked down at her belly and wondered again if it were Ben's…or…. A moment later she was drawn to peer through the large window and over the bay before turning her sight upward toward the billowy clouds. Gina dropped her head, then closed her eyes and began to do something she'd not done in quite a while. Gina prayed a prayer filled with her need of guidance in the decisions she faced, to help her make the choice she should.

***

Darrell walked in through the front door of the Big Apple on the Bay, Ben and Gina's newly opened restaurant and hot evening spot of Apalachicola. The place looked incredible, and he knew he was close to having a new reason for celebration. He should bring Mitz to dinner here. The back bank of windows facing the open bay caught his attention and drew him in. He heard sounds of people talking in what he assumed to be the kitchen to the right, but he continued toward the tables next to the wall of windows. "Yes, this table is the one I want to reserve—Mitz will love it. Just need to get a sitter for Katie…."

"Yes, on both accounts, Darrell!" Ben saw Darrell come in and apparently snuck up on him. Darrell about jumped a foot straight up.

"Damn…" Darrell caught his tongue quickly. "…I mean wow, Mr. Dane, you caught me off-guard."

Ben laughed. "Apparently so, my wife accuses me all the time of being a 'sidler' whatever the hell that is! I'm sorry if I took off a couple years off your life. I need to work on being louder on my approach."

"This place is spectacular! What a view, Mr. Dane."

"Darrell, it's Ben to you, and I'm glad you came today. I'm assuming it's with the wife's blessing?"

"Yes, sir. She is as excited as I am. She told me there is no way I should pass up such a gracious opportunity. I agree sir…um…Ben."

"Sounds better already, Darrell. Let me show you around and then we'll head into the office to get the paperwork, insurance, and all that necessary stuff done." Ben pointed in the direction of where Darrell assumed moments ago was the kitchen and he followed Ben's lead, remaining side by side. "So, I overheard your conversation..." Darrell looked mildly bewildered as Ben smiled and continued, "about making reservations for a specific table, but needing a sitter."

"Oh, yeah. Just daydreaming out loud." Darrell smiled.

"I imagine we could work things out. Afterall, you and your family have something to celebrate, and my wife and I could use some time with a little sweetheart like yours to help get us in shape with what's...I mean...who's on the way for us!"

"It's a bit of a shocker at first, sir, but I wouldn't trade either for all the money in the world. My life has definitely never been better!"

"I'm glad to hear it Darrell, no one deserves it more than you and Mitzi. I'm glad everything worked out and happiness stepped in. I share many of the same feelings. My life was a mess not too long ago. Hoping to maybe see you and your family on some Sundays at Reverend Gabriel's. Food for the soul because food for the body doesn't keep all our needs in check, if you know what I mean?"

"Yes sir, I do. I've been gone far too long. Thank you for reminding me. I have many reasons to give thanks and a few miracles to ask for too."

Ben showed Darrell around and after sitting down in his office, began to talk over what some of his responsibilities would be. Ben left him filling out paperwork while he tracked Gina down to see about babysitting tonight and reserving Darrell's table he'd picked out. "Gina, I want to give them the royal treatment tonight. You know, show them exactly how we can treat our guests."

"Perfect, Benny! And we get to watch sweet little Katie! I can watch how great of a dad you're gonna be pretty soon."

Ben hated when his brother called him Benny, but he'd grown to almost love hearing it from Gina's lips. He was glad to see her smiling again.

***

Joyce picked up the tab along with the piece of paper. She turned it over and saw a note that read: **(850)777-2228, CALL ME…anytime, day or night. Cali.** Mitzi looked across the table with questioning eyes. "Yes, Mitzi B, it's Cali's phone number. She turned it so her daughter could see the bold all capital letters that spelled out **CALL ME**.

"I hate to say I told you so, mom, but…."

"As much as I hate to say—when I do call and meet with her—I want you there, little missy."

"Indeed, Momma, yes indeed." She looked at her mom with sad eyes that were still mixing with the eyes that said, I knew it all along."

19

Ethan knew his world was changing. He'd decided to circle back home a couple of hours after he knew Joyce left and contemplate exactly what to do. It was only eleven in the morning but a tall glass of bourbon and ice called out desperately to him, and who was he to deny such a call? Filling the tall crystal glass with ice, he pulled a special bottle from the cabinet. A bourbon he'd saved back for special occasions and while this was no moment of glee or celebration, it was one that demanded the best. His brain along with his tastebuds needed to be roused with something other than the normal. He needed to think outside the box, so he needed the persuasion of a drink familiar but of a different savor. Blanton's single barrel black edition, which for some reason was only marketed for Japanese sales and consumption. He'd been served the smooth libation while over in Tokyo ten years ago on a defense law seminar and brought back a bottle. This was the occasion he'd now decided to crack the cork and pour. A double wouldn't do this late morning, so he filled it to the brim and carried it out to his chair on the deck. The chair he'd spent many hours planning his future and watching the gulf coast's best waves splash up the shoreline before retreating out into the salty vastness.

    Lifting the drink to his nose, Ethan took in its mossy scent before lowering the glass to his lips and sipping in its smooth rich flavor. He closed his eyes a moment and rested his head against the back of his chair. He attempted to shut all sounds from the environment from his consciousness, except the crash of each band of waves. Ethan's tensed shoulders dropped as his muscles released the tautness, they'd held seconds ago. The damp saltiness of the ocean filled his nose overtaking the caramel and oak smell that was just nestling in. The mixing of senses, from the chair in which he sat, was at present worth every minute of courtroom time he'd spent arguing his cases over the years. All the sweat and hours hovering over law books had brought him here to this exact point in his life where it all paid off. *And now...it was all on the fucking line. Would I be held accountable for everything I'd done to get here? So many years and details to align my life to overcome and build this personal Shangri-la...just to have it come crashing down on me now....* Eyes still closed, the glass of liquid relaxation found its way back to his lips and he swallowed a large gulp, bypassing the slow roll across his tongue to titillate the flavor receptors. A second swallow followed shortly, and he never heard the front door open and then close, nor the light footsteps that tiptoed to the open sliding door to the deck where he sat.

"Joyce, beautiful angel of my past, now treasure of my present—I don't want to lose you, again, my dear. I've waited what feels like a lifetime to obtain your sweet flesh that embodies my every desire." He spoke the words above the ocean sounds, while his eyes remained dimmed to the light, imagining images of Joyce and he together in nothing but their shared nakedness. So many years ago, the first time, but then again just before that gawd damned trip to Springfield. The place where everything changed in one evening of drug induced memory loss. "What the fuck did you put in my drink Aisling? Why in the hell did I ever go to Springfield? Like I ever gave a fuck about Billy Jay Cader and what he thought he could do to me. Gawd dammit all. Gawd damn you Aisling and Jaime."

Joyce stood quietly at the door taking in every word spoken aloud. Her face showed shock to no one, as the only other person in the room had no idea, she was standing so close. As Ethan continued to lament aloud, Joyce turned and quietly tiptoed back out the front door and steered her Volvo down the long driveway not knowing where to go. Of course, her car seemed to know the path it should take, and she retraced that journey back to her daughter's home.

Meanwhile, Ethan, never aware Joyce stood hidden hearing the words he'd spoke out loud, continued to pontificate his woes of feeling his empire built on sex, lies, and selfishness begin to crumble before him. In the time it probably took her to drive home, he'd refilled his tall glass twice and remembered the new cable news network that just became available last year. *Maybe I would be able to track any new updates on the Springfield, Missouri case of the murdered women. I'll need to be careful and not let Joyce know I have it. Maybe I'll see if I can get a satellite installed on the office roof and only pipe it into my office?* It was indeed, the not knowing that was eating at him the most. *How can I make plans to avoid or defend, if I don't know what the status of the case is? I certainly mustn't travel back to Springfield. The criminal always returns to the scene of the crime, and now I understand why.*

He looked down to his wristwatch to see what time it was, before he realized yet again, his watch was missing. Another fact to ponder on. *I know I was wearing it at the bar that night.* With that thought, his mind began to journey back to the evening he now regretted. He started with asking the concierge where he could get a whiskey and a good cigar that evening and went from there. The ladies were beautiful and seemed intent on taking him home—the two of them. It reminded him of the days the beach house room was regularly used—the young girls stoned on grass and pills. Being able to have as many as he could keep up with. Ethan swirled his glass causing the ice to make the clinking sound, which seemed to send his daydream even deeper. Another long slow sip and his eyes began to fade from the gulf's horizon and dip back under his eyelids where the darkness beckoned him. Less than a minute later, his fingers lost their grip on the glass they clutched letting it slip and fall to the deck with a smash, the vessel shattered into tiny shards while never stirring him, as he sank ever deeper into the grip of his chair.

***

Aisling's eyes were mesmerizing. Her reddish auburn hair smelled of some faint spice he wasn't familiar with. His body jumped a bit for a moment. Suddenly remembering a glimpse of being with Jaime on the roof, her naked body leaning over the railing, him nestled against her tightly while she bumped and stirred like a mare craving the stallion, their bodies moving together in unison. Hear pumping the lifeblood through his veins in surges. Hormones and pheromones bringing on the feeling like high voltage electricity stimulating the neurons in his brain; the synapses firing wildly and uncontrollably. A stroke was certainly on its way to force this madness to an end.

"Oh, Charley, baby!" After her last cry of his name, he heard a fading scream as if she were running away, and then a thud followed by blackness. He'd found himself chilled and he stirred, reaching for the covers, but instead he lay naked on a hard surface, the moon shining down on him. What the hell was going on? He got up, and in the moon and star-filled sky, he saw his pants and shirt—shoes and socks on farther towards an open door. A memory of Aisling, or Sarah, popped into his head. Where was she? He threw on his pants and grabbed his shirt, then walked through the door calling out both names. Sporadic dance music filled with booming bass rhythms and electronic synthesized sounds pounded against the walls, floor, and rattled the glass throughout the window-filled room, which smelled of patchouli oil and pot. It vaguely reminded him of his beach house room of the past. The city lights filled the large space with a subdued glaze of dimly lit color swallowed by gray and black shadows. Ethan spied a clump on a leather chaise in the farthest corner of the room close to the bar and he stumbled to it. There covered in a furry blanket lay Aisling. He leaned down and pulled the blanket away uncovering a beautiful almost ghostly white naked body. He ran his finger from her neck where it met her chin downward to her breasts. She stirred and reached for the finger that was now touching her nipple. Her eyes slowly opened followed by a sultry smile.

"Are you and Jaime finished?" She asked softly. "I'm sorry, I fell asleep. I was going to come outside and share with you two, but suddenly my knees felt weak...."

"I...I...guess...we...we are...I'm...not...sure where she...is?"

Sarah smiled. "She goes home sometimes when she's had enough." Sarah stretched and the blanket slipped to the floor, fully exposing her milky body to Ethan who suddenly felt very aroused again. "How about we go downstairs? Down to the warehouse floor—I think it might interest you and we can make it fun down there." She reached for Ethan's hand, and he helped pull her up. Once she was on her feet, she reached to the back of the chair and grabbed a robe that was laying across the back cushion. Throwing it over her shoulders, Ethan helped adjust it and then let his hands fall slowly down her sides until he reached around and tucked his hands between the robe and her bare skin on her bottom. He pulled her in to himself and leaned his mouth close to her ear, his tongue probing her lobe, searching for the opening, and dipping in it. Sarah's breath became deeper, and he could feel her heart begin to pound. She pulled back.

"Follow me Charley, we can continue this downstairs." She turned and led Ethan down a hallway and through an opening where there was a large metal door with a handle on it. Sarah pulled down on the handle and the door split open in the middle, one half disappearing into the floor as Sarah stepped on it, the top half traveled upward. It was a freight elevator covered in a metal mesh on three sides allowing one to see out, and around the entire open area of the warehouse from the top floor to the bottom floor as they stepped into it. Sarah pulled a strap that hung down from the top half of the door and it began to scissor back together, the bottom rising to meet the top in the middle once again.

Ethan squeezed the waist closer in. "So, Sarah…or Aisling…" She looked up and he whispered, "…I'm confused on which name to call you?"

"Oh, Charley, call whichever one gives you the desire to ravage me the most." She smiled wickedly but her eyes seemed to trail off from the concoction they's been drinking.

Ethan looked out into the darkness only lit by the glow of the outside, which shone through the oddly placed windows scattered on the outer brick and mortar walls. It gave him an eerie feeling, along with mild vertigo, as the elevator began to slowly move downward. Cables hanging from above began swaying, as clicking sounds and gear noises echoed loudly over the still pounding dance music heard throughout the large hollow building. It appeared as if there were car tops lined up in order below them. They looked like soldiers standing at attention. Different shapes and lengths but aligned. As Ethan stared out into the abyss, captivated by what he saw and heard, Sarah reached around him from behind and slid her hand below his waist, leaning in and kissing his neck at the same time. Ethan's heart raged once more as his body became prepared for what was about to happen again, but his first with Sarah.

She pulled her mouth back for a moment and withdrew her hand from under Ethan's waistband as the elevator very slowly and methodically lowered to a slow and growling stop. After stepping from the enclosure, she spoke, "My dad's collection." She held her arms open wide, her breasts glowing in the darkness, displaying them while she also drew attention to all the different automobiles surrounding them, as if she were directing an orchestra of combustion driven statues resting but ready to perform on cue. She was grandiose in her manor. "Some are even mobster's cars from way back. He even has Al Capone's last Ford Sedan...."

"That would be the one I'd be interested in seeing, Aisling." Ethan said. "I have a deep interest in Al Capone, a hero of mine with an unfortunate ending. This wristwatch was his. The only thing in 'my' collection of gangster's belongings." He held up his hand, the wristwatch glimmering in what little light reflected from it.

Sarah grabbed his hand, leaned in toward him and plunged her thin tongue into his mouth once and then turned. She began leading him through aisles of car after car, making turns both right and left as if journeying through a maze. A labyrinth she seemed very familiar with. Sarah finally stopped in front of what appeared to be a black coupe of some vintage twenties, and she opened the door. Turning with a smile, she hiked her leg up onto the door jam, her robe parted and showed her white glowing thigh, which led up to a small thin strip of reddish pubic hair barely accessible to sight but highlighted in its darker patch surrounded by milky flesh. She smiled, her auburn hair appearing even more red in the pointed light gleaming from the window that highlighted her. "Do you wanna fuck me in Al Capone's car? I hear people were even murdered in it."

Ethan's body jumped again suddenly, and he felt dampness on his lap. Running his hand over it, he half-expected to pull it back covered in blood, but it was only moist. He smelled bourbon and drew his damp hand to his nose, sniffing it before he got his bearings and saw the familiar sight of his beach in front of him. *Had I fallen asleep? It seemed so real.* He looked down to check the time on his wristwatch, only to remember once again, he was clueless as to where it was. He saw the tiny slivers of glass scattered on the deck beside him and the nearly empty bottle of

Blanton sitting on the coffee table. A sudden vision popped from his memory banks from the night of his recent past. A recollection that sent a shockwave throughout his body, and he looked at his hands in instant disgust. With his eyes wide open and the beach waves rolling up the shoreline, he saw Aisling's bright green eyes become empty and hollow in front of him, her face becoming crimson in color while his hands clutched tightly around her throat. He remembered now. He'd killed the gorgeous, quirky redhead as she had almost begged him to do by her own words. "Choke me Charlie, I want you to, or are you a pussy?" He'd killed the young woman in Al Capone's car as if she'd predestined it herself.

"I hear people have even been murdered in it...."

<u>20</u>

Georgie lifted her wine glass to her lips, eyes twinkling at me with anticipation of my sharing the story of why I was so late getting home. My face felt as if it were beginning to appear more relaxed after a third or fourth swallow of the fruity bottled elixir from the refrigerator. The chill of the liquid felt soothing across my tongue as I lie back into the softness of the overstuffed couch. I slowly began to tell Georgie about the start of my day until now. My story of the day needed to have some of my backstory told for the impact of what today really brought to me. I looked at Georgie after almost finishing my first glass of blueberry Moscato and stopped my story saying, "I may need more than what we have here to get through this—I only have one more bottle in the fridge…."

"If we need it, my momma has some sangria in our refrigerator. It's fruity like this, just no fizzy bubbles!" She giggled.

"Okay, it's a tough story to get through." I reached for the bottle and refilled my glass; Georgie was still working on her first. "It starts back to when I was very young, before I lived with my grandparents. I think I was probably seven when everything went from bad to scary, to horrible." I began telling her how my parents were addicts in one form or another for as long as I remembered, even though I held no concept that I lived differently than any other child at the time. "My momma was always either totally out of her head and passed out, or she was raising her voice at me.

Scolding me for I don't know—just being a child, I guess—acting rambunctious. I don't remember doing anything too bad or bothersome to deserve her harsh tones and words. My father drank whiskey, lots of it and constantly until he'd pass out on the couch. I remember there was always an open bottle beside him. Our house was very smoky. They both smoked non-stop, lighting one cigarette from the butt of the one about to burn out. It stunk inside. I coughed and choked so much, I tried to spend most of my time outside with friends. Sometimes when my friends would be called home for dinner, and I wouldn't know what to do with myself. We never ate supper or any other meal on any kind of schedule. I went home several times at my friends 'dinner time' only to find daddy passed out on the couch with an empty bottle on the floor beside him and my momma half naked asleep in their bedroom. I'd rummage through kitchen cabinets and the refrigerator to find scraps to eat. Crackers sometimes, Pop Tarts, anything."

"I'd thought it was bad, Amy Jo, but I am so sorry. I never could imagine growing up like that." She scooted in closer to me and began rubbing my shoulder as I continued.

"The worst is yet to come. One early evening, like I said, I was probably seven because it wasn't much more than a year or so when Grandfather came and took me away in his truck. The one I drive now." I nestled into the couch and clutched my drink, lifting it back up for another sip before telling the most difficult parts of my story. The story I'd told no one ever except my grandmother. I was certain she'd shared it with my grandfather though. "I came home from school one extra hot afternoon. I was sweaty and I went into my room to change into some different clothes before going out to play with friends. I didn't see my daddy in the other room. I guess he was watching me undress once he'd seen me come in from outside. I was standing with just my top covering me, getting ready to put new panties on when I heard someone at my door. It was him. He came into my room even though I yelled I was changing." Tears began to creep from my eyes and slid down my cheeks, as the story I was telling Georgie. It suddenly became all too real again after all these years of pushing it deep down and away from thought.

"You don't have to go on, Amy Jo. I think I can guess what he did, and I don't want you to have to relive it." She scooted in closer and hugged me tight.

"I've never trusted a man ever since, except for one, and one boy back in school."

"Your grandfather, am I right?" Georgie asked through damp eyes.

"Yes, my grandfather. People ask me why I always called my grandparents by the formal names of grandfather and grandmother. I think they probably believe they must have been extremely strict and demanded it—but that couldn't be farther from the truth. They showed me such love; two people who barely knew me before my grandfather rescued me. My momma never allowed them to see me. I think she knew they would disapprove of her life and the way she was raising me." I took another long sip from my wine glass and got up to grab the other bottle. I felt a bit woozy, but it was nerves and tension from the day, not the drink.

When I returned from the kitchen, I noticed Georgie finished the first bottle and I opened the second, filling both our glasses to the brim and then sat back down. Georgie nuzzled back into my side like a little one would cuddle into their mother at bedtime, waiting for the story to be read. This story, however, was not a pleasant one made for a child's night-time bed tale. "Back to why I'm so formal with my grandparents." I took a sip and accidently brushed Georgie's leg softly. I then patted it, as if intentional, before drawing my arm up and laying it across the couch back behind her. "I never knew what respect was, before my grandparents. My mom and dad certainly held none for me or even taught me the meaning of the word. Once I got settled in and watched how they took care of me, how they demonstrated love and gratitude and how they were so grateful they could keep me, for this alone, I wanted to show them my love and respect. I chose to call them Grandfather and Grandmother because at eight almost nine years old—they were all of what 'grand' meant to me. They were a 'grand' mother and a 'grand' father, so it is what I chose to call them. Their God-given names were only important to others, not me."

"What a sad, horrible story, but with such a loving happy turn. I'm so thankful they found you and were able to raise you as their own. I only wish I could have gotten to meet and know them." Georgie raised her brow as if she'd suddenly thought of something she wanted to know."

"You can ask anything, Georgie, anything at all."

"I was just curious if you ever saw your real mother or father again after that?"

"No. Not that momma didn't try, but Grandmother told her she must prove she was off the drugs and alcohol before they would allow it. My grandparents did tell me she left my daddy not too long after I came here. When I turned sixteen, my grandmother handed me a sealed envelope and told me it was the only letter she'd ever received from her daughter, my mother, since. The front of it contained my name, in care of. They'd tried to find her, but she'd moved away and disappeared."

"Did you ever read the letter?"

I hesitated a moment and brought my glass back to my lips and swallowed before answering. I got up and walked a bit wobbly to the fireplace mantle and picked up a handmade wooden box. I brought it over and sat back down close to Georgie. I lifted the clasp and slowly opened the lid, then reached in pulling a yellowed envelope from it. "No, I never opened it. I've thought about it hundreds of times and came very close, but I always stopped before the edge was torn, telling myself I don't want to know what she had to say. She could have cleaned her life up if she really loved me and then we could have been together. Being a stoned gypsy living on the street was more important to her than being with me and loving me like a mother should. So, I wouldn't allow her to be of any importance to me." I turned my head and faced Georgie directly before asking, "Does that make me a selfish evil and uncaring bitch?"

"No, no, no, Amy Jo. It makes you a grown-up girl who wanted her momma only to love her. You don't have a selfish or evil hair on your beautiful head. I wish things were different for you, that's all. It makes me love you more."

I looked into Georgie's beautiful brown eyes, seeing the glimmer dance in her pupils from the candles I'd lit earlier on the shelf behind me. Before I knew exactly what I was doing or realized the implication it would make, I leaned closer and put my lips on hers. She didn't pull away until my tongue searched the crevice between her lips, and I felt past her teeth and touched her tongue with mine. Our tongues danced a brief waltz together before Georgie quickly pulled away from me. I can't say how the moment made Georgie feel, but it was the first time I'd ever experienced a kiss other than a peck on my grandmother or grandfather's cheek or lips. It felt totally different of course. It was very warm and made butterflies instantly flutter throughout my body, but it also felt awkward after the heated moment ended abruptly. I looked at Georgie and saw she appeared shocked.

"I'm sorry, Georgie. I...I...don't know what...I...."

She interrupted me quickly. "It's okay, Amy Jo, I let it happen even when I knew it was about to. I never...."

"It's okay. It was the moment. It doesn't mean we are different, or...." I couldn't look at her for several moments, afraid she would now find me repulsive.

Georgie reached over and pulled me into herself tightly. I could feel her warm breath in my ear, and it reheated my interior. And then she began to whisper and the little bits of air that entered my ear gave me goosebumps up and down my entire body. I didn't realize what was happening to me, but I knew I wanted more, but shouldn't.

"It's okay, Amy Jo." She whispered. "It was the moment, the wine, the years of loneliness..." She gave me a small kiss behind my ear and then moved her mouth to the front of my ear again and continued to whisper, "...I felt something for a moment. I've been lonely and I'm light-headed from the wine. It's okay. Please don't let this ruin our friendship. I need you and I feel like you need me—maybe now more than ever." Georgie pulled away from me and took my cheeks in each of her hands and lifted my face 'til our eyes met. We both had tears dripping down our cheeks and a smile worked its way across both of our lips simultaneously. "Will you be able to sleep tonight? I should probably go home, if you can."

"I didn't even get to the part about Jay...."

"How about we both get some sleep, and we agree to talk tomorrow. Maybe we both deserve to take a break and go to the beach together to unwind and let this evening settle for both of us?"

"But I have work to go...."

"Amy Jo, it's Saturday tomorrow!"

"Oh, it is! Yes, let's do that. Let's go to Cocoa Beach! I'll drive!"

Georgie got up from the couch and walked to the kitchen to take our glasses to the sink. She put what was left of the second bottle of Moscato back into the refrigerator before coming back into the living room. "You know I love you back, don't you, Amy Jo? You've been my best friend ever in all my life. It's a blessing from God that you rented your grandparents farm to my family, and the home we live in now. And I'm so close to my best friend I can walk home so easily."

"The entire thing is a miracle. I'm very blessed to have you." I said with wet eyes.

As I watched Georgie go through the front door and into the night, I couldn't help but think to myself—*there goes the person I feel I was meant to fall in love with, I didn't know it until now, but it obviously isn't meant to be that way, and it aches bone-deep. I held no idea I would be a woman who wanted to be close with another woman. Jesus? Please help me....*

21

"**O**h, Mitzi B, I can't believe what I heard him say."

"Mom! Stay here with us. We'll talk this through and see what's best for you to do. What else did he say?"

"He didn't have a clue I was even there. At first, I thought someone else was in the house, so I tiptoed in to see, but he was sitting in his favorite chair on the deck, a glass of bourbon, I presume, in his hand and his eyes closed. Just talking aloud as if there were someone he was conversing with. He said two women's names. Something like Ashland or Ashling, something like that, and Jamie."

"Has he ever mentioned those names before?"

"I've never heard either. He's found someone else. I just know. But, why? He knows I'd do anything for him. He told me he'd waited his entire life for me..." Joyce's eyes sharpened instantly, and she perked up with a questioning look growing across her face. "...Wait a minute. He worded something else oddly. He said...let me think..." Joyce closed her eyes and mouthed words under her breath, too quiet for Mitzi to hear or understand. She tried to read her mother's lips, but baby Katie's movement caused too much distraction to watch close enough. "He called me his beautiful angel from his past and something about not losing me again. I don't understand what he meant because we never shared a past. A treasure from his past or something? And then he said, and I quote, 'What did you fucking put in my drink Ashlin, or

Ashling...something like that. He also said a thing about my sweet body finally embodying all his desires...or...I don't know, I just freaked. I wondered if this Ashlin was hidden around the corner where I couldn't see her, and maybe he was talking to her. I wanted to stay and see what else came from his drunken mouth, but his crazy words were scaring me. His demeanor seemed so...so...unpredictable, not like his normal...."

"You did the right thing, mom. You got the hell outta there and you're safe."

"Honey, my job...I have very little in savings...and..." Her tearful appearance changed drastically for a moment, just before an angrier side unleashed. "...he fucking cheats and my life has to suffer? What the hell is fair about that? Son-of-a-bitching cheater motherfuc...." Joyce covered her mouth and dipped her head towards the floor. "I'm so sorry, Mitzi B, and right in front of my precious granddaughter."

"Mom! She's like four months old...geez, don't worry about it. I'd be cussing like Capt. Blackbeard if I was in your shoes. Avast ye fuckin' maggot eatin' son-of-a...."

Joyce began to crack a smile. "Oh, Mitzi B, don't—just don't!"

"Mom, you know what you have to do now, don't you?"

"I know, I'm calling her tomorrow."

"Mom, it's Friday early evening, call her now and see what time we can meet!"

"You're correct, Mitzi B, no time like the present. I've taught you well. Can I use your phone and call from here?"

"Mom, you're staying with us, of course you can. Mi casa, su casa."

"Hello, Cali...yes, this is Joyce, my daughter and I ate lunch with you and you were kind enough to leave a card with your number...yes, I would love to meet, tomorrow would be perfect...do you mind if my daughter tags along...I can meet wherever you'd like, and then I can drive, we could go wherever you're comfortable…okay, we'll be there at nine in the morning and we'll find a nice outta the way place to have breakfast, on me of course…thank you so much, thank you, and we'll see you in the morning." Joyce hung up and looked at Mitzi, her hands shaking like sea-oats blowing on the sand dunes. "It's done. We're picking her up at Mac's auto-service on the east side of town at nine."

"I'm glad, Mom. We need to get to the bottom of this and straighten it out."

Joyce held her hands out for Katie. "Yes, Mitzi B, we do and we're on it now." Mitzi handed Katie to her mom, and Joyce snuggled her tightly into her arms, close to her chest, just like she'd done all Mitzi's young life. She looked away from Katie and to Mitzi and mouthed in silence, "I love you, baby-girl," and Mitzi mouthed back "I love you, Momma, to the moon."

22

I laid awake in bed unable to fall asleep no matter how much I needed it. I ended up going back to the refrigerator and refilling my wine glass, twice. I needed to feel close to my grandfather. He loved Willie Nelson, so I walked over to the stereo in the built-in cabinet near the fireplace. I stopped and briefly stared at the small wooden box sitting on the mantle containing the yellowed envelope. "Nope, not tonight, not ever," were sharp words I spoke, and then continued to dig through my grandfather's old record albums. They of course sounded crackly in places from all the years they'd been played over and again, but it was the way I loved to hear them, scratches and all. I'd been given the brand-new technology of compact discs and Grandfather of course, bought some of our favorites such as Red Headed Stranger. But tonight, those would be too perfect to the ear, and I needed to hear the album the way I grew up listening to it, with skips and crackly spots. I knew as I lifted the arm of the phonograph, placing the needle carefully at the beginning song, "Time of the Preacher", my grandfather was surely up in heaven smiling as he looked down upon me. Suddenly I became aware that he could also have been watching me as I foolishly leaned over and kissed my best friend, Georgie. I knew he'd understand and not judge me because he knew how hurt I'd been, being tainted and broken by my father. I didn't tell Georgie it happened several more times before I was saved by my grandparents. Once was enough to kill my trust and interest in boys as I grew up. I wasn't sure if I'd ever trust or loved one a way like marriage was supposed to bring. I'd been asked out by many boys as I grew older, but never agreed upon going out or dating any of them. I became labeled quickly, the tom-boy. 'Little Amy Tommy-Boy' or 'TeeBee' for short. It hurt and it lasted most of the way through twelfth grade. I also remember the boy who was responsible for my nickname finally disappearing for good. It was a blessing and a curse both mixed in together, but I'll never forget Cable Lee Johnson. First, because his name was a rarity, not to mention the way he stopped the name calling, which had previously haunted me for so many years.

Halfway through the last part of eleventh grade, Cable moved into town. His father was a steelworker who built bridges. They'd moved to town, so Cable's dad didn't have to be away from his family as much while he worked on the different dilapidated bridges all near the Orlando area. Cable's family had lived up near the northeast coast somewhere towards New York City and his accent was as funny as his name. His daddy named him Cable because he specialized in suspension bridges using steel cables. Cable told me one day it was because cables were strong and necessary and enabled bridge-making, bringing things together, which weren't possible before. "My daddy said I was flexible but strong like a multi-stranded cable in bridgework." He smiled after he told me. A couple of weeks later I noticed no one called me "TeeBee" anymore and he told me why. "Amy Jo," he said. "Don't be angry with me, now. Some of the guys noticed we talked, and they asked me why I wasted my time on a tomboy who will never drop her panties for me because she was a man-hater." He smiled and continued. "I told them I'd already seen what was in those "panties" and it was the most special treasure I'd ever found." He flinched as I threw my English book at him, nearly taking out his eye and right ear. He just smiled and laughed. "I was only thinking of you, Amy Jo, and trying to correct a wrong for one of the sweetest and prettiest girls I've ever met."

I reckon ole' Cable built a bridge himself that day, albeit in an odd use of construction. By the first half of my senior year, I found I was no longer an island. I could go anywhere and be a normal kid. The bridge he'd built for me gave me access to anyone I'd never been able to reach before that day. His bridge gave me confidence and self-pride. I never told Cable about my daddy and what he'd done to make me fear most boys. Cable moved off to the west coast about three weeks after our senior graduation. He got brave enough on the last day of school to tell me he wished what he'd said had been true. Cable looked into my eyes that afternoon and said without pause, "Amy Jo, I know your treasure is extra-special and I'm not talking just the physical. Someday you'll find the boy who will recognize your value and treasure what he's lucky enough to hold, I just wish it could have been me. Who knows though where life will lead us? Maybe we could find each other again someday."

I'm twenty-eight years old and so far, neither of Cable's predictions have come true. I thought for a quick moment tonight, I might have felt just a small bit of what that special value felt like, before the reality hit me. Now, I can't sleep and I'm listening to Willie Nelson and longing for my grandfather, the only man I ever felt a hundred percent safe with. I'd not thought of Cable Lee Johnson since that last conversation we shared. Funny how the human brain works. I now wonder how many other unique bridges he's built throughout his adult years—and if he still uses his talent, which gave me what I may never have found on my own without him.

***

Billy Jay laid on his cot in silence. For the first time in a long time, he felt worried. In fact, he wasn't sure he could remember struggling with the feeling of worry, least not in any time he could think of specifics. The last image of Amy Jo he witnessed, the guards tried to shield him from her as the medics came rolling in with a gurney to pick her up and rush her through doors, he'd never been past. Was she okay? Did she pass out or suffer a medical emergency like a heart attack?

Lord, I know I'm the last living creature on earth you expected to hear from or for that matter, ever wanted to. I know you say you never created anything bad by your hands. I seen proof your creations can turn evil and I'm one a those, I 'spect. A vile wolverine of sorts with little value to mankind. Spawned from my daddy's demon seed. Now I ain't prayin' for myself here. I'm prayin' for an innocent soul who carry's shelter in her heart for those in need like you taught her to provide and tried to teach me. She prolly needs your help tonight, Lord. While I ain't worthy to ask, I'm askin' anyway on her behalf to please make her right. Cure her of her ailment. She's a keeper and worth savin'. I'm tryin' to figure a way to quit judgin' and killin', even those here where I live, who ain't worth savin anyways. It's late in my final days and I realize in your eyes, too late to care ifn' I was ta change or not. But Amy Jo has already been dealt shit for livin' early on and still made a fine Christian woman without twistin' her arm or nothin'. Only 'bout four or five of them kinda' people I ever known of, and she be on the top of the list, just sayin'. Protect her from the likes of me and my failin's and other evildoers alike. Amen.

Jay was thinking differently these days. He didn't really notice it until Lyle had called him out on it. He now noticed he didn't feel like killing more inmates after judgment from the T-7. In fact, he wasn't certain he felt like being a part of them at all anymore. He did know there would be harsh treatment if he let anyone know he wanted out. Why did he have these feelings? Was Amy Jo changing him just by him being around her every week? Is this how Jesus works? He missed his good Book from Ms. Cela. Even though he hadn't ever really bought into it. He sure enough missed reading it. Or maybe—was his mind playing games with him again? *All these damned questions and worryin' bout Amy Jo....*

***

Georgie laid in bed having difficulty staying still enough to fall asleep. She tossed and turned while her mind spun in circles tonight. The apparent reasons were Amy Jo telling her about her awful past childhood before her grandparents stepped and saved her. There was of course, the brief surreal moment that was shared between them. There was now a circumstance she'd never-before been faced with. Never imagining any feelings like those that Amy brought about tonight, made sleep impossible. There was no doubt in her mind she'd felt something odd. She'd experienced some sexual urges spurred on by seeing young men she'd been attracted to, but rarely. She also noticed beautiful women she'd wished she looked like, but women never stirred such thoughts as tonight. This kind of thing was of course not even close to being accepted. Laws have been passed stating the military was no place for non-heterosexuals. She held no desire of enlisting, but…. The Vatican, her leadership of the Catholicism she practiced, attacked such behavior as abhorrent to God's word. Would she now be out of God's favor and graces for the brief unexpected moment with her best friend? *I don't feel any different or dirty. What I felt was a warmth almost as soothing and tingly as the way I felt as a high-school girl on my first date with Joshua Reynolds, a ghostly, white-skinned, awkward boy my parents weren't sure they approved of whom I shared my first kiss with. Fireworks! Almost the same explosions I felt tonight but became frightened of. The thing with Joshua didn't last long. His parents didn't want their boy to be dating a girl of Spanish heritage of any kind. The mixing of races was impure in their thoughts. My God, we were sixteen, not planning a future of pumping out grandkids! This thing with Amy Jo and I would be explosive in other's eyes if we even thought about pursuing it any further. If I was. Even Amy Jo acted as if the act was embarrassing and obscene.*

Amy Jo was her best friend. As much as Georgie fretted over something that only lasted seconds, there was no way she would let it affect their friendship. Amy Jo was a gracious and kind young woman. She alone was the reason her family was able to farm the land on their own behalf for so little money. Being a first-generation American citizen, opportunities like the ones Amy Jo provided, were not a common occurrence for people like her. Amy Jo saw no color, no specific brand of faith, and apparently no sin too great to withhold compassion from someone as she'd witnessed in the stories shared with her from her Billy Jay Cader interviews. She seemed to be able to look past every stigma or peripheral difference in everyone she came across. She was certainly a one-of-a-kind woman, who stands up boldly in this world filled with self-centeredness, greed, and a lack of compassion for humanity of any brand. *I love her for everything she is, I just never saw ahead of time this being part of her. I never imagined the necessity of confronting such feelings. My heart is aflutter, and I now think I'll need a late-night glass of Sangria to settle my thoughts. Morning will come quickly and while I look very forward to it, there will also be a bit of self-consciousness along with the sun rising.*

23

Morning came and nine o'clock was closing in fast. The sofa wasn't comfortable and spacious like her bed at Ethan's. Joyce missed spooning but now the thought brought anger bubbling up. Joyce wasn't sure about anything now Her thoughts bounced around inside her head with sporadic confusion. *Do I have a job? I'm certain I no longer shared a bed with my boss who'd just recently sold himself as my knight in shining armor, coming to my emotional rescue.* "Oh, shove it Mick! I couldn't ever stand your song anyway." She said aloud while she finished folding her sheets. "Mitzi B! We have to roll soon!" Joyce hollered out to her daughter.

Mitzi poked her head from the bathroom door. "I'm just about there, Mom."

Darrell opened the bedroom door and quietly shushed the two of them. He pulled their bedroom door to a silent close before continuing, "If either of you wake Katie up…I'll…."

"Sorry, babe. I still forget sometimes." Mitzi blew him an invisible apologetic kiss through the air.

Ten minutes later, they were in the Volvo heading out to the east side of town, one nervous as a whore in church, the other visibly ready to kick some attorney's ass with devastating evidence. "Mom! You're not the bad guy here. He is. Did you write down what you heard him say yesterday so you don't forget?"

"Mitzi, I'm a gawd damned paralegal and a damned good one who works for a high-powered attorn…well, I used to anyway, and yes, I wrote every damned word down, in my version of shorthand so nobody else knows what the hell is on it!"

The Volvo was slow to start, slow groaning before kicking over, leaving the two wondering if the battery would suffice in getting the job done. Just another wrinkle in her life thought Joyce as she steered the tired old auto east toward Mac's. After pulling in, Joyce realized she hadn't asked what Cali drove. It didn't matter though, she suddenly popped out from behind the old garage building. She waved as she walked towards their car.

"Morning y'all. Looks like it's gonna be a scorcher for bein' late in the year and all."

"Hello, Cali." Joyce said as she opened her door and climbed out to greet her. She glanced over and asked Mitzi to move to the back seat, which she did with a mild eyeroll.

Cali climbed in the passenger side and quickly turned back and smiled at Mitzi. "You look even prettier in the morning, how do you do it?"

Mitzi flipped her strawberry blonde hair and said, "What, this old doo? Took me all morning and I still look like yesterday's news." She spied her momma as she climbed in when their eyes met in the rearview mirror. Momma's eyes wore a "you better be nice" scowl in them while Mitzi's eyes sported a "I hate fake bullshit" look.

"Well, where should we go to eat, Miss Cali? What sounds good and where?"

"Out west leads us towards Ethan's house—not good, and head out east it takes us to Port St. Joe, also not good because Ethan is out thatta' way a lot of the time too. Main street is out of the question because of his office. The son-of-a-bitch has us pretty buttoned up, I'd say, which is why I'm nervous about talking. But I have so much you should know before you get too involved with him." Cali's eyes held concern within. "Look, y'all don't have to feed me. I can eat at Poppy's later before my shift. I say just start driving and we can pull over if we spot a place. I think better when I'm moving anyway."

"I'm not sure I can drive with what I'm afraid you're going to tell me." Joyce responded with a hushed tone of sadness.

"Oh, my Lord, you've already fallen hard in love with him, haven't you? I thought maybe I saw it when you were with Ethan the night at the restaurant, but I see it for sure now. You got a broken-hearted look. I'm sorry." Cali reached over and touched Joyce's arm. "I'm afraid what I say ain't gonna help with any mending of your heart."

Joyce barely backed up and pulled from the parking lot at Mac's before her eyes began pooling. She stopped. "Mitzi B, you're gonna have to drive. Maybe you and I can sit together in the back, Cali?"

Mitzi got out and walked around to the driver's door while mumbling.

"What honey?" Joyce asked her daughter.

"Nothing, Momma, I just said I would love being the chauffeur for today's outing." It took a couple of minutes for everyone to get situated before Mitzi pushed the pedal down and headed to a place, she knew would be private. She knew one thing. Ethan wouldn't be caught dead there. The name of the place was Old Woman's Bluff up on the Apalachicola River. She and Darrell used to go talk and drink Pabst Blue Ribbons with the gang—before Kyle crashed his car ending up operating a wheelchair instead of a muscle car.

***

Mitzi grew agitated trying to listen to the hushed voices between her momma and Cali. The babble was pushing her anxiety to an all-time high. The sides of the car seemed to close in around her tighter and tunnel vision narrowed her sight through the windshield ahead. She tried to focus, but her brain was causing her thoughts to rattle and bounce sporadically within her head. The drive up to Old Woman's Bluff quickly drew memories of her recent past and all that had happened in her life so quickly. She played the story reel in her mind as she retraced the road to the bluff....

I feel as if I've grown up instantly in the less than one year's time since my momma and I first pulled into this little Peyton Place. I started a brand-new school in a town where I knew only my estranged father-- none other than the sheriff of this one-stoplight dust speck. Somehow a respected man, but one who personally never even sent me a frickin' Christmas card, birthday balloon, teddy bear, phone call to say hello or even just one to say fuck off, little missy. Funny now in retrospect, since he ended up not being my birth father after all. My new first real boyfriend, Darrell, whom I love with all my heart, got me knocked-up after the first time we made love, and it was on a damned beach! You know, sand! Oh, we'd only known each other less than two weeks. PS, we have a four-month-old baby girl named Katie now, and she's frickin' beautiful, but I digress.

I then find out Darrell could possibly be my brother, of course, what girl wouldn't want THAT news—sharing the same dad, Sheriff Roy Burks, with the boy you've fallen in love with, let alone had sex with. Luckily though, the disgusting thing didn't pan out, thank God. Too bad for ex-daddy-o though; we found out his and my blood types were all wrong makin' it biologically impossible for him to be my dad. It was of course, too late to save him the ass-beating of a lifetime by the son he still denied--the love of my life and Katie's daddy!

Then my boyfriend, Darrell, got to go to jail for beating the sheriff, his newly discovered father in a moment of shock and violent assault of passion from the news making us brother and sister. Ewe, disgusting moment in both our worlds! You see, I'd found out a day earlier I was pregnant and needed to let him know about it, but wasn't ready to tell him, being how all our friends and my mom were all there in the living room along with the not-my-daddy-no-more-sheriff, layin' all beat up on the floor with Kyle holdin' the sheriff's own gun to his bloody, swollen face. This part of the story transpired because the words, "I'm pregnant" fell unexpectedly from my gaping mouth after Jay, Darrell's supposed father, yelled out to Sheriff Roy that ole Darrell was in truth the sheriff's son, making the two of us, me and Darrell, a tightly woven family bloodline. Sick backswamp drama and thankfully mainly untrue!

Mitzi mentally drew a deep, deep breath from the exhaustion of reliving this mental life reel rolling like a twisted movie inside her head.

Later in this crazy out-of-sequence story, which was continuing to unfold in my head, comes a horrid tragedy. I know, the whole damned thing is tragic, but this part really sucks. Kyle and Vio, who were coming back from the beach where Darrell and I did the wild thing and the two of them unfortunately ended up wrecking his pride and joy. Kyle's car, which sported a kiss-my-ass bright red, black pinstriped, paint job on a 1970 Chevy four-fifty frickin' four cubic inch LS6 Chevelle SS, factory horsepower clocking in at 450hp, spun out of control and crashed on the bridge coming back from Eastpoint. It left Darrell in a wheelchair and his girlfriend, Vio, my best friend, on the TBI (Traumatic Brain Injury) patient list. Mine and Darrell's two best friends now live in the apartment next to us, because they need help getting around and they truly are our best friends for life—no matter what.

Another deep breath for Mitzi and a moment of much needed personal reflection.

And then there's Jay. The crazy psycho who Darrell, my boyfriend, originally grew up thinking was his mean-ass father.

The one and only, who Darrell tried to kill with his preacher's shotgun loaded with two 20-gauge shells, unfortunately filled with only birdshot. This happened about two months before I moved here. Vio warned me about Darrell's background and family and how dangerous he was, after I told her he was cute, the very first day of my senior year at Apalachicola High, home of the Bull sharks. I didn't listen and it turned out Darrell wasn't the bad kid she'd warned me about. It was all because he thought Jay was attacking his momma, Cat, in the cemetery when he saw them together. Cat was being held tight in Jay's grip, and then Darrell thought she was trying to get away from him. Believable because three and a half years earlier, Crazy Jay killed his oldest boy by stick in' an eight-inch butcher's knife into Billy James' chest during a scuffle. But later, Jay was the one who ended up shooting and killing Darrell's real father, sheriff Roy Burks, with three bullets after he stumbled onto Kyle's car wreck on the bridge. Imagine, Mom told me the day we arrived here, and I quote, "Apalachicola is a quiet little beach front town where we can start over and get away from the hustle-bustle of Birmingham, Ala-damn-bama." Right Mom!

Mitzi's brain was growing more frazzled by the minute, and she looked in the rearview mirror, spying the two still chatting in the back seat. Her momma's world collapsing behind her, being reflected in a two-inch by six-inch mirror attached to the car's windshield she was driving. Her eyes shifted back and forth between the road ahead and the mess of tears behind. Mitzi lost count already of all the many crazy things that fell like dominos around her in an out-of-sequence tornado, dropping them in no particular order. She'd always turned to her comedic talents to make people laugh when she felt overwhelmed and insecure. She knew this was her poker-like tell and even attempted using the diversion on herself occasionally, just like now with the life tragedies she played through her mind with an attempt at added humor. Sometimes it worked…and sometimes not so much.

Let's see, she gathered her thoughts back to the internal countdown of events.

That's right—Chubbs, one of our original pals in our clique, disappeared only to wash up shark-eaten twenty-some miles away from Apalachicola after Vio swore she'd seen him running away from my home. Or possibly Crazy Jay's, who lived next door. All while Momma and me were hiding from Jay at her boss' beach house, afraid Jay might possibly kill us after going nuts the night of the scuffle between Darrell and Sheriff Burks.

This led up to the reason all three of us girls are now headed to Old Woman's Bluff, a comically inappropriate spot I would think, to talk about Ethan, Mom's boss, who holds some sordid history with Cali, the bitch sitting behind me causing my mom needs to bawl like a baby. It would all be too fuckin' whimsical if my momma wasn't sittin' in pain and betrayal alongside the bimbo tramp from Ethan's past who probably brought all this shit raining down on her. All ending in a chance meeting, bringing us together today because Ms. guilty-ass, I'm sure, feels the need to heed a warning of impending danger. So, I mash the friggin' gas pedal to the floor in this pathetic old Volvo just prayin' we will be able to get up the slightest incline to the landmark spot of this shadowy, esoteric powwow. A meeting like I'm sure General Custer held with Sitting Bull or Crazy Horse the night before the Battle at Little Bighorn rained a brutal end to his slaughterin' ass.

In the mix of some of this whacked small-town hospitality to newcomers like us, my mom and Crazy Jay, our next-door neighbor, the guy we were hiding from, got in a shoot-out with two Florida State detectives; killing one and wounding the other, leading to his arrest and conviction then receiving the death penalty. Oh, yeah, our principal Charley Bingham disappeared only for his corpse to wash up on a beach close to the same spot and in the same awful shape as Chubbs' body did a couple of weeks after disappearing. Coincidence? I think not. Safe little town? Again, I think not. And now, my mom finally meets the man of her dreams, a wealthy good-looking fifty-something successful defense attorney, but who is more than likely up to something no good and happens to be her boss too. Inconvenient, I'd say. And finally, if I haven't missed anything other than I'm driving my mom's beater Volvo to an undisclosed destination so a strange waitress can fill my mom up on dirt about her lawyer-boyfriend, slash ex-boss—this is life in a quiet, little out-of-the-way, beach-front community. Apalachi-friggin'-cola, Florida.

Oh, and I did overlook one last important snafu. I don't know who the hell my real father is now, because the doctor says the blood type makes it impossible for the dead sheriff to be my dad, but I'm happy about it, because it means the father of my baby isn't my brother after all! My mom swears though, she's never slept with anyone else but Roy Burks, the now deceased sheriff! And somehow, I believe her even with facts refuting this. My mom never lies. She follows the law to a "T" after all, she's a paralegal and she's, my momma.

The Volvo rolled to a stop on the gravels edge facing the Apalachicola River on Old Woman's Bluff.

I Mitzi B, chauffeured my momma and Cali, the spy, here to a clandestine place, now wondering just what the hell could life deal us now as we sit here in the middle of nowhere fucking Florida, the state full of snowbirds from Everywhere-Elseville, USA. Salute!

24

The sun began to burn off any early morning dew left enclosed in tiny beads clutching onto the orange fruit in the trees. I looked out surveying the calm beauty before me, grasping tightly my morning dose of lifeblood in the largest coffee cup available. "Hmm. Nothing like it," I peered out at the green trees with the tiny orange dots sprinkled throughout, reminding me how beautiful this place is. Along with relishing the fresh smell of the blackest brew of java known to man, and the feel of the rough sawn planks under my toes, I'm reminded just where I was blessed enough to wake up every morning. "I love the way this floor feels." I spoke aloud even though I was alone, scrunching my toes downward and dragging them on across the wooden planks, remembering how Grandfather would act as if someone was scratching their fingernails down a chalkboard as he saw me. "Missy, you're gonna cry loud when a splinter gets shoved up one of those pretty painted toes!" He'd say.

I wished to hear Grandmother rattling around in the kitchen, spatula clanging against the pan followed by the scent of peppered bacon, fused with the scrambled eggs. A familiar scent, which usually hovered on the cross-breeze of morning air wisping through the open windows. Rituals of my past still cling to my favorite memories. It used to be a morning affair that happened every single day until the one day it stopped in an instant.

Grandfather would always be tinkering with something at the kitchen table that couldn't possibly wait until breakfast was eaten.

It wasn't unusual for the conversation to begin something like, "Awe, dammit, Maggs. Did you see where that confounded spring sprung off to?" followed by a reprimand from Grandmother. "Jeffrey William Langstone! There's ladies present in this household!"

I smiled. I played in my mind what Grandfather would probably say next. He spoke similar words many times when he didn't see me in the next room. Little "naughty words", as Grandmother would call them. Although, I imagine he sometimes spied me from the corner of his eye; likely smiling to himself at his verbal display of the mild rough edges a working man's reality brings. "Maggie Mae Langstone—you know I coulda' spoken something far more harmful to the child's ears, but I didn't, and dammit, I love you madly." I couldn't fight the urge to grin again, thinking of how their love for each other showed in tiny little ways and words throughout their day. My mind heard the nonexistent conversation so plainly in my head, I turned from the window back to the kitchen to make certain I hadn't woken up from a long hibernation to the time they were still here. But I didn't and they weren't. The kitchen was silent and vacant with no odors of a nearly prepared meal tantalizing my sense of smell. Neither of them was anywhere in their house any longer, just me and my memories. And now along with those past reflections from afar, were more recent ones. Like the elephant in the living room from last night. The empty Moscato bottle we shared. Georgie and my awkward moment of confusion entangled with sparks like a fourth of July celebration. A brief bright explosion, which fizzled to the ground and quickly burnt out from lack of gunpowder. A dud, but one that still smoldered in my insides, baffling me why I still smelled the sulfur and charcoal from it yet this morning.

I somehow managed to break a smile, anyway, allowing warm coffee to miss my mouth and drizzle down my chin. It burned just a little bit, though. Sometimes I think Grandfather's ghost is responsible for the little mishaps of mine. Just to let me know he's still by my side. I swear I feel the tickles of his beard on my chin occasionally, like when I was a little girl sitting on his lap making funny faces and bumping our chins together. God, I miss those times. The memories are a wonderful gift from our maker, but still not an adequate replacement for the real thing.

Enough reminiscing, I tell myself. I've got to get ready for Georgie and the trip to the beach. I took another sip of my morning adrenaline boost, this time without Grandfather's help dribbling it down my chin. Moving onto my bedroom dresser, I rifle through a drawer filled with swimsuits I haven't worn in years. Will the two-pieces still fit without making me look pudgy? I giggle slightly, which quickly grows into an absurd laugh. I suddenly feel like I'm readying myself for a date. But it's Georgie, and I don't know why I suddenly have these funny tingles in my stomach and whimsical thoughts invading my brain. I tell myself aloud, "I'm not that way. I haven't ever given in to these kind of feelings for anyone—not men or boys—and especially not other women. It's preposterous."

My thoughts make a one-eighty turn and Jay pops into my mind. Jay, who all but admitted yesterday he'd done horrible things to young ladies. The thought chases away the butterflies in my stomach that fluttered mere seconds ago. Now chills were what I felt. Like warm winds blowing through the house and then suddenly freezing in an instant because it brushed across my shoulders like I remember the calloused skin of my daddy's cold and rough hand on my back before he let it fall downward where it never belonged. An instant memory reminding me why I may never be attracted to a man or his touch on my body. I started to think and use the word 'again' but it made no sense because I've never experienced those feelings before. Mine were emotions of fear, dread, and panic. I've never felt any kind of desires that were good from any man. I shook my head to clear the thoughts from sticking around, letting them fall back to the deep crevasses of my mind. The blackest part where I can bury things forever that I don't want to think about or see behind my eyes when they're closed. Jay would understand how I felt, but then again—what kind of horrible feelings did he lay on young girls. I told my mind to stop going there, it wouldn't do any good at all. Easily drawn in, easily defeated. Not me, not today.

I try on a couple of different swimsuits and look in the full-length mirror, which hung on the wall on the side of the room where Grandmother readied herself. I'd put on a few pounds, but I looked dang good I thought. Comfortable anyway. I started to get undressed, quickly taking my top off when there came a rap on the front door. *Georgie*, I imagined. Butterflies flickered their way back to my insides again.

Grabbing the white dress-shirt I'd worn last night I began buttoning it while making my way to the door. Swinging it open, Georgie greeted me, but wore a thin vail of embarrassment I read right away in her smile. "Hey, Georgie! I'm almost ready." I said as I pushed the door wider and stepped away allowing her entrance. As I turned sideways, I caught her briefly staring at what seemed to be my chest. I looked down and the fabric brushing against my bare breasts had caused my nipples to become hard and push against the lite translucent fabric. Georgie quickly looked away when out of sudden shyness, I wrapped my arms around myself covering them almost in shame. With the action to hide the display of my breasts, it pushed my cleavage together, making my top gap open even further. She brushed past me with more determination.

"Georgie!" I blurted. "This is crazy! I'm sorry about last night, but we can't let it make us act awkward around each other—not and still be friends!"

I always seemed to face problems head on. Never felt like they should be glazed over and forgotten. Probably because I'd never been afforded the chance to face my mom and dad with the situation, which led me to be taken from them. I detest confrontation, but even more the avoidance of working things out.

"Oh, Amy Jo, I've not slept all night. Part of me looked forward to today and seeing you again, but another side of me dreaded every moment in between then and now." She looked down to the floor, appearing afraid to face me, and it hurt instantly.

"Georgie, I feel like a sharp knife just sliced my sensitive skin. I never wanted to make you feel uncomfortable—never."

Georgie slowly lifted her head, then like a magnet drawing metal to itself, her teary eyes lifted and looked decidedly into mine. "It's not just you. There's something I have no idea what it is that caused this…this…well, shit, Amy Jo, I don't even know what the hell I'm…I'm just babbling and rambling and…."

I turned back again and touched her shoulder to give her comfort, which caused her thoughts to fade into silence. "Georgie, I would never do anything to intentionally cause you any…."

Georgie suddenly moved closer to me, and I saw her hands reach to my cheeks. I pulled away, but suddenly felt drawn back. Her hands met my face at the same time I drew toward them. We stood for a moment in my entryway with the front door still swung wide-open into the house letting the sunshine brightly inside. We looked at each other with question, but also a strained unknown yearning. One that begged to seek answers yet at the same time fearing what the solutions may bring. Georgie pulled my mouth to hers and our lips met before both of us parted them, pushing into a deep passion-filled kiss, full of exploration and discovery. The uncomfortableness quickly materialized into clumsiness as we fumbled together, one wrapped in the others clutches. Not only were we lost in the moment wondering what we'd almost tripped and fallen into, but I also attempted to kick at the door to close it before anyone spotted us in this fortuitous experience we were sharing. The pleasure mixed with my embarrassment of thinking who could be watching us. Her parents? A farmhand? My grandparents from above looking down in disappointment, as if shutting the door would hide us from their heavenly watchful eyes? Then it hit me, all the sudden I didn't give a flying …. THUD, as the door slammed closed.

I stopped my internal conversation instantly, like flicking the lights off with the switch. Not only wanting to avoid my grandmother entering inside my head to chastise my use of foul language, but I also did not want to invite her in to find me in the sexual quandary I now found myself…no matter how impossible such a thing would be. So, I instinctually self-corrected and returned my focus on exploring this crazy happenstance occurring between Georgie and me. Attempting not to second guess how long this moment would endure, but also never wanting these new incredible sensations to find an end. I focused my mind on shutting off the normal self-rationalizing decisions and over-thought "what ifs." Those words always seemed to dominate the background inside my head. Instead, I relished every goose-bump and twitch my body continually fed my brain receptors.

Her skin felt so soft to my touch and her voluptuous body jiggled slightly while we both gracelessly caressed each other, toying with passions we neither one ever experienced in this way before. We were like two high-school lovers fumbling with something we didn't understand but were headed toward losing our virginity without a handbook of instruction. Yet somehow, we both instinctively knew how to fit the puzzle pieces correctly.

I believe we both understood our friendship could never go back to before last night and the first kiss we shared, but I also suspected after this morning, neither of us wanted it to.

***

My eyes blinked several times. The room slightly lit from the sun coming up mixed with the blurriness of the sleep still in my eyes. I quickly looked over to the empty side of my bed. *No Georgie—it must have all been a dream?* My temples began aching and with the dry raspy cough, I remembered the second bottle of wine I'd polished off after not being able to sleep. I felt disappointed and relieved at the same time. *It was just a dream.* There was a wrap at the front door. I glanced at my clock on the nightstand. Nine. *That's Georgie.*

I hopped up too quick forcing me to grab my forehead and squeeze with one hand as I quickly headed to the door. It was a fast and crooked pace until I reached the handle and pulled it open before I realized I was still just wearing my nightie. "Good morning, Georgie," I said as I tried to cover myself as best I could.

"I didn't wake you, did I? I can come back. Or I could make you some coffee while you get ready?" Georgie asked.

"Yeah, that would be great. You know where everything is—I'll take a quick shower and be right out." I smiled uncomfortably and turned to head back to the bedroom, talking as I continued, "I'm so sorry I overslept! I couldn't get to sleep with all that happened with Jay…." Knowing I was only speaking partially of the real reasons.

"It's okay, we can talk about it later, after you're wide awake and we're on the road!"

"You bet, Georgie. I'll be out in a few…."

25

Ethan woke up for the first time in a long while with his temples pounding to the beat of thunder. His eyes focused on the table beside his favorite chair. As the blur began to clear, he saw two bottles standing boldly upright as if happy to see the morning come. His Blanton Black bottle appeared empty. Pinching his eyelids tightly together helped straighten the fuzziness to a point he could read the second bottles label. "Son-of-a-bitch! I drank almost two-hundred fifty dollars of bourbon last night." He said aloud without reserve. The other bottle a Basil Hayden containing a deep rye and one he would normally enjoy slowly. Apparently, he'd enjoyed almost three quarters of the bottle—along with the Blanton. Ethan rubbed his temples and applied pressure as if cranking the handle of a vice. "I'm too old to win battles of drink and pity. If only I could keep the good fight going." He thought of an old Abraham Lincoln quote. "tell me what brand of whiskey Grant drinks. I would like to send a barrel of it to my other generals." He sighed. "I feel like ole Abe considers me a general and sent his barrel of Grant's favorite, expecting my being due a good hoorah, before sending me to my final destiny." *Damn, it hurt to hear myself speak words aloud.*

A fleeting thought rushed through his brain like a lightning bolt strikes without advance notice. *Had Joyce come home?* Panic entered the mix of thoughts, and he turned toward the backdoor leading into the house from the deck. It sat wide open. He looked down, finding the same clothes he'd worn yesterday. She'd certainly be disappointed if not angry with him for the state of intoxication she would have found him; if she did make it home last night. Grabbing both arms of his chair, Ethan struggled to pull himself up to a vertical stance. He stumbled as soon as the room began moving. He bumped the chair, which jiggled the side-table enough to topple the bottles, spilling the small amount left from the Basil Hayden. "Well, fuck! There goes a great tasting fifty-dollars of Kentucky's finest high-rye recipe right down the shitter." He watched its contents pour over the side of the table and onto the deck floor, most spilling between the gaps of the planks to the sand below. He paused a moment, thinking he almost wished he owned a dog, at least the whiskey wouldn't have been a total loss. He'd rather share a good buzz with a four-legged companion than see expensive bourbon go to waste. Small steps along with hands on the walls, Ethan worked his way slowly back into the house and down the hallway to his bedroom. If Joyce laid asleep in bed, she'd certainly be awake now. Ethan wasn't stepping quietly or with concern of whom he may be disturbing. "Sweetheart?" He questioned as he pushed the door open and peeked in. Empty. Looked exactly like yesterday before they both left. *Where could she be? Have I lost her for good after all these years of searching and planning how to obtain her?* He turned back around and stumbled to the hall bathroom to relieve himself of the nights now filtered alcohol. He felt certain his liver suffered from his love of whiskey. It surely pushed the limits of his bladder also. The ache from holding it became so great, he felt it may burst at any moment.

Ethan peered down at the toilet, expensive spent liquor splashing loudly from the night of heavy drinking. He held his shriveled penis between his fingers, remembering how just weeks ago it stood firm and proud when he'd tucked it inside two beautiful young women's bodies in a single night he now regretted horribly. Springfield, Missouri. Who would have thought such crazy sex-starved women would live in such a small town, the buckle of the Bible-belt. Especially who lured him to a warehouse and practically forced him with their carnal sexual whims without the asking. It sounded so unbelievable he knew his defense would never stand up in court. Especially a jury with even one woman sitting in the box prepared to judge him. He spoke a plea of defense aloud, "It can't be my fault. I would never..." He started to follow with the word kill, but he knew he'd not only be a liar, but a defendant's attorney in a murder case, let alone a double murder, would never allow him to speak the word "kill" while testifying. It's the single damning word, which would most likely cloud the courts eyes with visions of a sex scandal gone awry and brewing the rage it would require for such a horrendous act of violence. It could then all but seal the verdict of guilty on all counts immediately on cross examination. Besides, he'd never be able to hide his guilt on the stand. He'd killed before. He'd killed recently. He'd even killed old friends. The prosecution could certainly unmask his facade showing the rabid dog he hid deep inside.

Even if he'd been given a dangerous mixture of drugs, why wouldn't he believe he could be capable of murdering two women who could ruin his world with their scandal? After all, the accusations would have been born from bitches he didn't know, much less didn't care anything about after the sex was done. He resigned himself to the fact he'd more than likely committed these acts. In order to justify his own conscience, he told himself they'd chosen him, risking some strange concoction they dosed him with. Again, certainly their fault. They were their own collateral damage, he the victim in the long run.

Glancing back down into the bowl he'd finished urinating in, he visualized the moment Jaime leaned over the railing, her ass bumping wildly against him—the flaccidness began to give way to something more like a granite obelisk in his hand. A thought conjured up inside for just a fleeting second. How could he still become aroused even after knowing she'd lost her life, most likely by his hand. Aisling also. Without hesitation, he spoke his self-assessment aloud while he stared into his own eyes reflecting at him from the mirror. "You're a sick dangerous fuck, Ethan William Kendrick. You deserve every horrible and painful retribution the dark-cloaked horseman brings you. He will choose the time to trot his mammoth Clydesdale out of the charred remains of Hell's entry to drag you back into the flames." And with that, he held a soft shrinking implement in his hand. Poking it back in and zipping up, he considered his dagger sheathed, his battle near its end.

He knew for certain, as if he'd received some sort of mystic calling that Joyce would not be coming back to him. Not ever. And he deserved it. She most certainly did not deserve the wrath that would eventually fall like rain on her for being with him. *Is this guilt I'm feeling? Joyce is this important to me? Am I putting her good in front of mine? Who are you? I'm staring at a stranger in the mirror. A living contradiction, because you aren't the Ethan, I've been accustomed to being. Not the man who clawed his way through the mire and built all I enjoy in this life at whoever's expense it would be costed out to.*

He still puzzled over one piece of his and Joyce's story. For a moment he hungered for the possibility that the mirror before him held magic. Sorcery, which could expose a definite yes or no question, like the magic eight-ball a child could ask and then turn up to find their answer inside the small dark triangle. He wasn't certain if it were gospel truth, or for that matter, if it would change any outcome for the better. But it was a missing piece. he believed he'd figured it out the first time he met her. He could see it in her eyes, her demeanor, her beautiful skin tone and structure. He felt certain within himself but wanted the assurance of a definite answer. Was Joyce's sweet daughter, Mitzi, born from his seed.

After all, she looked nothing like Roy. She owned mountains more sense than Roy, smarter, natural humor and street smarts. More like himself, less the evil greed. He prayed so anyway. Or at least he would pray, if he only believed there were a God who would save him and allow his love and possession of Joyce to continue.

The single time Roy brought the prize to the party, Ethan became elated. He remembered how he didn't even want Roy to touch her, sensing how special she was from the moment the car door opened. And then Roy stepped around into the picture, blocking her extravagant beauty with his sloppy backwoods arrogant cop attitude. Type-A personality that he'd dealt with in courts all his adult career. And he could barely stand it, even when they were kids growing up.

But as he watched Roy touch his wife, Joyce, on her curvaceous ass, pretending to steady her as they walked up the steps to Ethan's house, that's the moment his jealousy began overtaking him. She was already tipsy from the roofie Roy had slipped her unknowingly on the drive out. Roy was itching to share her goodies without his wife offering on her own accord. Roy obviously wanted to watch another man with her, knowing she was his to take back home. He was acting like a little punk bitch gloating with his new toy, which no one else received from Santa. He acted smug about it, Ethan noticed the look in Roy's eyes as his hand pawed her bottom and then ran those fat stubby fingers between her thighs when she attempted each step she took, needing his shoulder to lean on for balance. She couldn't even walk, and her new husband was copping cheap feels from her barely conscious body. If Roy would have looked back at him, he would have seen it. Written boldly across Ethan's forehead, 'murder' in big red letters.

He'd wanted to break Roy's fingers with a pair of rusty pliers then and there for starters. It'd taken every ounce of his patience and tolerance to allow Roy to be a part of this sexual scenario.

Ethan wanted this three-way to be minus one boisterous, self-indulged pain-in-the-ass cop—forever. With Joyce there, the desire finally surpassed Ethan's abilities to suppress his urges. He would have killed him then and there that very day—no Charley Bingham there to be a witness, Joyce was almost completely out of her head and no other young girls present like usual to see anything or talk. It was gonna fuckin' happen. Roy certainly didn't deserve this beautiful princess. He wasn't much of a friend anyway. Just a disgrace to his badge, a maggot who would burrow in and feed off any living creature who didn't either flick him off or couldn't reach to remove him. Even worse yet, afraid they'd bleed out if they pulled him from sucking their blood like a dog tick anchored in for the long haul. *Well, I wasn't afraid of Roy Burks, not then or up to the point he was killed.*

***

The moment I saw Joyce, I knew her to be a precious find. The way we were introduced happened all wrong. Recently married to a deputy who didn't have the honor to keep her treasure sacred and the hell away from Phuck-House. Yeah, I'm gonna kill him and feed him to the sharks. I told myself. *Right after I got his ass drunk on the cheapest whiskey I owned. Jack Black, his poison of choice and I always kept a bottle, so I didn't have to waste vintage bourbon on his blue-collar tastes. Who could drink that over-marketed crap anyway? Roy's white trash ass would lap it up like a puppy, mixing it with Coca Cola because he held no taste for finer libations. He's too cheap of a tight ass to spend money on quality. He's loud and obtuse. Sitting there seeing him in his drunken state, his overweight body even when he was young, standing naked at the foot of the bed, offering his wife to share so he could participate in our club. He made me sick as I felt forced to allow his revolting personality and body parts to chastise his beautiful princess like she was a cheap cut of meat at an all you* can eat buffet—I planned my revenge. I fed drinks to Joyce hoping to keep her numb enough to be oblivious to Roy's horrible demise. Everything was about to come to fruition, the quickly drawn plan in place. The three-some now over—Joyce lay sleeping in my bedroom, Roy was shit-faced drunk on the deck. I'd come from the garage with the hammer at my side. I remember hearing his loud incoherent babbling when I walked out to begin my plan of execution, knuckles whitened from my firm grip on the wooden handle. I'd crack his head open with the claw end of the hammer and then push his ass off the deck and onto the sand. Wheelbarrow ready nearby underneath the deck, handy to load him up and wheel his bleeding carcass out to the surf where the bull sharks would enjoy a tasty meal of lard.

I heard another voice. Then I saw her. Fuck! She stood at the base of the stairs down to the beach. The hot little blonde. Cali Lea Jenkins. I thought she'd overdosed and wandered into the surf, becoming shark bait too. But no, there the little druggie stood yacking to Roy, listening to him try to get another piece of ass off her. Fuck! Plans aborted.

I remember slipping away hoping Roy would at the very least be tied up with Cali while I went in and shared what time I could get away with, alone with Joyce, the sweet princess I'd fallen for. When she kissed me, she seemed clueless that I'd now become her prince, a part which I played so well that evening. I also must have left my fertile swimmers inside of her. One penetrating her egg and growing a pretty, little life inside. Our encounter creating our little baby who none of us knew about at the time. The next thing I knew, Roy divorced her, and she disappeared, never to be seen again. I never knew about Mitzi. Never knew Joyce became pregnant after our shared night. Roy wouldn't talk about her. I pried. His lips sealed. When I think about it, I never saw Cali either, until the night with Joyce at Poppy's. Now, the chance meeting makes me wonder about a lot of things. Could Joyce and Cali have talked?

26

There was nothing more to say. All Mitzi could do as they sat around the picnic table was listen with her mouth gaping open as Cali explained to her mom the connection she and Ethan held in the past. She couldn't possibly feel the daggers in mom's heart in the same capacity, but watching her mom's reactions, tears, and shock produced sharp pains of their own. Twisted lies one hundred and eighty degrees opposite of the façade Ethan somehow created and projected outwardly.

"I'm so sorry, Joyce. But you see why I wanted to talk to you. He's a dangerous man who abused young girls in his past. Who knows what he is capable of now or who else he's hurt? He has so much power around this area. His foot was strong in the door of the sheriff's office before Billy Jay put an end to it. I'd been waiting for year's wondering if Billy Jay would ever do anything, and then he just disappeared after he killed his oldest boy."

"So, Jay found you on the roadside way back when you were manipulated into going with some school friends to Ethan's house?" Joyce asked. "Because my impression of Jay is fear and uncertainty. Mitzi and I thought he was going to try and kill us."

"Oh, Jay's not a nice man, I'm not implying innocence at all. But I was out of my mind back then when I woke up. I was struggling to breathe. My chest was heavy, and I was hallucinating. I don't know what drug they gave me, but I felt lucky Jay found me by the highway. Back then there was nothing out past

Eastpoint. Nothing but dead-end gravel roads and swampy-alligator land on one side and ocean on the other. I'd ran after Ethan became busy with another girl and found myself in the middle of nowhere, no idea where I even was. If he or one of the others looked for me, they could have found me and killed me." Cali reached across the table and held Joyce's hands. "...Jay, as scary as he is, saved me that day. He told me he'd fix them one day. He'd judge and punish each one involved. He never tried to hurt me or force himself with me. With all those scary tattoos, I was surprised he didn't rape and kill me. I couldn't have defended myself the shape I was in."

Mitzi spoke up. "So Crazy Jay didn't try anything sexual with you, but Ethan, a prominent attorney, and Roy, who was a deputy back then, along with Charley, our f'ing principal, who taught at Apalachicola High..." She paused and looked at Cali with a perplexed look. "...these early pillars of this town, drugged you—and other girls from school—and forced themselves on you—altogether in the same room in sex parties?" She looked to her mom and said, "Oh my gawd, ewe," and then back to Cali. "That's just disgusting. At least Roy and Mr. Bingham, argh...Charley the perv, paid high prices for their parts. Bullets and bull sharks, and I hope it was horrible and painful for both." She looked again to her mom. "...I'm so gawd damned glad Roy isn't my dad—and I'm sorry as hell you ever were in the position to think he was, Momma." Mitzi shivered. "Now it needs to be Ethan's turn to face the fiery consequences. Painful, lingering ones!" Mitzi paused, remembering Crazy Jay watching her couch-show through the window. "...actually, maybe they could cook 'em together like a two-slotted kitchen toaster and we could share popcorn while we watched—that'd beat any movie on the big-screen!"

"Oh, Mitzi B, don't talk like that, don't even think like that..." Joyce pulled her hand away from Cali's to wipe the tears from her eyes. The sorrow she felt seconds ago from being betrayed, transformed into a bitter anger mixed with thankfulness that Ethan and her relationship hadn't gone any farther forward. "...and to think I wanted to marry the son-of-a-bitch!" A look of panic passed across her face. "I'm jobless now. He'd said I could stay, but I could never face him again...."

"Momma! We're puttin' that motherfucker in prison!" Mitzi halted her words too late as she glanced over at her mom. "Oh, I'm sorry, Momma, for the cussing and my lack of your feelings. You have a place to stay, and you'll be okay. You'll get another job. We've started over before, you and me..." But Mitzi realized it wouldn't be the same. She had both Darrell and Katie. Her momma other than sharing her family, had nobody. No parents, no real friends yet, other than Ethan and Addi, his assistant. She reached over putting her arm around her mom's shoulder and pulled her in close. "It's gonna work out, Momma, you'll see. I love you—to the moon, Momma."

27

Damn the luck of losing such a great employee, Ethan thought. He suddenly felt swallowed up with paperwork and pre-trial needs. Files scattered across two desks. He never really realized how pertinent his paralegal was to him. He couldn't believe things like this could happen so unexpectedly. Just days before, life was promising. His clients were pretty much happy with his representation. The law firm's reputation impeccable due to all the wins in court. Now, one of his biggest, most publicized cases, was close to taking a big turn. Certainly, there would be blowback from the town, but since he lived outside its proximity—the winning would outweigh any negative press. After all, all press was good, even if was mixed with some outrage, it was still notoriety and notoriety brought new clients, which brought in the money. It was a circle all neatly tied together. Once a defense attorney was proven enough to become part of the circle, well round and round we go…. "Unless of course, a damned link breaks in the chain that propels the continuous loop! Dammit, she held such promise! Why now? Son-of-a-bitch."

28

I was disappointed, and yet knew it was the right thing. At least I wasn't worried like before. The feelings between us had been like lightly touching against a beautiful flower you can't keep. You enjoy the feeling of it, the aroma that surrounds it, and the beauty it holds; but you realize, pulling it up from the ground for yourself to enjoy would shorten its time together quickly. You'd never be able to keep her.

When Georgie pulled back, it hadn't been because she was being smart or even full of caution or question; it was because the feelings were one-sided on my part. I'd surprised her and in shock she'd responded. At least she wasn't acting awkward towards me.

If we had crossed that threshold and into something more defined, it wouldn't have mattered how strong the feelings of passion were on my end. And that's what hurts. Knowing the moment things went any further would have been like stepping onto a swinging bridge leading over a deep and scary chasm. The cautious inspection of the bridge's strength would have overshadowed ever stepping onto the swaying bridge to begin with. Examining the cables and the wooden planks for their safety would instead become the insight showing us the dangers lying ahead. I would have looked back into her eyes with willing adventure, and she surely would have nervously looked away. Stepping onto that bridge would have become more than hesitant, it would have been an embarrassing mishap. Both of us feeling the sway. I would have been willing, but comfortable, while she likely experienced vertigo with the awkward movement. Would the abyss of the unknown have swallowed us up whole; even though it was only a wine and circumstance induced mistake?

Georgie would have sputtered the words out first. *"I...I don't want...I don't want you to think..."* She would be nervous I imagine. *"Dammit, Amy Jo...I'm...I'm just going to spit it out! I'm not sure I want this...I...I do...but..."* She'd squeeze my hand tighter before loosening her grip and step back towards the safe and solid unmoving ground.

And in my cautious attempt to keep the door open, I'd say, *"Georgie...It's okay. Applying the brakes doesn't mean the vehicle has to stop completely. Sometimes, it's better to slow down by taking your foot off the pedal and coast, moving forward slowly with caution...."*

We'd both probably would smile at each other, as we each stepped back from the bridges swinging motion and instead, we'd turn and slowly make our way back down the hallway towards the kitchen in a flushed silence. The coffee on the stove would then save the day.

The warm water sprinkled over my face and down my body to the drain as I acted out the scenario in my head. I was so damned confused. This scenario would never happen, and I'm okay with that. I told myself I could be satisfied with the friendship we shared and leave it at that. *Don't we always tell ourselves this bullshit, to convince us we can really achieve this farce? Is it ever possible to put the surprise back into the box and pretend you didn't see it?*

It was just the fleeting moment of circumstance that brought this whole thing between us anyway. Well, and a bottle of wine. I smiled. Now I would just work at deleting the entire episode from my memory, after all, this was the first time these kinds of queer feelings had taken hold of me. I was good at suppressing things and burying them deep in the darkest recesses. I'd had early practice at it. Thanks to my mother and especially my father.

***

The waves roll up the shore wetting the sands, turning it into a soupy cement before racing back to the salty world it momentarily fled from. Tiny fiddler crabs pop up and scamper about in crazy circles as the frothy water washes over them; quickly draining away from their homes burrowed underneath the sands surface. The sight reminds me of the way people rush around for no apparent reasons in life. Was this what life was supposed to be for us as well? Running in pointless circles, wasting our time instead of settling down with someone to love. My life seems to continue in this same way, the crabs mocking me with their madness, without change and never ending. The hamster wheel I now ride as an official adult, I guess. Is everyone content with this?

My mind continues its toying and twisting of my thoughts even as I sit on a towel soaking in the warm rays from the sun. While the heat seems to pull the tension from my body, I'm unable to turn my brain completely off or nudge it onto a different subject. Its direct rays do leave me slightly more relaxed as I hide my eyes behind the cover of sunglasses. Oh, they're not only for the brightness of the day, but more for hiding myself like a masked marauder not allowing anyone who may be watching the ability to decipher my self-pitying thoughts. I held up the cheap romance novel in front of me as a backup, pretending to the point of turning pages occasionally, which I haven't read, nor do I plan to attempt to today.

My thoughts were too deep, much like the ocean waters before me, and at times my contemplations tired me much like treading water does. I wanted to keep my head above the surface, but then again, should I let it sink below—did I really want to be saved from my torment today? I forced my brain to persevere, keeping me from mentally drowning.

Jay and Georgie. Two polar opposites in my life who were presently battling for my focus. Interviewing Jay for my book and Georgie worried about my trip to and from alone. The two of them were the present purposes of my life that I felt I knew. From our times spent together, in some crazy way, I felt I was in control of them and how they affected my life.

Jay, a man whom I thought had some characteristics in common with my grandfather, but I now believe that was only because I missed my grandfather so horribly. He is the only man who was ever a positive influence on me. My rescuer, my hero.

Jay most definitely now lived on the opposite of the spectrum of where I'd placed him. Hindsight truly is 20/20.

And then Georgie, my sweet friend who watches nightly for me to see I make it home safe and sound. Her smile always greeting me with excitement. So alive and vibrant. Who wouldn't be attracted to a woman with so much life, loyalty, and love in her? She can't contain it or hide it without spilling over the edges to anyone nearby.

Jay, it seems, turned out to have a nasty hidden past he was about to confess, shattering any imagery of a salvageable soul to me. An example of polar opposites of humanity.

Something in Georgie awakened a spirit buried deep within that I never knew existed, but was it with the cost of confusing an innocent angel? I now felt guilty of somehow trying to convert her into something she wasn't made to be. Who really knew if I, myself was this person I now found myself debating about? If I truly was, was I applying pressures to someone I'd called friend for my own selfish needs? I thought I was better than Jay, but maybe we all have our price for self-preservation in life and love. Do we all do whatever it takes to pump the adrenaline into our hearts to harness the power of drunken desire?

I've never felt my heart pounding so strong, my skin tingling so fluttery, my body wanting to be caressed and kissed. But why last night? What was different in the way I saw her? She wears the same short dark hair she wore since we met, the same brown eyes with the identical sparkle and soft milky light-brown skin. Infectious beautiful smile that showcases her loving soul. So, what transformed her from being the caring friend next door, to the object of my new appetite?

Just what happened to me at Lake Correctional when my internal lights went out and I woke up fuzzy headed and blurred eyed? Was my brain invaded by aliens? What happened to make me now wander if I could I ever feel the same goosebumps on my arms or butterflies in my stomach she inspires from the hand of a man if I force myself to deny my feelings? Aren't the desires I feel this very instant, while I sneak peeks around the pages of my book to watch her playfully frolic at the surfs edge, socially unacceptable? *Dammit Amy Jo!* I yell to myself in a loud internal scream. *Don't mess with your friend's head. Back away. Don't leave her a broken mess when you know it's not right.*

If I do refuse what I feel my heart is calling, will I live life alone? I picture myself sitting in a rocking chair contemplating my worth to the world, listening to the squeaks and groans as I move back and forth. Only going inside to heat another frozen dinner so I can remain alive for another empty day.

I fear without someone to love, this will be the future I grow into. I need you, Georgie, and I don't understand why. Help me, Lord. I suddenly feel isolated and alone in a place I was perfectly content living alone in only a day ago.

<u>29</u>

Kyle rolled across the sidewalk out for an unusual ride, because he was completely bored of being alone in his apartment. He now sat in the driver's seat of a different kind of vehicle. He missed his life before the crash, and he beat himself up daily when he needed to remind Vio of the simple things she'd somehow forgotten. It was his fault after all. He knew it. Kyle also knew Darrell and Mitzi blamed him, even though they never said it directly. Their anger would be rightfully so. In a way, he was responsible for breaking up the group and before they'd reached the end of their high school careers. The world they once shared together as best friends was now like a distant planet from where they were not long ago.

The sun seemed to burn extra hot on his neck and shoulders as he threw his arms forward. The act of gripping the wheel on either side of his wheelchair and then thrusting himself ahead at a snail's pace was a relatively new chore. The thoughts of how the doctors seemed to think Violet was improving drove him to dig deeper on the wheels to exert more energy to build speed. He wanted it to be true—what they told him. He prayed constantly that she would return to her normal happy and beautiful self. The girl he fell in love with. If she woke up cured and decided for a different life other than the one, they now shared. It would destroy him if she left, but it would also relieve the pain from all the self-blame he kept wrapped tight inside.

He wasn't sure where he was wheeling himself, he just answered the call to get the hell out of the lonely house. That call he answered out of nowhere that led him down the sidewalk. Anger propelled each thrust of his arms the more he remembered the minutes up to the point of losing control of his car on that damned bridge. His biceps and forearms now burned. He'd noticed the increased strength in his upper body along with heightened muscle-tone. What good would it do though. He didn't feel anything below his thighs except for tingles and sharp jolts occasionally.

***

"Those spasms below your waist in each leg could be good signs, Kyle. We need to keep up with your therapy. Are you getting help with the techniques we've shown you?" Doctor Mendle had asked the last time he'd been examined. The truth was, he'd given up on ever being able to walk, even though the specialist told him there were no severed nerves. Pinched and injured, but not severed. His specialist also asked about Violet and how she was getting along.

"Her doctors say she's improving, I just don't see it."

"Are you encouraging her?"

"Doc, I try, I really do—but how can I when I feel like shit all the time? I have all this blame inside my head, I can't escape it. I get up at night after waking and look over at Vio, knowing I did this to her. And then as I drop my dead legs to the floor to wriggle into my chair, I just shake my head in disbelief."

"The way I see things, Kyle, you were given another chance. Both of you. I saw the pictures of your car—you should both be dead. You can't give up when you've been given the gift of a redo. Are you still talking openly to Dr. Shandice? She's a very good phycologist, one of the best in Florida. But you need to keep the channels open with her for anything worthwhile to come to fruition."

Kyle's face dropped leaving his chin resting on his chest. "I meet her every Tuesday morning. It's part of weekly 'routine' of life," he said as he held quotation marks beside his ears. "I do all of this, and it adds to the guilt because Mitzi wheels me here and drives me there like my sled dog."

***

As he forced each hand to grab onto each large wheel and propel himself forward in perfect timing again, the thoughts of his visit to his doctor and those words he heard, now churned something inside he couldn't decipher. He'd also seen the pictures of his Chevelle. She'd been his girl since he was sixteen. He'd fought with hard discussions to convince his mom he would be a responsible driver in it.

"Son, that car has over four-hundred horses I'm told, and while I don't know what that means exactly…."

"But Mom! Look at her! Aren't you still disappointed with your mom and dad for not letting you have that Ford Mustang you've told me about?"

"Yes, but who's to say I'm alive today because they chose to say no to me…."

Kyle realized as he began to tire from venturing so far off without resting, he'd won the battle with his mom back then, but that last night driving the prize he'd won, he now realized he'd lost the war and taken collateral damage with him. Almost beyond coincidence his mom died only one year and four days before his accident. With his dad running off with his mom's best friend before he was old enough to remember, he didn't have any family left now except for Vio. And they weren't married. Hell, even if they were, she'd only remember it occasionally. He'd been successful in messing her life up too. For that matter—Vio's parents also. He'd noticed how difficult it was for her mom and dad to look him in the eye when he was around. Who could blame them though, I'd taken their daughter away from them, at least the one who remembered them every day?

He drew the strength to push forward again, increasing his speed. It was like he was back behind the wheel of his Chevelle. Pushing it close to beyond its limits. The wheels and frame began to shake and wobble as he sped down the decline. His wheelchair began to veer toward the street into oncoming traffic. Seconds before he was about to jump the curb, he tightened his grip with every ounce of strength on the left wheel, causing it to bring the right wheel quickly around to the left, dumping him onto the grass and sandy ground. The wheelchair rolled over to a stop as Kyle rolled four or five rotations before sprawling out in some scattered weeds. He lifted his head to survey his new girl. She was in better shape than his Chevelle after her roll and all he could do is lay back down and laugh hysterically. Hell, he couldn't feel anything anyway, he was already damaged goods.

A truck slowly pulled to a stop beside the road and an older gentleman crawled out from behind the wheel, leaving his door wide open into traffic. "My gawd, son—you alright?" He bent down to give a hand after rushing over to Kyle's side. "I can't believe you're laughin', son."

Kyle continued to chuckle. "I didn't realize this baby had so much power! Guess she got away from me...." His chortles quickly turned to choked cries as he strained to look behind him, remembering seeing Vio's hand lying motionless and not being able to make his body turn to check her status.

"Should I call an ambulance?"

It took several seconds before Kyle answered. "No sir, if you could just help me back up...."

"Son—your ride ain't goin' nowhere without some tinkerin'

and repairs on that ride. I can put it in the back and take ya home if you don't want no medical attention."

A couple of cars honked at the open truck door as traffic backed up. "Let me load your wheels up really quick." The man glanced at the driver that just honked and flipped him off before he slammed his door and walking around to the back to open his tailgate. "Ain't ya got no concern for people in need?" He yelled at the driver. The old man turned the wheelchair upright, then drug it to his truck bed and hoisted it up and in. He slammed the gate and walked back over to Kyle, holding out his hand. "I'm Jake Hodges, what be your name, son?"

"Kyle." He held his hand up for Jake to grab. "Kyle Jones, sir." And then he groaned as Jake pulled him up to his feet, grabbing onto the old-timer. It took all Jake could do to get Kyle over to the passenger side of Jake's pickup. "I just live up the road a bit, mister Hodges...."

"Just call me Jake, Kyle. And no problem, let's get you back home and make sure you're okay."

30

The manila folder fell to the floor with a slap, scattering the enclosed papers across the aisle to the desk where detective Blane sat staring at a computer screen. The loud slam and clatter were preceded by a subtle bang, which grabbed his attention. The detective quickly looked down, then over to where Tony stood. This all happened within mere seconds. The detective's eyes backtracked from Tony's face and downward, using his investigative senses. Working things from the end and following an obvious trail toward the beginning to deduce the original cause. This trained reversal process, nudged the recruit to continue his survey of following the papers, the ones beginning wide apart and at his feet, until the papers distance became narrowed from the one in front to the next and so on—as if a dealer at a poker game had fanned the deck of cards out onto the table. When the papers grew closer together, the file soon appeared in his sight, which lay at the foot of Tony's desk. This sight drew the detective's scrutiny upward to the top of the desk where the file would most likely have resided before the spill. There was a leaning stack of files that appeared to have tipped past the point of angle allowing the folders to remain straight and stable. Detective Blane scanned the area quickly but thoroughly before feeling confident he'd solved the case of what just happened mere seconds ago.

Blane began his internal narrative, or audit, of the events leading him to his deduction of what had just happened. A form of double-checking his final analysis. It was good practice to help stay in tiptop form.

Tony's phone dangled from its cord until almost settling on the floor. It still swung slowly back and forth from the initial momentum. Looking again at Tony's face, there was an evident look of frustration. Possibly outright anger. His chair was also sitting crooked and awkward to where no one could have been sitting seconds ago. The thought process was pointing out evidence and potential circumstances. Considering different options was critical to ensure the accuracy of the initial assessment. Surmising Tony was on the phone in a somewhat recumbent position. He must have heard something that upset him enough to throw the phone receiver onto the desk. This action possibly bounced the receiver off the stack of files that then shifted the pile enough for the top file to slide over and fall off the edge of the desk. The slipping files thereby instigating the action of the enclosed papers heretofore once housed within the folder to land across the aisle and spread across the floor to my feet. There were two distinct sounds separated by a rattle. First a louder bang, which could only have been the phone smacking onto the desk, followed by the phone rattling about as swung back and forth. The latter disturbance being the smack of the chair after being shoved into the table. This would explain the shocked and still angry scowl on the suspect's face! Case closed! The suspect of course, was Tony Rawling. The department's best damned detective that the state of Florida employs.

Instantly, the recruit, Detective Blane, realized he'd named Rawlings his suspect within his mind. *Was it written all over his face too? That he'd mentally declared Tony's guilt of the incident?*

"What the hell are you lookin' at Blane? Go back to your own business."

"Yes sir, Sargent Rawlings." He turned away and began stroking the keys of his computer, as he had before the disturbance.

Hank rushed over to Tony and asked, "What the hell is up?"

"The fuckin Governor is ready to give Cader clemency because I...dammit! I didn't announce who Sam and I were when we went to question Billy Jay. The son-of-a-bitch is gonna skate from the chair, and it's my fault."

"But we still got him if we find prints or his blood type on the barrels, don't we?"

"I don't know, Hank. I don't know a damn thing anymore. We work our asses off to keep the state safe and this is the gawd damned thanks we get. Some prick defense attorney screams foul on the murdering asshole and we end up being the bad guys." Tony kicked his chair again as if to put an end to its misery.

Blane started to look over but decided to stay busy with his own case and keep his head down until his words slipped out, "Just wait 'til we can use DNA matching—we'll nail 'em then...."

Tony responded even louder, "Bullshit! The fuckin' attorney's will still find faults in our evidence and get these killers off. It's pointless!" Tony kicked his chair a third time before storming out of the office.

***

Georgie ran up from the water's edge and stood in front of me, water glistening on her body from the bright sun. I folded my book closed, the one I hadn't read a single sentence from for over an hour, too busy thinking. "How's the water?" I asked.

"Amy Jo, it's so refreshing. You should come out with me and cool off. You look like your red. Do you need some sunscreen? I have some in my bag."

Before I could answer she'd dropped to her knees and bent over her bag, rifling through it. "No, really, Georgie—I'm fine. If you wanna go back in, I'll come with you this time."

"Let's go then!" Georgie stood up and held her out hand to help pull me up. The excitement across her face re-energized me and I bounced up quickly as I tossed my book to the side. We ran off towards the surf, hand in hand like young schoolgirls playing in the water for the first time. My mind cleared completely of my sorrows and worries about Jay the minute my legs hit the first wave. Listening to the laughs and giggles of not only Georgie, but the others including children, took me back in time. Time when all my worldly problems seemed resolved. As we both squatted below the surface, keeping our heads above the surf as it rolled in steadily, I grinned at Georgie with what must have been a huge smile. She immediately looked at me, her lips turning up on their outside edges also.

"What, Amy Jo? Are you laughing at me?"

"No, no, it's nothing like that. I'm enjoying watching your excitement. You don't carry a single sorrow on your face. I love that about you."

"What's to be sorrowful about on a beautiful day like this? The sun is shining, the water is perfect and I'm spending the entire day with my best friend! Everything is happy today!"

She began to work her way closer to me, keeping just her head above the waves as she moved in.

"You should smile more too, Amy Jo. Be happy! No worries, we have each other!" She reached out for my hand and of course, I held mine open because I couldn't stay away from her any more than a honeybee could resist a beautiful flower.

I smiled back. "You're right, friends forever, Georgie!" But inside my thoughts were the feelings that took over last night. I smiled through my woes though, not wanting to cause any friction. *I'll admit, I love this feeling, but I don't like feeling the lack of control over myself. I'll get over it, this whole thing has got to be a passing fancy. Our friendship will endure. It simply has to. She is almost the only person in this world I have left.*

***

Billy Jay was already counting the days until next Friday. He needed to see Amy Jo. He knew she was smart enough to know where he was headed in the discussion before.... What the hell was he thinking? *Gawd dang that girl's gotten inside my head. Lyle and the boys were seeing things more clearly than I'd given due credit. Maybe I am growing soft, maybe, just maybe it's finally time.* The summer was gone, and winter would be upon him. *Thank God I'm not in that gawd forsaken New York City. I don't know if I could make it another winter hustling the street.*

The sounds of a bull coming down the hallway broke his thoughts. Billy turned and saw the guards stop abruptly in front of his cell.

"Warden wants you upstairs, Billy. Right now." He used his club to tap on the cell rail with each word spoken. It seemed 'the boss' was serious so he got up immediately. He thought his cell must be gettin' a shake down.

"Yes sir, what Warden Wilkerson wants, he gets." Billy Jay couldn't stand Warden Willy, but he knew they were gonna be together for a long time. *It was just the way life was drawn out now.* He'd seen plenty of "incidents" between the guards and inmates before. This house wasn't known across the state for assaults on inmates just for shits and giggles. It was known as number three in the state and that was just on the inside. You didn't give lip to the bulls unless you wanted pay hell in return. "He wants to see me on a Saturday mornin', boss? Kinda' unusual ain't it?"

"Now, Billy—don't start with the twenty questions. Warden wants to see you for breakfast—just not sure if it's to be shared with you—or if you're gonna be the meal...." The Guard snickered to himself, the other bull just blankly stared with a look of meanness in his eye, ready to charge for any given temptation to do so. Almost as if he were daring Billy to challenge him. *I chose to go quietly without incident though.*

A plate of donuts sat in the middle of Warden Willy's large desk. I could see them the minute I stepped through the entry. I no sooner got inside before the warden began to address me, "Billy—Jay—Cader. So far, you've been a model inmate, especially for one that is under our care for killing two law enforcement officers." Warden Wilkerson sat behind his sprawling wooden desk with scrutiny and judgment wailing from his face. "Sit down, Billy Jay."

Hmmm. Maybe I was getting served donuts for breakfast, instead of "being the meal?"

The guards led Billy to a single chair sitting directly in front of the warden's chair and about two feet from the front edge of his desk. He sat and began to scoot the chair closer to the desk, but the guards put their hands on each of his shoulders putting the kibosh on his forward movement.

"Billy Jay, you'll have to forgive my feeling a need for some extra space between the two of us, but you see, I'm a man who enjoys life as a free human being and well..." Wilkerson pivoted in his large, overstuffed leather desk chair, each elbow resting on an arm, hands folded together propping his chin as if in prayer. "...I'd like to remain a free and living man. The men I meet here in this office, that the great taxpayers of Florida pay for privilege to babysit, are not ones who generally hold respect for my place in life here within these cold gray walls. They also don't seem to have the same reasons to live as I do." Wilkerson rolled his chair close to the edge of his side of the desk and then leaned towards him even closer as if he were to tell Billy a secret. "For that reason, I have a 12-gauge shotgun mounted to the undercarriage of this beautiful handmade walnut desk and it's aimed squarely at your balls—at precisely the perfect distance to spread them all the way back to the door you were escorted in through..." His smile broadened as he continued after a brief pause. "...if you should make the poor choice of attempting to get up or scoot your sorry ass towards me in a way that I would feel threatened. It would be a shame to have to send another cleaning and repair bill to the state for those good citizens to pay for. Do we understand each other—Mr. Cader? Consider this your last courtesy of a warning to sit perfectly still and talk only when asked to participate—again, are we both on the same page?" Wilkerson, still leaning forward waited for a couple of seconds. "This would be your cue to participate in the discussion, Mr. Cader."

"Well, I suppose those delicious lookin' donuts aren't for me after all, and yes, we are definitely on the same page, Warden Willy."

Wilkerson sat back into his chair with a disappointed look washing across his face. "I suppose that is what I am called back on the floor between the animals—but in this space, the one we are sitting in—this is my personal domain—and I'm afraid I just won't accept that brand of disrespectful bullshit in here without repercussion. You might want to rethink the way you address me. I'll give you about ten seconds to come up with a more pleasing reference to me and an acknowledgement that you won't be making the same mistake again."

Billy looked squarely into the eye of the warden for a full five seconds, almost daring him, before he spoke, "I do apologize. I meant no disrespect—Warden Wilkerson. It won't happen again, sir." Billy's eyes never quivered or faltered in any way.

"Now look at that, I just love it when one of society's throw-a-ways—can be taught so quickly how to maintain a common courtesy. Much like teaching a puppy to sit and roll over. Maybe beg for dog biscuit. It warms the cockles of my cold, cold heart and gives me the satisfaction of doing my due diligence of what's expected of me." Warden Willy sat back with a look of pride mixed with self-righteousness. "Billy Jay, you're never gonna see the light of day outside these walls and barbed wire fences as long as you live, but you'll be molded into a cordial, humble, and respectful inmate within these boundaries as long as I serve the great state of Florida as your keeper." He motioned for his guards to go back to the far corner of his office. "Now that it's just between you and myself, Billy Jay..." The warden's demeanor appeared to relax a bit having set his perimeter of power. "I received some news. Several different bits of news—that I need to converse with you about. The first concerns a young lady you have become familiar with, a Ms. Amy Jo Whitenhour...."

Billy's eyes perked up.

"I see by your expression that you are cognizant of whom I'm referring. It seems she suffered a mishap here in my fine facility yesterday and while she was in fact—in a discussion with you." Wilkerson reached over to a square box sitting on his desk to his right. He reached up and opened it, pulling out a long narrow cigar. He then reached in his drawer while he continued to look at Billy Jay, pulling out a cigar nip as if driven by memory muscle to where in his desk it resided. He never pulled his eyes from view of Billy's as he inserted the tip into the nip and sliced the blunted end of the cigar into a flat smooth surface. This was done in mere seconds. He then placed the cigar into his mouth and reached for the table lighter, pulling it to the tip and flicking the steel roller causing the spark against the flint, igniting a bright flame. He held the flame to the tip of the cigar and drew in several puffs, expelling the smoke from the sides of his mouth until the tip was well lit.

"Billy, I need something from you..." He paused and drew in a long pull from the cigar, enjoying its flavor as he rolled the brown leafed tobacco cylinder around in between his thumb and finger before slowly blowing the smoke across the table towards Billy's face. "I need to know exactly what the conversation was about that you two were engaged in when Ms. Amy's mishap occurred. And I mean the exact words. And if I don't feel compelled in my thoughts that you are being honest, well, these little 'interviews' between you two every week—will be brought to a halt. So, answer carefully, Billy Jay."

Silence overtook the room. Billy sat quietly with little movement while he appeared to be contemplating his answer carefully.

"While you are cautiously preparing your answer, I'll go ahead and let you know some other news I've been made aware of. It seems the fine democratic governor of this state, and I say this facetiously about our present state of leadership in case you were remiss of my demeanor…" Wilkerson guffawed before continuing, "…the governor has apparently found fault in your trial and is prepared to grant clemency, therefore withdrawing the state's ability to—put you down like the rabid dog you truly are." He took another long slow draw on his stogie, letting big puffs of gray smoke escape in between sucking, but never inhaling. "What a fuckin' pussy he is—as you can surmise—I don't agree with him politically—or morally. Not that you will ever leave this facility in any way other than in a body-bag…" A cloud of cigar smoke hovered as if it were a stagnant fog in the valley of the Smokey Mountains of Tennessee. "…which brings me to another call I just received this morning. This one is a bit more—of an ominous subject matter, and one that could possibly nullify the governor's poor choice he seems hellbent on following through with…."

Billy Jay sat still in his chair. "Warden Wilkerson, I'm guessin' you have a pretty good notion what we were talkin' 'bout." Billy's voice was matter of fact, without so much as a skip like a brand-new record album, still wrapped and virgin to having the needle laid to its vinyl. "Ms. Amy Jo was askin' if I ever killed anybody other than those two cops I was convicted for. More specific—she asked if I ever was responsible for any atrocities on any—young girls."

Wilkerson's eyes lit up briefly before the question washed across them. "And what was your response, do tell?" He asked.

Billy sat still but his legs moved back and forth, and Wilkerson spotted it quick like a poker-players tell. "I told her it was more complicated than an answer as simple as yes or no."

"I suppose your response was indeed one she wasn't prepared to hear. I also would imagine you are reluctant to say any more to me also?" Wilkerson questioned.

Billy Jay gave in to a brief smile. "Your perception would be correct. What would be in it for a man either facing the electric chair or at very least a life term in your—little kingdom you reign over? Life is over for me as I once knew it. I see no pleasant future value under your 'keep' here at this glass house no matter which way that wind blows." Billy paused a moment for either dramatic effect or to prepare for what would certainly quickly follow. His eyes gave no tell of which answer was correct. He just drew in a slow breath and continued, "So, you go ahead and pull your little trigger. Blow my balls, sir, or whatever other little sexual depravity you might have. I've been beaten and raped by inmates and guards alike as if I were some nickel and dime whore just a beggin' to give freebies and samples, so I'll bet you couldn't come up with anything new I've not been forced to do already. I've been threatened by bigger and scarier men than you to a point I just don't give a tinker's damn no more. I ain't got shit to say—sir, other than this puppy don't sit, or roll over no more. Not for nobody, and especially not the likes of wanna be somebody more than the piece a shit you are."

"Do you think you're the first nut that was mistaken about me crackin' open?" Wilkerson laughed. He motioned for the guards to take Billy away. "Henry, take this worthless trash down to the hole and give him two weeks in solitary. Tell Emma Sue to get a hold of Amy Jo Whitenhour of the Orlando Beacon first thing this Monday morning. I'm gonna wanna talk to that sweet little tart and give her my love from Mr. Cader here."

31

Georgie rested her arm on the door frame as the wind blew her short hair across her face each time, she turned to face Amy. "Are you going to tell me about what happened with you and Billy Jay?"

I looked over and smiled, noticing the strands of hair in her face. It was all I could do not to reach over and brush them behind her ear.

"What Amy Jo? Why are you smiling? I thought it was serious stuff with Billy Jay."

"It was, or is—I just…" I turned away and looked ahead in front of me, my hair also blowing in the cross winds between each window. Every time I turned, my hair flew one direction or the other. The skin around my eyes and my forehead felt tight and radiated some heat. She'd been right when she asked if I was sure that I didn't need sun lotion. I had. My fair skin felt burned now, even in the shade of the truck. "My face feels flushed with heat—I just hate admitting you were right, that's all." I smiled again, feeling like I'd just landed a nice save. I'd need to be getting better at this because it seemed my feelings weren't fading away very quickly. After a couple of minutes filled with small talk and silence, I began to tell her the conversation Billy and I were sharing, and then my incident of fainting or passing out.

"So, he admitted to hurting or killing young girls?" Georgie asked.

"Not exactly, but he seemed on the verge, and he offered no

outrage at the question. He told me he needed to set up the background behind what he was going to tell me. The look in his eyes told me what I suddenly suspected. I think he knew he'd been caught in a trap. I don't know...." I pulled my hair back and tucked it behind my ear for the umpteenth time. "...kind of like a wolf with his paw snapped tight in a snare. He looked like he knew he couldn't chew through it with me there watching, so he was preparing to confess. My damned mind just shut down on me. You know me, Georgie. I was beginning to see some of my grandfather in him. The whole idea of him being so evil like my daddy..." I reached up and gently wiped my eyes, trying to avoid the tender spots on my face. "...I just never saw it coming. I'd convinced myself he'd acted out in self-defense killing those officers, refusing to see the other side of him. The dark, evil side he'd kept slightly hidden or camouflaged."

I could see Georgie turn to her window from my peripheral view. She was quiet a moment or so before I caught her turning back towards me. I turned and looked at her—square on, our eyes locked. "I warned you about messing with that devil. He's trying to kill you from the inside since he can't from the outside. He's doing it, Amy Jo, killing you softly and slowly."

"I know, Georgie, but...."

"But nothing, Amy Jo. You need to stay away from him and that prison. It's not worth it. It's not even your boss that is making you go, is it?"

I tried to smile. Suddenly I felt like no one in this world would understand my purpose. I wasn't sure I comprehended it now, myself. I just watched the road as the white stripes came rushing at the truck and then disappeared briefly underneath before becoming a white blur trail behind us.

My thoughts began to drift back to before my grandparents passed, like most of my trips back home driving in my favorite vehicle ever. I could never bring myself to sell or trade my grandfather's pickup. It's my connection to him. The only one that still gives me the feeling of sitting with him—able to talk and share my thoughts. Who could possibly understand the attachment that an old blue pickup was able to be—between two people who have no other physical ties anymore? Some of my colleague's chuckle when they happen to be in the lot as I come or go. "There goes little miss farmer frugal!" They sometimes jokingly holler, but I'm used to the name-calling. I know deep inside they don't feel my truck matches the persona I should give off as an investigative reporter. Yet, I seem to be the one who brings the big stories to the headlines, so I guess it's not what you drive that gives you the drive to succeed. I'm happy with my lot in life. I don't need a convertible or fancy BMW. I've seen what kind of happiness those things buy in life and its emptiness on credit terms that slowly rob you blind because they know the hunger for bigger, better, and newer only grows. It doesn't subside and you can't consume it. It consumes you.

My eyes wandered over to Georgie just long enough to see her head kind of wedged between the seat and the door with her eyes closed. Had I been daydreaming that long? The sun did the same for me. My eyes were wanting to drift but my brain kept me going with broken thoughts here and there. We were getting close to Green Swamp Wilderness, not far from the farm, maybe twenty or thirty minutes. Glancing over at Georgie again, my thoughts swam back to the beach and watching her enjoy the waves. I knew I would sleep well tonight. A thought popped into my head that it had been quite a while since I'd gone to my grandparent's church. Church of God in Dade City. I'd go tomorrow. I may even ask Georgie when she wakes up. Lord knows I have a lot of woes on my mind. I felt warm inside, like after Grandmother's fresh from the oven chocolate chip cookies. Her way of approving my intentions, I told myself.

Once I turned off Highway 98, the road became bumpier, and

Georgie soon stirred back to life. It's funny to watch someone who fell asleep while on a trip start to wake up and try to pretend that look of not being asleep. Caught from embarrassment and in a state of denial not only from anyone else in the vehicle, but themselves. I kept quiet, not making a deal of it, but I did snicker to myself while I snuck little glances of her performance. When I pulled into our drive, the first thing I noticed was my porch light lit. Just as Grandfather told me. "A visitor or stranger in need can easily find our door for help with the light burning bright." *Indeed,* I thought to myself as the truck rolled up to a stop.

"I'm tired, Amy Jo! The sun and water always wear me out." She let out a big yawn.

"Are you coming in or heading home?" I asked.

"Oh, I want to come in and chat, but I am so tired…."

"Well, I'm thinking of going to church tomorrow if you are interested?" I asked. "I'll be leaving by seven-thirty in the morning."

"If I get up in time. If I'm not at your door, it means I couldn't get out of bed!" She giggled.

"Okay, sounds good." I hesitated a minute before saying, "I had a good time today relaxing with you."

"Me too, Amy Jo. G'night."

"Night."

***

There was no light except for the edges around the tray slide on the cell door. It wasn't even bright enough to light the cell to see his own hand in front of his face. His stomach growled. It was going to be a long two weeks. Wondering what all was happening behind the scenes. He'd never been to the warden's office before. The entire day was out of the ordinary. *Clemency? What did that even really mean? How was Amy Jo doing now? Did she know any of the things that Willy was talking about? How was I able to remain so calm being questioned and treated like that pompous ass talked to me? Where was my anger hiding these days?*

Without warning Jay suddenly grew the desire to have Ms. Cela by his side. Her frail old body seemed able to show and give such strength. *Did her words really contain the power she spoke of?* "I need you Ms. Cela! I give in! I submit!" Billy screamed at the top of his lungs into the thickest darkness he'd ever experienced. "I'm sorry for all the evil I done to others. Gawd damn you Satan!" Jay's cold bones instantly began to feel heat within the marrow. Tears streamed down his eyes as he sat up and then maneuvered onto his knees. He waited a moment with anticipation of the demons taking his body and mind over once again. The thought scared him this time instead of just becoming entertainment for his thinking. "I feel so warm...." Such a feeling had never happened when he'd claimed to seek forgiveness before. Had Jesus reached inside his heart and soul tonight? He knelt on the cold damp concrete floor, but he felt warmth. He held his arms in front of him with palms open and facing up. "I'm yours Jesus. Take me and do what you will. Forgive me...."

Jay's entire body shook from his head to his toes, but he held no fear. He cried as he asked forgiveness for each person he could name or picture that he'd brought harm to or death. His last sentence he spoke even surprised himself as the words left his mouth. "I forgive you Daddy, I forgive you...." Billy Jay dropped to the floor and curled up in the fetal position and whimpered until he fell asleep.

32

Monday came quicker than normal to me. My Friday with Jay was extra rough. My evening when I got home was, out of the ordinary, leading the weekend to an interesting, but fun beach trip with Georgie and then a Sunday spent in church. Something I'd been meaning to do but hadn't followed through in months. Georgie decided to come with me. It was a quiet ride there, followed by a quiet ride home. I'd never experienced Georgie in such a way. She was always beaming with smiles and very talkative. I guess we all have those days occasionally and I feel certain my reactions to her helped put her in the mood she seemed caught in. I never questioned and she never offered any explanation. We shared glances and simple safe typical "the weather is pleasant, etc." conversation. Nothing with any deep substance. I tried not to mentally dwell on it. In fact, I tried to leave my mind open for God to speak to me. It was his day today and I wanted to give him the chance I hadn't been gifting him. If he found a way to fill me with what he saw was needed, I would accept it.

    I woke up refreshed. I woke up earlier than normal. No smells of bacon in the air or coffee until I performed the duties myself. This morning, I almost felt ignored by my grandparents. It was nothing unusual for little things or incidents to nudge me into thinking they were nearby. Watching, smiling, maybe giving me a warm nudge her or there. Today was different. Not bad, not necessarily good, just different. I felt more aware. I heard the birds clearer, appreciated the sun a little more. The soap on my skin in the shower even felt fresher, the smell richer. It was like I was brand new today. *Yes, that's what I feel. New.*

I tossed my work bag and purse up in the truck onto the passenger seat and twisted the key. She kicked over immediately, and I'll be damned if she didn't purr differently. She sounded new. *What the hell is going on?*

The orange groves smelled sweet this morning as the citrus-filled air blew in through the rolled down windows. For such a mundane daily drive into the Beacon, today seemed exceptional. Pulling into the familiar parking lot made me smile. My life was pretty good. I'd certainly weathered my share of storms, but all things considered, I was very blessed. So many others in this world were dealt much more difficult hands to make something of themselves. I was living my childhood dreams. How many people can honestly say that and mean it? I'd always wanted to write, to be a reporter. To be able to tell the stories that mattered in this world. There were fluff journalists, but I'd never been expected to write fluff in my entire career so far. My editor-in-chief always seemed to let me weed through and pick up on the vibes I'd felt and go with them. I'd exposed some bad apples, reported on hard crime and human-interest stories that brought light to people who help others on the front line. I'd seriously thought about joining the army to be a journalist or a war correspondent, but I just couldn't pull myself away from the farm. It's home. I don't see myself ever leaving.

Just after walking through the front door, I was nailed by our receptionist. "Morning, Amy Jo. You've gotten two calls already. From the secretary to Warden Gerald Wilkerson himself over at Lake Correctional. Who did you piss off over there?" Cassie asked as she gave a wicked grin. "Could there be a story here?"

"Wow! I was wondering when this call would be coming in.

Get the attorneys lined up, Cassie. I think this a-hole is going to try and bar me from coming back to finish my interviews with Billy Jay Cader."

"I'll patch 'em through to your desk when they call back. Better skip the powder room, it'll probably only be five minutes..." The phone rings and Cassie picks up the call. She begins to wave her hands towards me, before she covers the receiver and holds it off to the side.... "It's for you sweetie, I'm going to put it through, good luck!" She turned her attention back to the phone, "I'm putting you right through."

"Warden Wilkerson, Amy Jo Whitenhour of the Orlando Beacon will be on shortly...Yes sir, I'll put her on through."

I hurried with dread, threw my purse on the desk, and barely got seated before my line buzzed. "Good morning, this is Amy Jo, how can I help you this beautiful Monday morning?"

"Well, good morning, Miss Whitenhour, it is Miss, isn't it?"

"I'll answer to that, or you can just address me as Amy Jo, that's what most people call me."

"Well then, Amy Jo, that has a nice ring to it. I imagine you are curious why I would be calling you."

"Oh, I have a bit of an idea. I'm sure you've gotten word about my Friday night fiasco. I've never passed out like that before."

"Yes, ma'am I was informed of the incident. It's partially why I wanted to touch base with you. I know you've been a weekly regular in visiting Mr. Cader for quite some time now."

"Yes sir, I've been coming for about thirteen or fourteen weeks. I've been interviewing him on his past and of course, his death penalty conviction."

"I must admit it brings a curiosity to why you—fainted, or lost consciousness? Was there something said to you by Mr. Cader that would have caused such a thing?"

There was a brief silence on the line between us. I wasn't sure how I should answer. I felt I was being set up or probed. "I..." I started but hesitated again. "...I'm going to have to plead confidentiality, Warden Wilkerson. I'm writing a book and I certainly don't want any information released before I publish." I paused again. "I'm sure you understand my dilemma. I'm fine. It could have been the heat, possibly the smell in the interview room. Does anyone actually perform any cleaning in there? It always has a strong smell of urine in the air."

"Now, Miss Whitenhour—I called to check on your welfare after I saw the report of your accident. I certainly didn't call to spar with you about the accommodations we afford you for the 'ability of interviewing' one of our most dangerous responsibilities we are charged with housing. An accommodation we have allowed most graciously, I might add."

"Warden Wilkerson, this conversation is beginning to take a turn and sound more like a threat of 'removing' that allocation you've granted. I am an upstanding member of the press with awards and letters to show. I've followed every rule I was given and done nothing wrong. Mr. Cader has been nothing but kind and helpful. There have been no problems in the weeks I've been spending in your facility. Am I to be made to feel my future visits are being threatened? I hate to return an inauspicious response, but we at The Orlando Beacon are well represented with a very qualified legal team..." I wanted to pull the words back from my mouth, but it was too late, they were dumped on the desk he most likely was sitting behind. "I'm not finished with my questions of Mr. Cader. I have a substantial amount of time and resources dedicated to this interview. The people have a right to hear the possible reasons for such an awful set of crimes against law enforcement."

"Miss Whitenhour...."

I swore I heard a pen drop on his side of the line. After that, a long deep breath taken in. I could feel the tension attempting to be quelled within him.

"Miss Whitenhour—at this time, we will not be able to allow the continuation of your visits. Mr. Cader has been moved into solitary confinement at this time and his status will be totally upon his responses...."

I interrupted, "Just what did Jay do to deserve this? He did nothing in my presence to be put in solitaire...."

"Miss Whitenhour, Billy Jay Cader is a very violent and dangerous criminal charged and found guilty of two felonious murder counts for which he will face the electric chair. It is solely under my authority as the caretaker in charge of this facility to decide what is in the best interest of all involved. Specifically, the safety of my staff and inmates—and most assuredly civilians allowed to enjoy any visitation privileges."

"I'm asking you not to force my hand, Warden Wilkerson. Please."

"And I am asking you to refrain from threats that will get you nowhere, Miss Whitenhour. As of now, your visits are suspended. My office will be in touch when changes to the situation become different than what they are at present. Thank you and I'm sure we'll talk soon. Good day."

The line went dead.

"Son-of-a-bitch!" I said rather loudly as I slammed the receiver down. Twice! When I looked up, I saw everyone in the office staring at me. Granted, my reaction was not typical for me. I felt deep in my gut that I would not be able to see Jay again. I was being punished, as was he, for some strange reason.

My editor's glass door opened, and he began to weave himself through the desks sitting willy-nilly throughout the newsroom. Our office wasn't set in rows, they were scattered like a rat maze and now walking towards me in the middle was the tomcat of the neighborhood. As he approached my desk I blurted out, "I'm sorry Malcolm. I lost my shit."

"So, what's the scoop?"

"The scoop is, I lost my story. There is no scoop. The f'ing warden is locking me out and Jay is in lockdown solitaire."

"Jay? Are you two on a personal level now that you call the crazy cop killer, Jay?"

"Malcolm—you don't spend four to five hours one day a week in a tiny interview room for fifteen weeks and not come out either friendly or so filled with fear and hate you only call him motherfuc…" I stopped short and covered my mouth. "You know what I mean, Mal. And you know me. I'm generally a friendly likable kind of girl. Sad I can be closer and kinder to a sociopathic killer than the full-deal asshole warden in charge of housing that killer. I wouldn't squat to piss on Wilkerson if he were smoldering in hot coals and beggin' my urine to quench his thirst. Pardon my man-talk."

Malcolm smiled big before the laughter broke through his grinning lips. "Amy Jo, I love you, girl. You are one-of-a-kind!"

"Yeah, I wish I had a quarter every time some guy in a suit said I was a keeper. I'd be worth about a buck seventy-five by now."

"Should we go talk to the law department?" Malcolm asked.

"Billy Jay is in total lockdown. Wouldn't do any good right now. Let's see if the old warden cools his attitude. I already threatened him with having our lawyers look into it."

"Hey in the meantime, Amy Jo, there's been a string of interesting bank heists in some surrounding small towns—I need somebody like you I can trust to dig deep. You interested? At least 'til we see what the hotel manager is gonna do with Cader out there at Lake Correctional?"

"Sure, Mal, give me the info and I'm on it."

Everyone still grasped on to a surprised look in their faces like they were expecting a showdown between me and Malcolm. What they didn't know or understand was that Malcolm was my grandfather's best friend when he was alive and as a favor to a friend, he had taken me in under his wing and coached me through the ropes. I'd fall on a grenade for Malcolm and all he gave my grandparents. He gave me the freedom to interview Billy Jay once a week on company time. Not for a newspaper story, but for my book. I'd told him my interest about writing Billy Jay's backstory. Malcolm probably knew most of my backstory. He knew this was important to me. I think he knew it would also give me some much-needed internal healing. I'm certain he realized the frustration of being shut down by a bureaucrat.

I suddenly recognized I openly told many people I no longer had family since my grandparents passed. I'm mistaken. I have people who might as well be considered family because of our close ties growing up. People like Malcolm Kingsman, who practically lived at Grandfather's home up until the day Grandfather died. And of course, now I have Georgie who is my best friend and confidante. I'm sure I could think of more if I wasn't so pissed off at a government official who bested me today. One thing for certain—I was gifted with digging up dirt if dirt was what I was looking for. Wardens may not be elected officials, but they still answered to the state at a state-owned facility. I'd just gained a hobby to work on—dirt digging. I'm a loving Christian, hardworking girl who tries her best to reach out and do for others that can't do for themselves. I pride myself in keeping the mission ethic among the important things in life to give. But if you cross me in an ill-intentioned and calculated way—my hell offers no quarter. My ornery side has always told me it's easier to ask for forgiveness later than permission before.

"Mr. Wilkerson, I'm a bettin' girl, and I'm lay money you got secrets buried in shallow graves all across this state." I looked up and realized I'd spoken out loud and drew some attention from co-workers. "Go about your business folks, nothing to see here—yet!" I sat down with a snicker and booted up my computer for the day's work.

33

"Good morning, Ethan." Addi, his office manager said, as her normally cheerful boss walked through the door. He appeared solemn. It was a common look Ethan began wearing ever since Joyce stopped coming in or calling. His face showed sorrow and she knew something wasn't right but didn't feel like it was her business to pry. She'd thought Ethan had finally found not only the right person to work into a law partnership in practice, but also in his private life. In her eyes, the two looked to be made for each other.

For days now, Addi kept the office open and neither Ethan nor Joyce had come in or called the office. Whenever Ethan did come in, he lacked the happiness for life he'd recently shown overwhelmingly. He now wore the face of a broken heart and Addi worried. She'd molded her life around Ethan's practice, but now she felt that life slipping away quickly with nothing to grab onto and nobody to talk about it with.

"Ethan, what can I do to help you?" She asked him, trying to broach him in a caring way.

Ethan looked at her and the edges of his mouth briefly turned up slightly. "Thank you, Addi. I appreciate you asking. You've always been a sweetheart to me. I believe I've gone and messed everything up." Ethan paused and looked down to the floor in submission.

Addi watched him wither before her eyes. She'd never seen the great attorney, Ethan William Kendrick, wilt under any circumstances. He was rock solid in any scenario. A vicious Pitbull in the court room, yet a man who would go to any lengths to help a friend in trouble. The man before him now seemed to hold none of those typical attributes that once drove him. He now wore the look of an abused puppy. One who'd just had their nose rubbed in the mess they'd made. She felt sick to her stomach at witnessing him in this way.

"There's nothing anyone can do for me, Addi. I appreciate you showing concern though. I have some cases needing my immediate attention, so I'll be in my office. Please disturb me only if something pressing comes your way. Thank you again, for asking about me. I'll snap out of this; it'll just take some time."

"I hate to ask, but—I'm assuming Ms. Bonham isn't returning?"

Ethan looked up and turned as he opened his office door. "I don't believe so. I told her she was welcome and needed, and there were no strings attached between her job and our personal life—but we haven't talked for several days. Her things are still at the house undisturbed since she left. I just can't say for certain what will happen with her and the firm or with me."

"Oh Ethan, I'm terribly sorry. Please, let me know if there is anything I can do." Addi stepped forward as if to console him with a rub on his shoulder or a hug, but he moved through the entrance to his office and slowly closed the door behind him, avoiding any contact. He sauntered over and sat down behind his desk, then swiveled his chair to the large window that faced the docks. He loved this view of the Apalachicola fishing marinas. He'd been raised around the waters of this area and the familiar smell of fish from the nets and saltwater were what brought him back after law school. His practice grew quickly due to his gift of representing the criminal clientele that seemed thick in the area. Ethan was good at what he did.

Ethan looked away from the bay and scanned the entirety of the room, taking in the benefits he'd learned to enjoy from the fruits of his work. One side of his large 1888 produced Hocking Valley bricked office held windows, which faced the downtown main street of highway 98. He also shared a view of the old Chestnut Cemetery and Trinity Episcopal Church. Two places he enjoyed looking out his window at but avoiding any more than observing them from his elevated office view. The large windows beside his desk on the opposite side of the room showcased the docks and the still waters of the bay. He could also see the Franklin County Courthouse where many of his trials were held and also Battery Park and the fishing pier. These were the sights he loved admiring the most from his view.

After spending some time peering out at the calming water, he swiveled back and observed the interior collections of different oddities and gifts he showcased throughout the office he'd spent his life building and now enjoyed. An immediate eyecatcher was a seven and a half-foot, long two-hundred and twelve-pound Carcharhinus Leucas, or bull shark, which hung by thin steel cables just six feet above the conference table. The table's glass top was dark blue and lit by tiny can-lights dimly shining downward on the low resting table. It was an ominous visual enhancement to his office setting. He'd considered himself not only a graduate of the Apalachicola High School, home of the Bull Sharks, but also a likely representative of the predator world in the courtroom in the same like fashion of his school mascot. He admired their ways of hunting and clearing their dark domain from unsuspecting trespassers. An unforgiving force that dominates its territory.

To the left and opposite corner of his office sat the long black leather couch and four overstuffed chairs and ottomans surrounding his regulation-sized pool table. A wet bar stood on the other side of the dark-blue felted game table. The bar top was custom made of wooden ship planks retrieved from the alleged ship of outlaw pirate William "Red" Tanner that had sunk out in the bay. Red was believed to be friends with Billy Bowlegs, another pirate with some local history. Spaced sporadically, in no sequence on the wall behind the bar, were deep indigo blue glass shelves that held bottle after bottle of Ethan's exotic collection of bourbons from around the globe. The deep blue shelves were lit by strips of small bright halogen spotlights, which cast varying shapes of blue colors on the brick faces, looking like flashes of sun lit colors of the gulf. Elegant in appearance and impressive.

Original paintings hung on the twelve-foot-high walls, which dead-ended into solid oak twelve by twelve rough sawn beams that ran the span of the room. The pieces of artwork, mostly painted by various well-known artists of the area, were each lit by its own fixture as if hanging in the Guggenheim. His art collection was an eclectic mix in style and mediums. From stark charcoal drawings and abstract oils to assorted watercolors in brilliant hues. Each painting held a story of its own and Ethan loved to talk about them with anyone who would listen.

An open framed staircase made up from the same type beams as the ceiling above, led up to a loft where comfortable seating was spaced out around a television. It was Ethan's relaxation spot where he could sip bourbon and unwind to Florida Gators football or NFL's Dolphins and Buccaneer games. This room was dimly lit to invite a cave-like feeling overlooking his office from above. A circular staircase in the corner led up to the roof, which held outdoor furniture and a view of the small town's rooftops. A view that no one else held. Most people weren't even aware of its existence. A skylight, which could be cranked open by electrical motors, sat in the middle and a good portion of nighttime stars and moon could be seen from inside his office. Nothing was spared to create the perfect environment for him.

Ethan tilted back in his chair, fingertips touching each other together as he lightly bounced them in unison while he contemplated where all this surrounding grandeur had truly gotten him. The nine-foot-tall by six-foot-wide abstract painting on stretched white canvas, seemed to sum his life up in a mixture of colors and textures. Bright yellows and burning oranges along with varying degrees of creams and whites boldly mixed with each other in the top left corner of the painting. To Ethan, it almost seemed to portray a birth or beautiful sunrise splashed over an azure blue thin line dribbled across the top toward the right side of the painting like an ocean wave. Where the orange, yellows and creams mixed, a tiny slit of bright red puddle-like drips spilled over the bottom edge of the mixed warm tones and broadened as it fell from top left to bottom right of the large vast whiteness of the canvas. Blood red. Deep and glossy as if there were life trapped inside its bold color. As it spread out half-way down the nine-foot height of stark white, it poured into a dark vast jagged shape of black. The deepest black one could imagine. It looked violent and bold as if the blood red liquid of color splashed back upward from the darkness, caused by the red hitting the solid black with such momentum it exploded. It was beautiful and hideous all at the same time. The artist, Stephen Bassett, who painted the piece, called it "The Death of Innocence" and Ethan knew he must have it from the moment he'd seen it in Savannah, Georgia on a conference trip.

The price tag was a healthy nine thousand and eight hundred dollars. He'd asked the artist if he would deliver and help install it and he agreed. It brought the price tag to almost twelve thousand dollars. It didn't matter though; Ethan would have paid much more. This painting spoke to him from first sight. As a new defense attorney, he'd struggled with using his talents to dash convictions of guilt from murderers and thieves, takers from the innocent. At least in the beginning. He in fact quickly realized he was nothing more than a pawn in the game of "The Death of

Innocence" in the real world, and he was born a master. He'd now become a living version of this painting almost as if it were a premonition of what was to take shape in him and his world. The guilty clients he'd freed on technicalities were his first introductions to his talents until he'd really looked back at himself. It of course started way back early in his youth, before his admission to Stetson University College of Law, his father's alma mater. The beginning of his aggression of innocence had first knowingly appeared when he was a mere sixteen years of age. It began with Veronica. He'd stolen her virginity by telling her lies he knew were bold untruths. Ethan told her he loved her. It was the only way to manipulate her into having sex with him. And oh, how badly he wanted her to be his first. She'd given him tingles and questionable thoughts while in class. He couldn't study, he couldn't listen to his teachers. All he could do was sit in class filling his thoughts with carnal lust as he pictured her naked in every movement she made. He wasn't mistaken, thinking he loved her. No, he knew it was an act of animal desire he was craving. Like a shark smelling blood in the water, he could barely keep himself from an instinctive salacious frenzy.

The entire feeling of lust came over him almost like a virus. One minute he knew he liked girls, but the next minute, he craved them. He knew the moment he'd spied her from across the parking lot that one hot sticky morning as he got out of his car. He nonchalantly scanned the lot and there she was, being let out from most likely her mom's car. He'd known her since the beginning of his sophomore year. It wasn't like she was a new girl to the area, but today she appeared different to him. Her white thin legs against the red fabric of her shorts. Whoever came up with short shorts was his new hero, and she wore them very well. He suddenly had an erection and had to hide it with his book bag. Ethan walked a little faster so he could be in perfect view as he followed her into the school building. He told himself quietly—she was to be his first conquest. Not his first and last, he wasn't foolish enough to want to be tied down so early in his youth. But she was going to be his first. Veronica Kaye Mallory, a blonde-haired, fair-skinned, and blue-eyed virgin. He was certain of that. Of course, he was too. Ethan knew he had to possess her and would not stop at anything to obtain her. The cost? It wouldn't matter.

He quickly found he could link his words together so eloquently it was like music and in such a way Veronica was almost of no challenge at all. His sentences were almost hypnotizing and held such convincing power it was like drug induced poetry. He'd told her everything he imagined she wanted to hear. Davy Crockett may have been able to grin down a grizzly bear, but Ethan Kendrick could whisper a fifteen-year-old girl out of her panties with a slew of single lines, chocked full of flowery adjectives. Lines like, *how sparklingly beautiful her lips were and how her fragrance was like pleasantly drowning in a garden of roses and ambrosia. Her ability to steal his breath and turn him into a fountain of desire seeking only to please her.* He knew he held talent for persuasion at the young age of seventeen, which happened to be the age he lost his virginity along with fifteen-year-old Veronica Kaye Mallory. The experience was invigorating and intoxicating. He now felt like a kid in a candy store. No single flavor would ever suffice again. He must try them all and compare. After that passion-filled night up at Old Woman's Bluff overlooking the Apalachicola River, Ethan couldn't dump Veronica quick enough.

The thing Ethan had not thought out before hand was the effect his selfish and self-serving lies would have on the sweet young virgin that he'd spoken those words to. When the act was over, Veronica was planning their relationship, while Ethan was planning his getaway. She was crushed. She couldn't just let him go at the easy whim he'd written her off. She was devastated. What became of her world after she'd just given herself to him, to be her first and what she'd thought her last, was nothing but devastation. After all, he'd said these things to her almost verbatim. She was certain he was just scared. Ethan surely wasn't through with her. She'd win him back. She called him relentlessly. She stalked him by today's standards, although after what he'd told her—even promised her—it was probably what he deserved. Ethan even knew deep within; he owned the pursuance she was attempting. He finally realized he had but one option to stop the situation.

It was a Friday afternoon. It was the last hour of school before the weekend would come. There was a party that was going to be at Charley's house at nine o'clock that evening. Charley's parents would be gone for a long weekend. A trip to Charlotte, a getaway to celebrate their anniversary. Charley had been planning the party for weeks. Ethan, in the meantime tried to move on to another girl he was now interested in. Tavin Marieza. Her look was as sultry and foreign in appearance as her name would suggest. She was the hot new foreign exchange student from Spain. That wasn't important. But what was crucial to his plan for the party, was getting her drunk or high and then alone, where he could sample sex with the hot vivacious foreign girl. He'd persuaded Charley to set it up where she would be attending. But damn the luck—so would Veronica, and there lie his quandary. He couldn't have her in the way of his attempts to "get to know" Tavin, so he told Veronica he wanted to go to the party and enjoy both together in bed, a three-way, hoping it would cause her to realize he wasn't going to stay loyal to her, and she'd just go away. Veronica was in English class with him when he sprang his plan on her. She didn't believe him and couldn't react in front of everyone as they watched, even if she did. The look on her face was as if it were just a mean-spirited joke. She reached for his arm to pull him into her so she could silently plead her love, but the bell suddenly rang. Ethan shrugged and said, "Well, hope I see you tonight!" And he winked at her with an evil grin.

In Ethan's memory, now in the present moment, he sat looking up at the expansive bright and dark painting, which swallowed his wall along with his attention. He concentrated again on the brightly mixing oranges, yellows, and creams. He could picture the hot foreign exchange student, Tavin being that medley of bright scorching oranges, vivacious and steamy. Veronica was the lesser flashy creamy color with tiny bits of yellow attempting to amalgamate together and overpower Tavin's provocative orange splashes of paint strokes. The two together at once—hmm. Ethan was becoming aroused with his orchestrated daydream.

He alternated between staring at the painting and closing his eyes attempting to eke-out some pleasure from all the recent pain; trying to relive the moment of at least his past and feeling his heart pulse and pound inside his body as it had back during the time of his youth. He compared the near experience of sharing two girls to his recent experience with Jaime and Aisling. Jaime wanted him, she wanted to be in the middle, he'd quickly figured that fact out from her forward dialogue, and of course her body language. Jamie was trying to mix in with Aisling's bright orange paint strokes from the start of the entire evening from first glance. He hadn't craved the yellow paints as much as the oranges though. But now he wondered what colors would have been created had the three gotten to share the experience together as it was planned either time, way back then—or recently in Springfield. The bright blood-red paint that splashed into the jagged dark blackness on the canvas was a replication of the feeling he'd gotten when Veronica walked in and found Tavin naked and on top of him, bouncing wildly and gyrating; the look on Veronica's face bore hurt and shock like he'd never witnessed before. It was beautiful and hideous all at the same time as she ran off crying. He, the untamable maverick he knew he was, explained his way out of the outburst to Tavin and then they continued their sexual tryst, which was far too heated to end.

He should have felt guilt over what had just transpired. But he didn't. Not even the next day when no one could find Veronica. Much like realizing the outcome of his exploits in Springfield. He believed he bore no real guilt. Veronica showed up on her own accord even though he'd told her what he wanted and the two women in Springfield had drugged him with some crazy concoction and brought it all on themselves. He was merely giving them what they'd asked for.

After his lengthy reflection, Ethan studied the painting again, "The Death of Innocence," he spoke aloud as he opened his righthand top drawer.

There it was. It sat in the same spot he'd always kept it in. Protection is why he purchased it. After all, criminals get upset and vengeful if you fuck up in representing their case or things don't go like they expected. The type of clients who bore a "you fuck up my life and take my money—it's owed back and with interest." He lived both sides of the story; so, he figured he should own a firearm. He didn't want to be caught needing one and not having one within easy access.

Ethan's face changed as he picked the cold black revolver up in his right hand. He studied its simplicity. He hadn't gone for the shiny chrome version. Normally though, he did like to stick out boldly in most ways, but a shiny handgun just didn't feel right. Dark, cold steel, that's how an implement of death should appear, not like a girl at a party dressed to kill. Just plain cold harshness—created to kill, to do the job without pomp and circumstance or pizazz. Pull it out, point it, and pull the gawd damned trigger—problem solved. The only real challenge in using the damned thing, was finding the correct problem that needed solved—otherwise, you've just created additional troubles.

He turned the snub-nosed .38, or "Saturday Night Special" around in his hand, watching the reflections of the light that landed on it bounce around and roll over the smoothed edges as he leveled it toward his large bright, blood-red painting hanging on the wall in the background. Pulling the cylinder rod, it released and rolled outward exposing the bullets held within each of the five chambers of the circular cylinder. With his left hand he reached over and spun it like a roulette wheel, causing a whirring, clicking sound as the bullets brass casings blurred into a flash of a circling shiny ring. He quickly snapped the revolver to the right causing the cylinder to slam into place. Ethan watched it move around in his hand and then he re-pointed it at the bright bold red splash on the white canvas, just as it touched the deep, dark black of the painting.

Silence. Reminiscing silence. Bold colors blurred behind the wheel gun he held pointed at the painting that he should resent but instead loved.

Ethan suddenly lowered the weapon and placed it on his desk. He got up and walked around past the black couch and then circled slightly past his pool table, reaching out and rolling the cue ball into the racked balls with a slap and crack. The balls scattered about across the blue felt. He continued behind the bar grabbing a high ball glass. His eyes slowly scanned his bourbon collection. Today was special. A rebirth within. It should be celebrated with the best bottle owned. His eye moved directly to the upper left bottle. A twenty-five-year-old vintage, Old Rip Van Winkle. Distilled in 1959. Its price was too outrageous to speak out loud. His memory of what he'd paid caused his cheeks to swell into a grin. He reached up and grabbed it, held it under a spotlight shining from above to admire the bottle's beauty and the caramel-brown colored liquid residing inside. He'd saved this acquisition for years. It had been purchased in celebration of the fact he was able to afford purchasing it. The payoff of his first big win on his own. His firm brand new. The government surely hated him for his win against it, the state's prosecuting attorney certainly did. The little rich prick's banker-dad had practically worshiped the concrete steps of the courthouse he'd walked down to face the media after their winning verdict.

Yes, this was the correct choice today. Celebratory. He tore the label seal and uncorked the bottle. He decided not to dilute the contents with ice, adding water in any form would be an atrocity. He'd drink it as it was distilled to be drank. Straight. He tipped the bottle to his glass and poured a very strong double-shot. Setting the bottle down and recorking it, he lined the bottle back up on the shelf, twisting it slightly to perfect alignment with the others on either side. Lifting his fresh pour up, he held the glass in his hand as he turned to admire his beautiful surroundings once more. He slowly walked around, admiring each beautiful artifact displayed between the bar and his desk while he sipped from his glass of Kentucky's finest bourbon ever produced. He made his way back to his desk and comfy leather chair. After sitting back down, he drank another sip and eyed the black revolver lying motionless on the rich walnut top. Ethan lifted the glass up to his face studying the caramel-colored whiskey cling to the crystal's interior surface as he swirled the glass. The motion causing its oaky scent to be released.

After swallowing the last sip of whiskey, he placed the empty glass on the table beside the gun and in one fluid motion, Ethan's hand swapped from grasping the glass to gripping the revolver. Without any dramatic flair or emotion, he pulled the barrel up to his chin pressing it into the loose skin underneath and positioned it by twisting his wrist until his grip was comfortable and he felt able to pull the trigger.

The bright painting of "The Death of Innocence" hung silent and boldly facing him from the wall opposite from the chair he sat in. This was the comfortable spot he'd spent many hours admiring the colorful story the painting had spoken to him many times. It's outline and outcome never varying but remaining true to the way he saw his life. Its veracity to the truth was why he felt so drawn to it. The facts no matter how they were painted, were always pointed from the canvas outwardly to him and his actions. Ethan felt as if the artist, Stephen, had painted it with his very own life in mind and now, its creator was calling out to him to complete the final act. The last brush stroke of finality. Ethan's fingertip touched the trigger, which was encased in the guard ring. He felt his muscles begin to respond to what his brain communicated to them. "That's right Ethan, follow through with the muscles' response it will take to apply the proper pressure to sedate the pain forever. Pull through." Ethan was certain he'd heard the paintings creator direct him out loud. Stephen's last words he heard spoken to him were, "It's the only way to expunge your failures, Ethan."

BAM.

The blood-red color splashed as if hitting the dark black with such momentum, it exploded....

34

Jake Hodges pulled his rusty old brown GMC truck onto the gravel parking lot in front of the old Tanner place. Its springs creaked and groaned with each dip in the uneven ground. "Kyle, there is some history to this old place. Did you know you lived in the Tanner house?"

Kyle lifted his head and turned to face Jake. "Tanner house? I'm not sure what you're talkin' about, Mr. Hodges. I just moved here from up north. I don't know much of anything 'bout this town or its history."

"Willy "Red" Tanner was a pirate back in the 1800's and some say he befriended Billy Bowlegs a fellow pirate of the area. Florida historians generally claim Billy died in 1864 of smallpox. He's supposedly buried over in Oklahoma, which always seemed peculiar to me." Jake's eyes gleamed and sparkled at the telling of the lore he'd grown up learning. "Before Billy died, he refused to sign a treaty with the confederacy and instead joined the union to fight pro-confederate Indians. Some say he never died and Red Tanner took him in as a partner in crime. Others say he never made it much farther east than Fort Walton. There are all kinds of rumors 'round here."

They were still sitting in Jake's truck and Jake saw the excited and quizzical look across Kyle's face. "You interested in Indians—or pirates?"

"Well, Mr. Hodges, I reckon I didn't know I was interested in either one. But you put the two together mixed with the mystery in your voice, and somehow' it's peakin' my curiosity. Especially if you're gonna say I'm living in a possible past home of an outlaw pirate!"

Jake's wrinkled face crinkled up tighter in his eyes as he smiled. "Well, son, I don't wanna bore you or nuthin' but I got stories and local lore 'bout both." His eyes lit up with a new sparkle. "You see ole Billy Bowlegs was a Chief of the Oconee tribe of the Seminoles. His name translated down to the 'Alligator Chief.' There's a lot of historical stories here, but right now I imagine we oughta' get you inside and outta this heat, let you rest a bit. You wait here and I'll come around and get you out. Anybody home I should let know I'm helpin' ya inside?"

"You can't start a story like this and then stop all the sudden! But yeah, my wife is probably inside with her best friend, our neighbor."

Jake grinned quickly and snorted. "Is that why you were drivin' your buggy like a racecar driver? Makin' a run from the wife's best friend?" He chortled.

Kyle grinned. "No sir, it's really nothin' so bad like that. I like her friend and her husband too. It wouldn't matter anyway 'cause she's over all the time—not like we can really get caught doin' anything—with me in that damned chair.

Jake shook his head a moment with a frown washing across his face.

"What's that look for Mr. Hodges?"

"I'm just thinkin' son. Seems you may need a little more than just some history of pirate and Indian lore from around here. You been in the chair long?"

Kyle looked at Jake with question. "Just what are you talkin' about?"

"Son, I can see you're slowed up, bein' in that chair and all—but you ain't dead yet are you?"

"No sir." Kyle looked away. "Might as well be, though."

"Wife still alive, right?"

"Well, truthfully—we ain't exactly married yet. I just wasn't sure what you'd think about our situation. I was gonna ask her—after we graduated school this year—before the damned wreck that put me in this predicament—but who'd want someone like me now?"

"Your situation of marriage ain't none of my business, but if I'm gonna be your friend and finish tellin' you my stories—I'm gonna be offering my old-timer advice along the way. That's just the way I operate. A tit for a tat kinda' thing—you get what I'm sayin'?"

Kyle started to wiggle towards the open truck door on his side. "I think I know where this may be headed." His eyes bore a tinge of resentment in them.

Jake stepped right up to the door causing Kyle to look at him square and eye to eye. Kyle appeared to wear a look of confusion. Was the old man blocking him from getting out, or getting ready to help him?

"Son, just consider me an old man whose lived a lot of experience." Jake smiled. "One who's tryin' to pay it forward by befriending a young man startin' out in this difficult world. A boy who appears to have some serious questions of his life. And maybe—just maybe, some dangerous tendencies towards doin' things he don't quite get the jest of exactly." Jake put his hand on each of Kyle's shoulders for a second. "Consequences to those actions. That's what I'm talkin' 'bout son." Jake squinted as if the sun were in his eyes even though it was on his back. "I think we could both use a friend, someone to talk to—maybe each keeping the other from doin' something neither one has actually thought through to its end..." Jake hesitated. "... and of course, what outcomes those snap decisions leave behind in their wake to those we love or love us." He leaned in moving his hands from Kyle's shoulders to underneath his arms to help ease him from the truck seat. As Jake lifted, Kyle groaned out. Jake continued as if he knew Kyle needed verbal distraction to distort the pain level he was about to experience. He lifted and, "I think you might have been on your way to hurtin' yourself with some intention…" Kyle gritted his teeth as the pain overtook him again and he moaned, but Jake continued, "…to maybe escape some mental pain. Maybe pain you think you're causing your fiancée?"

Kyle let out a whimper as he slid down and tried to use his legs and feet for balance to no avail. Jake lifted Kyle's arm and hurled it around his neck to his shoulder as he slightly lowered it to accommodate. Kyle cried out a little, once more.

"Kyle, I think the good Lord placed me on this highway at just the time you wheeled your hotrod big wheels towards traffic—that's what I think."

Kyle turned and he was face to face with Jake. "No, no sir…."

"Bullshit, young man. But it don't matter 'cause I'm here and I think I need you just as much or more than you need me. Now let's go inside so you can introduce me to this young woman insane enough to obviously love a young rebel of a man like you."

The two staggered over to the front door and before either could knock, it swung open wide to a beautiful young lady with a shocked, worried look upon her face. "Kyle! Are you okay? What happened?"

"I crashed, baby, but Mr. Hodges helped me out. My chair needs some work, but it'll be okay." Kyle reached for Vio, and she moved into his arm instantly as he struggled with hanging on to Jake.

"I love you. I don't know what I'd do without you." Vio cried out as she hugged Kyle tightly. Jake continued to hold him up as Vio slid under Kyle's other arm and helped Jake move him inside to a chair.

"Let's get you sat down, buddy." Jake said. Mitzi B came out from one of the rooms down the hallway.

"Kyle? What happened? Where's your chair?" Mitzi asked.

Kyle tightened his mouth in pain as they helped him back into the couch. "It's in the back…oh…aw…hmm…back of Mr. Hodge's truck, Mitz." He looked up at Jake.

Jake finished lowering Kyle into a seated position and Vio quickly sat next to him and fussed.

Mitzi looked at Kyle, "Looks like we both got stories to finish tellin' each other."

Kyle answered. "Well, you can just sit yourself down Mitz, but it don't mean I'm tellin' ya nothin!"

Kyle and Mitz grinned.

Vio threw in a "Mr. Hodges, is it? Don't worry about them. They do this all the time!"

Jake returned the grin. "So, you are as pretty as Kyle was telling me."

"Why, thank you…."

Jake nodded. "Yes, ma'am.

"I think I'm gonna like you! How about dinner with us tonight? I bet Kyle would whip up some mean smoked gator and taters on the grill." She winked.

Jake looked over at Kyle and then turned back to Vio, "That'd be great. Sounds really tasty." He turned to Kyle. "Maybe we can talk about the Tanner house while you're cookin'?" Kyle nodded and smiled. Jake continued, "I'll grab your wheelie and my toolbox and see what we can do 'bout getting' that ride fixed up first."

35

Two weeks pass by very fast for most folks, but for some…the seconds become hours; days feel like months….

Jay was one of those folks. Solitary confinement for two full weeks.

It might as well have been two years. Jay's mind already lost track of what day of the week it was. Fourteen days and thirteen nights were melded into one infinite timeline. He felt broken. His mind drowning in a sea of emptiness and time that had no beginning and no end each day.

The light felt like it seared his eyes as the steel door opened with squeals and clangs. The sudden blast of light appeared as an explosion and Jay snapped his eyes shut quickly covering them with his hands, unable to withstand the pain. It was too sharp.

"Get up, Billy Jay, your time in the hole is over." The bull said loudly. It smells nasty down here, you shit yourself, Billy Jay?"

"What? What the hell, I can't see, too damned bright. Shut that light off."

The guard kicked at his side. Lightly at first, but harder each time Billy wouldn't move the way he wanted him to.

Billy Jay reached out for help. "Can I—can I get a hand?"

"I ain't touchin' your filthy damned paws. Get up. Warden wants to see your worthless ass again." Barely a second went by until the guard continued, "Get the fuck up Billy Jay, before you piss Warden Wilkerson off for having to wait. He'll throw you back in the hole." He lightly kicked him another time.

Billy crawled up to his knees, his eyes still locked tightly closed. He was still about the same mess by the time he was escorted into Wilkerson's office when he was walked over to the warden's desk and ordered to sit in the chair. The chair wore a plastic sheet over the top and sat on another sheet covering the floor. It was in the same spot with the shotgun aimed at the person's balls who sat in it. Just in case. Billy Jay's eyes were still closed tight and couldn't see the plastic but heard and felt its slippery and crinkly texture as he was positioned on it.

"What...where am I, I can't see?"

The guard looked down and offered a word of advice. "Shut the hell up and let the warden talk. He'll let you know when it's your turn to open your trap."

"Billy Jay Cader. Well, well, well. I sit here in wonder if time has affected your attitude in a positive way?" Willy seemed to wait upon bated breath for Billy Jay's answer, but only silence followed. The warden drummed his fingers impatiently atop his desk before lifting the box lid and picking up a cigar, reliving his daily routine with the nip and lighter. "Billy Jay." Wilkerson said in a slow but direct tone. "This would be the appropriate time to converse." He lit the end after nipping it, puffing the smoke and then exhaling it across the table to Billy Jay. Déjà vu.

Billy tried to crack open his eyes, but the light was still piercing and was bright behind whom he assumed was the dark silhouette of Warden Willy. He wobbled back and forth on the chair, obviously disoriented from being in solitude and darkness for fourteen days. "I...I don't...know what...you...want...want...me to say...Willy...." Jay parted his eyelids as he looked to the spot the warden's words came from. He tried to open them enough to see the warden's response. He must have seen what he wanted because Jay smiled. He smiled big. That brief glimpse of light was the last thing Billy Jay remembered as the warden's soldier, Henry, slammed Billy in the back of the head. The force caused him to fall forward into the warden's desktop and then slide down onto the floor in an unresponsive crumpled pile.

"Remove this pile of shit from my office and send maintenance in to clean up this mess and deodorize my office. When I return, there best not be one reminder or leftover stench of this worthless dreg's presence…" The warden's face boiled from Billy's total disrespect and outright obtuse response. "…and wash him down with a firehouse outside where his "friends" can be spectators to his humiliation.

Billy woke up cold and damp on what appeared to be his own cot back in his own familiar block. He was still somewhat disoriented not only from the time alone in the dark, which he was used to, his daddy had taught him well. But also, from the whatever he was whacked in the back of the head with. His vision blurred, but he did see several figures standing around—above him. One was much taller than the others. Lyle. It had to be Lyle.

"So, boys. I presume I'm correct in who is standing here. Happy to see me back? Or—is it my day of judgment?"

The tall blurry shadow moved closer. "Jay, I don't know how to tell you this…."

Silence followed Lyle's words.

Jay began smiling. His lips spread wide with no control. He knew what was happening. The T-7 (Trusted 7), but only six of the remaining had made decisions through a vote about him while he was away. "So, brothers, I'm only seeing blurry outlines, but I'm seeing intentions that are very clear to me. When you drop the tile—I'm gonna have to trust you with what the punishment is, 'cause, I can't see a gawd damned thing but fuzzy bullshit." He smiled. "I've heard the rattle before, believe me, I'm okay. I'm ready. I don't know if you boys have ever met the Lord, but he's been beside me now for several days. I don't fear no more. Shake that fuckin' jar and let it spill her out!"

Lyle began to speak, "Billy Jay." He hesitated and looked over at Louis. "The vote was passed to us, and after hearing the charges—you already been found worthy of the Mason Jar's judgment and punishment—unanimously." Lyle hesitated. "You got any questions?"

Jay squinted as he strained to open his eyes once more and face his accusers, his judges, his executioners. "What's the charges? I mean—I know I'm guilty as fuck for a lot of things, but what say you?"

"Warden says you tortured and killed young girls." A voice Jay couldn't recognize, stated.,

"Rape and torture of at least seven young women they have evidence of! T-7 could rule no other way!" Another voice responded.

"You denying this charge, Jay? This is your chance, your last one at that. Speak up." Lyle said.

"I'm just curious who the lucky individual is that all you worthy men of judgment chose to replace my position with? I did believe I heard the pipsqueak a minute ago but can't seem to put a lion's face to such a tiny mouse of a voice? Who is he? Not that it matters, of course. I just would like to face my accusers, each and every one. Only seems fittin'."

Lyle spoke up. Tommy Smith is his name, Jay. You don't know him. He's fresh in glass house from Tallahassee. Life without parole for murder one, a trooper."

"Well now, at least my replacement is a man of honor..." Jay chuckled. "...pretty impressive crime from such a small-voiced man...." Jay laid still,

Seven charges judged by seven men with a Silent Seventh or SS taking Jay's place in the vote. It almost seemed biblically appropriate and symbolic. "Won't take much to prove to you I'm no disciple or anything special." He paused. "I've sinned against man and God my entire life. I'll make no plea of innocence. I'm far from it. I've lived a life of sufferin' no doubt, but I've also lived my life judging others with no right of ownership in doing such a task. God is my judge, not criminals and scoundrels like what we put together in this unholy house." Jay's eyes began to see past the fogginess in small areas. "I've committed horrible acts that I ain't felt no pain for. My conscience sat firm and clean for most my life. I don't know if it's age or like you, Lyle, claiming—maybe my visits from the outside with the reporter Whitenhour be makin' me soft...."

"Awe, for the love of gawd, let's just get this shit done. Guilty! Shake out the fuckin' tile, already." Hollered Tommy, the one of the seven.

"We give all defendants the chance to talk." Lyle said firmly.

"I've said all I need to say, other than yes, yes—I killed them seven young ladies and more. I've had a horrible demon inside me, and my Lord has sent him away now, exiled from my soul forever. I go to my sentence knowing where I will be. Ms. Cela's good Book says my Lord will forgive and I'll see my Heavenly Father moments upon leavin' this hell." Jay paused a moment. "Shake that Mason jar boys and deal me my fate. I'll accept it and go willingly."

There was a muffled sound of clicking, making the sound of rattlesnakes hidden under a thick blanket of leaves and then there was silence followed by some gasps.

Jay felt the outcome of the roll was most likely not GRACE. He could hear it in their quiet tones and see it in their blurred faces. The form of punishment was not yet apparent to him, the lettering far too small for his light sensitive eyes to make able for him to see it. It wasn't until the word was spoken, he realized what the "roll of the dice" bestowed on him.

"HANG" was quietly spoken by the SS, or silent seventh. The tiles were passed back from each member of trusted seven (T-7) and the red cloth was ceremoniously rolled back up. Each member now had seven seconds to dissent the Mason Jar's outcome. Each inmate of the group gestured one by one to the SS and either gave a thumbs up or down. No one present gave a thumbs down or spoke the word GRACE. With the thumbs up from the six of the judges, the decision was unanimous. There was no need for the SS to break a tie.

Jay was quietly walked out of his cell and toward the laundry room. A room off limits after hours, but each inmate knew the route the bulls took on their evening check. Each inmate also understood the price of being caught carrying out the execution. Jay walked out of his cell staunchly without any words or pleas.

Bobbie uncoiled the strips of bed sheets, which were twisted tightly together and inner-woven with a blue electrical cord. He threw one end up and over a pipe directly above a small laundry folding table. Lyle pulled Jay's hands behind his back and tied his wrists together tightly. Bobbie placed the noose around Jay's neck and snugged it up close to where his neck met his chin before Jay was hoisted up and onto the table. The rope was pulled taut and tied off to one of the steel levers of an ironing press. There was nothing more to be said. No inmate found guilty by the Trusted Seven ever got any kind of special treatment or last supper. They got the punishment the Mason jar gave and that would be that.

William Rogette III, or Billy Boy, was the member who was given the responsibility of pushing the table out and away from under Jay. Jay wasn't even afforded a blindfold, so he was fully aware of what was just about to happen.

Jay stood tall on the table and looked over his fellow members of the now, new Trusted Seven, an organization and the brainchild that he was responsible for putting together. After squinting to see each face, Jay looked to the heavens and began to speak softly to his Maker.

"I'm sorry Father for all the sins I've committed. I've wasted my life choosing all the wrong paths. I'm especially sorry for what

I did to that young boy Chubbs." Jay hesitated as he saw movement from his peripheral vision. "Please help Amy Jo to be able to forgive the evil I was about to confess to...."

Bobbie shoved the table midway through Jay's prayer and said, "Fuck you, pervert, get on with the death dance!"

And that is exactly what Jay did. His legs began kicking as if he were trying to swim his way up towards the ocean's surface and get his head above the waterline. His arms attempting to pull away from the bed sheets they were tied, which created a sound surely none who witnessed would ever forget, along with the muffled gasps for air. After about twenty or thirty very long seconds, Jay's arms and legs slowed down to less frantic wiggles, eventually sporadic twitches. The gasps from his mouth faded into silence. Jay never cried out for mercy or begged for any help in any way. He may have been a demon sent up from hell, but he left this earth a strong silent angel even though his mouth remained unimpeded by any kind of gag.

Lyle eyed Bobbie with a wink as they quickly headed back to their cells leaving Jay's body slowly winding down after swinging in the mocking motion of the pendulum arm of Ms. Lila Pasternack's old grandfather clock. Jay's futile attempts to climb the air mere seconds ago slowly came to a halt. The death dance was complete.

36

Each of the seven members made it back to their cells quickly and got into their bunks just before lights out and cell checks.

There was a sudden ruckus of bulls headed down the hallways as the alarm lights flashed. The footsteps of boots ran by the cells quickly and towards the laundry room. Lyle managed to change into a guard's uniform that was purchased from one of the prison guards on the take. At just the precise moment, the tall inmate slipped away from his cell before it was locked down and he quickly moved down the hallway and towards the laundry room.

Bobbie smiled as he watched him disappear around the corner from his cell. He said under his breath, "I'll be gawd damned if it may just work...."

In another cell block, Lloyd Ruby, Lyle's brother, slipped his prison orange suit off that covered the paramedic uniform he wore underneath. He now just needed to slip out through three locked doors he held the keys to and out onto the grounds where the ambulance would be parked. The sharpened shank in his hand, prepared to stop at nothing, he proceeded with the plan. His heart was pounding, legs throbbing, and hands tremoring from the excitement, but he thought to himself, *this plan just might damn well work—my brother is a genius....*

37

Cat woke up from a fog. She felt like a different person. One whose been asleep like Rip Van Winkle. Three important names were settled in her mind. Jay—Billy—and Darrell. She thought about the names, letting them roll around in her mind before she got up out of bed and charged the memories head on. *Billy. Hmmm.* Billy had passed. It clicked. Passed was the wrong word though, *Jay killed him. Stabbed him in the chest.* Her eyes watered immediately at the thought, retrieving the pain of loss to relive it again. It was murder, or at least manslaughter. Her tortured oldest boy attempting to settle the score his dad had plagued upon the family.

The thought led her to the next name, and of course, it was Jay's. Her process was like mentally turning the pieces of a puzzle in different directions until she found the spot the piece, she wrestled with would fit together snug. She mentally scuffled with the next piece of the missing puzzle in her head, Jay's. *Hmmm. He'd killed her boy Billy and deeply scarred Darrell. She'd been afraid Darrell's mental damage was permanent. But this year he appeared to be changing, growing up, becoming a man. The process almost appeared to be happening too quickly for a normal boy who'd lived through all the hell he had. Would Darrell grow into being the right kind of man? Or would all this drama and loss be hiding deep down only to bubble up in unexpected moments? Afterall, Jay started out seemingly normal at first sight.*

The memories of her past almost felt like the thick morning fog that hovers inches above the ground and roads of the Smokey Mountains. Her mind began to clear, mocking the fog slowly burning off with the rising summer sun. Sorrow hit her momentarily before happy thoughts of her youngest boy and the granddaughter he'd recently given her began to overtake the negative memories of Jay. Jay and her struggle with the bottle. Her two demons she was made to defend her last son from. "I'm strong." Cat spoke aloud. "Jay has been removed from our lives and the bottle is dead to me forever. Praise God, Lord almighty over all!" She admitted she held no idea why God's plan for her held so much pain, grief, and tragedy. But in accepting Him as her Savior, she knew she held no right to question. It was hard to accept sometimes, but Cat's will to do the right thing was now deeply embedded in her heart and even deeper within her soul.

***

Warden Wilkerson was awoken at 9:28 precisely on the Monday evening of Jay's hanging. "What the hell?" There was a short pause before Wilkerson asked the next question in a tone his wife wasn't familiar with. "Just where the fuck did they go?" He instantly jarred himself from the confines of the bedsheets and began to swing his legs over the edge and to the floor. "I'm coming in and they by gawd better be found and lined up in shackles in my office when I get there. All damned three of 'em." His wife June watched her husband as he got up from bed and swore some more. "Gawd dammit!" Wilkerson said as he slammed the phone back onto the receiver.

"What's wrong Gerald?" His wife, June, asked with a concerned look escaping her face.

"A fucking lynching and prison break is what's wrong! I don't know any more details than the body is gone along with a very dangerous pair of brothers from two different cellblocks. Just how in the hell they managed that..." Gerald Wilkerson was swearing and stomping around as he dug his clothes from the closet and dresser drawers in a complete rage. "This is my ass, June! This shit can't happen on my watch!" Another drawer slammed as June sat in her bed watching her husband fly around the room like a scalded cat. "Nobody is gonna vote for a new governor of this state who couldn't keep control over a gawd damn prison! If that future opportunity isn't already dead and buried now."

***

It was weeks since she'd witnessed her husband in any kind of mood close to the one, he was in now. The only thing she remembered was it involved a prisoner named Billy Jay Cader. The prisoner caused so much anger in him, he'd put him in solitude for several weeks. She sometimes wished he'd never taken the job of warden at Lake Correctional. Gerald told her it would further his climb up the career ladder to governorship. They both had their sights on a big political career for him. *He certainly couldn't be held accountable for such a mishap as this could turn out to be.* She thought to herself. She was already making plans for their future.

This anger he was portraying scared her though. It always caused question and fear on the back burner of her mind, wondering if it would ever happen again. There'd been only one time when she bore his wrath from his outrage, and it left a blackened eye that night. But it never happened again. *Not after Daddy talked to him. Gerald came home a different man from Daddy's house.* His blackened and swollen face showed what her father thought about a man who relieves his anger on a woman. Especially his own daughter.

***

The warden's car was stopped at the gate. "It's me you simple-minded dumbass! Open the gawd damned gate now!"

Gerald appeared disheveled, his hair a mess and clothing seemed wrinkled and unkempt for the warden's usual state of dress. The gate guard didn't recognize him at first. "I'm sorry sir, Sargent Valli told me to stop everyone and check IDs, even if they claimed to be the Jesus of Nazareth himself." He pushed the button to begin the gate sliding away from the guard shack. "You can pass on through, sir. I'll radio ahead to the other gate."

Warden Wilkerson never looked back at the guard as he stepped on the gas toward the main building's entrance, blowing past the second gate before it was fully open. His car's front end almost sideswiping it. He wanted to talk to his main man in charge, Sargent Henry Valli, and he better-by-gawd have some correct answers to give him. Wilkerson's Mercedes barely came to an abrupt stop before the driver's side door swung open and a leg hit the parking lot. Sargent Henry Valli came flying out through the front door and down the steps to meet his boss, who was already halfway up the stairs.

"Henry! You'd better have some damned good answers, son. Wake me up in the middle of the fucking night with news like this! What kind of incompetency are you running while I'm away? First off, how did—or who did the hanging of Billy Jay? Are you sure both the Ruby brothers are missing? Anyone else?" Wilkerson was firing questions in a demanding tone quicker than it appeared Henry could comprehend. His face held the look of someone trying to dodge bullets from a firing squad of ten. "Henry! Dammit! Say something for yourself. Tell me you and your men have a line on the Ruby brothers! If Billy Jay is dead as you say he is, show me his gawd damned rigor mortised corpse."

The entire facility of Lake Correctional was lit up like the county fair. Search lights dancing across the yard, walls, and wire. Prison guards dressed in riot gear combing every square inch. Dogs running with their masters attempting to pick up any scents left behind.

Warden William Gerald Wilkerson's eyes appeared worn and tired, but he wasn't leaving without bodies or answers. He didn't want to inform the Florida State police, but as he eyed over his campus, he knew he must do just that before the media got a hold of this and did it for him. Instead of the muscular rage-induced bull in charge of the ring, balls swinging with each step, Warden Wilkerson bore the look of a broken milk cow holding onto shattered dreams—watching them crumble to the ground and scatter like dust in the wind.

Six hours later, Wilkerson was informed the ambulance used as a getaway was found smoldering in a Piggly Wiggly parking lot in Live Oak, Florida. It was abandoned and the gurney in the back was empty. Florida State Police had sent a crime scene unit to dust what was left of the ambulance for fingerprints. Warden Wilkerson was overheard on a phone call saying resources were being misused. "We know whose damned fingerprints will be on the ambulance. Send the resources to go hunt down those three fuckers. Every hour wasted on dumbass shit like that is an hour they go deeper into hiding and further away.

The hours turned into days, days into weeks with none of the escapees turning up or being arrested. Warden Wilkerson was watching his political career get flushed down the shitter. He'd more than likely be fired or at least so scrutinized and micromanaged he'd resign. There wasn't a day the gawd damned media let the story rest. Lake Correctional was being dissected by every news channel and report that aired.

The governor's seat at the capitol building in Tallahassee wasn't looking like it would be his anymore. He was an embarrassment to the state prison program. Two murderers and a dangerous armed robber were at large and constituents looked to him for the blame. He might as well of gotten hung beside Billy Jay Cader, because his career was close to dead on arrival.

***

That thought was most assuredly reminded to Warden Wilkerson one early afternoon when he received a call that was patched into his office unannounced. "This is Warden Wilkerson...."

"Well, Warden Willy..." There was a brief chuckle heard in the receiver before the familiar voice continued, "I guess prayers are answered and karma truly is a bitch—'cause I certainly am enjoying the headlines these days. Would you be open to sitting down to an indepth interview for the Orlando Beacon?"

CLICK.

Amy Jo Whitenhour of course couldn't see the look on Willy's face, but she sure as hell enjoyed the visual, she pictured in her mind.

38

I was devastated when I saw the news. Billy Jay Cader had been found hung in the laundry room at Lake Correctional by a makeshift noose of sheets and electrical cords. Two other very dangerous brothers were now on the lam after strong-arming an ambulance meant to haul Billy Jay Cader's body, convicted murderer of two law enforcement officers, to the hospital.

My editor-in-chief, Malcolm Kingsman, called me himself to give me the news knowing I would be reactional about the story. I was indeed. I wasn't sure what I should feel. Part of me feels like I'm such a fool, while the other part wants to believe it is all a big misunderstanding and that it's the demons in his heart that should be held accountable. Or his gawd damned father. Why can't all men be like my grandfather? Loving, consoling, and full of compassion for everyone.

**

It's been almost two months with no word and no body. Georgie's been my faithful friend every evening, coming over and helping cook dinner and talking. Even though I'd sworn I ran her off with my whole leaning in to kiss her thing that I brought on out of nowhere. "Georgie, you are such a sweetheart of a friend." I said aloud even though I was alone this evening at this late hour, wine glass in my hand for the third or fourth…I don't know how many nights in a row. I did know there were far more bottles of Moscato held in my fridge than there were meats or veggies or things of that nature.

Tomorrow would bring another Saturday morning. This was now just another Friday in a string of them, I'd not been allowed to see Jay at Lake Correctional and now that chance had been erased for good. I lifted my glass to a toast of tribute to him. "Here's to wherever you slipped off to…heaven or hell, I wish you well. A more damaged man I never knew." I lowered my glass to my lips and swilled what was left down in one final gulp.

There was a knock at the door, and I looked that way from where I sat on the couch. "Come on in, it's open" I hollered. The door began to open with a squeak, reminding me I needed to oil its hinges. Malcolm peeked his head around from behind the open door. He held up a bottle of wine. "I thought I'd come check on you and maybe share a drink or two." He said solemnly.

I held my empty glass up and answered, "Just in time, Mal! You'll need to catch up with me though, I'm ahead of the game tonight." I giggled. Yes, I'd already drank two glasses. "You remember where the wine glasses are don't you?" I knew it was a stupid question. He'd practically grown up in my grandparent's home like me.

"Unless you've done some rearranging?" He looked around noticing the place looked exactly like it did five years ago when ole' Jeffrey and Maggie were still alive. "Yep, some things never change, right Amy Jo? The place looks as if time hasn't touched it." He let a somber sigh escape his lips from the memories he made right here in this room with them. He walked over to the kitchen cabinet, far top door on the left and reached up grabbing a glass. He spoke softly, but I heard him clear as day. "I sure miss 'em Amy Jo, I can't imagine how much you do."

"Mal, if we're gonna visit those times—I'm gonna need a bottle for myself alone. I'm already swimming in self-pity. I've not only lost the two people I loved most—but now one that I have no idea why I'm feeling the loss I do—I also tried to kiss my best friend several weeks ago." I waited for it. Of course, Malcolm didn't disappoint, He jumped on my last statement like a cat on mouse dipped in milk.

"I thought your best friend was your neighbor. The pretty Spanish girl?"

"Yep, that's her." I stopped and said nothing more to explain—just to play the game of making him feel awkward and to see how long he squirmed with my answer. I sat grinning like that cat who ate the mouse.

The room swallowed the silence making the quiet even louder if that's possible. Malcolm walked back to the living room with a glass and full bottle of wine. I watched him intently as he ponderously stared back at me. One could hear a thread fall quietly onto the floor from his sport coat, if one would have fallen. It was that silent. I winked at him and smiled.

"So, how about those Gators this year." He asked facetiously.

"Mal, really? You'd be that surprised? I mean, I've never dated anyone. From high school days until now. This fact didn't ever make you try to figure a reason why?" I mischievously asked. "Hell, it surprised the crap out of me too. Don't sit and look so…so…shocked and quizzical. It didn't go anywhere. I think I scared the hell out of her, maybe made her question her own sexuality for a moment. I was weak. I'd had a horrible experience up at Lake Correctional—she met me at my truck like she always does, as if she were responsible in keeping me safe. We shared a bottle or two of wine and…well…" I looked at Malcolm squarely in his eyes, not letting his eyes wander away, challenging him to remain focused and intent on my answer. "…hell, she's gorgeous, Mal. I just leaned over and kissed her. Tongue and all. It didn't last but a couple of seconds. I thought I was falling in love for a minute, not that I'd even know what that felt like." I let my eyes shift to the glass in my hand and swirled it as I watched the liquid splash against the sides. I held the glass to my nose and inhaled the bouquet, giving Malcolm a chance to break his vision away from me. "...I think maybe I'm designed to be alone. It's in my makeup. More than likely from my childhood. I don't think I could ever trust a man and it would take some kind of an extra-special woman like Georgie to pique my interest in a woman ever again. I believe a woman is more capable of breaking a girl's heart with more pain than a man is." I sat back and then drew the glass to my lips and sipped from it.

"I'd hate to think you're never going to find a soulmate, male or female; I don't have a care about which. It's not mine to judge other's actions or needs. I just don't want to think of you being here, in this wonderful but very memory-filled home, alone. Jeffrey and Maggs would not want that for you. In fact, you should change this place up and make it yours. It's been yours now for almost five years, Amy Jo. It's a damned museum of your grandparent's memories. While that's nice for a while, they'd want you to move on and make it comfortable for you."

"It is comfortable for me. I don't want to change a thing. I don't sit around and mope all the time about what was! Hell, Malcolm, I tried to seduce my female friend right here, wondering if they were watching! I'm fine, I promise. I just don't see a future with me and—well—anyone. But I'm okay with that. I'm just in mourning over the loss of someone I was interviewing and became oddly attached to. Like he...like...like there was some kind of...spiritual connection between he and my grandfather, which ended abruptly when he almost confessed about killing those poor girls." I looked into Malcolm's eyes again. "I've not seen him since that night...and...and well...like my grandparents...I...lost...him...without...getting to say...good...goodbye. And it hurts. Especially to still have that last conversation we were sharing—just hanging over me, with him never being able to finish." I hated it, but I started crying. I felt foolish and vulnerable. Like a child again.

Malcolm got up from the chair across the table from me and worked his way around to the couch, sitting down close within my space. He put his arm around my neck like a father is supposed to do when his child needs comforting. He knew how to give warmth and security when someone needed it. He'd put hearts at ease before. Malcolm leaned back so he could see my face. He took his finger and gently wiped away the tears that were spilling over my eyelids and trailing down my cheeks. He then pulled me into his chest and said just three words that lifted all the pressure building up inside myself, like a pressure cooker ready to blow. When he said them, I broke down again, but it was from relief. "I got you." That was all I needed to hear at this specific moment in time. My friend was here beside me to help me pick up the pieces I hadn't even known were broken inside.

I don't know how long I laid nestled within his arms, I was certain they were probably becoming numb, but I didn't want him to let me go. Afterall, he'd said, "I got you" and I knew he did, no matter what.

***

I don't know what time Malcolm left in the night. I saw a note on the table after I woke up from sleeping on the couch. I assumed he'd put my grandmother's old wool blanket over top of me and I'd slept more sound through last night than I had in months. I slowly got up, my first thought was how much I wanted to smell bacon and eggs from Grandmother's cooking and hear Grandfather bantering with her as he fiddled with something at the kitchen table that was giving him fits. But I didn't want to spend the morning reflecting in this kind of a way. It was a new day and I'd treat it as a gift, brand new from my father. My real father, my Heavenly

Father.

I looked at the note that was left for me, and I smiled. It read:

Sweet Amy Jo,

I decided when you began snoring you would surely sleep through the night. I hope you know I love you like a daughter or sister. I've got you and I'm not going to let go. You call me whenever you need anything, sis. We're family, and family takes care of each other through all our hard times.

Malcom

And then below his writing was an added note from someone else:

Amy Jo,

I wanted to check on you after I saw your friend's car leave last night at two in the morning. You looked so peaceful, I didn't want to wake you up, so I covered you with a special blanket. Hope you don't mind I let myself in. Love you and I got you too!

Georgie

***

I suddenly felt warm all over. I may have lost the two people who were my rocks, my foundation, but I now knew I'd gained two that loved me just as much.

I walked into the kitchen to start my morning coffee, my lifeblood—feeling very blessed on this Saturday morning. It was indeed a new day, a new beginning. It was as if the months had passed silently without notice between today and Jay's death and disappearance.

After that first careful sip of piping hot java—I made peace with my feelings of Jay and decided to pack those thoughts away. It was like gathering up Christmas decorations and storing them into boxes, taping them up closed, then pushing them back up the drop-down ladder into the attic, neatly tucking them in as little space as possible. The difference was, now that I'd finished my novel, I wouldn't need to retrieve these memories ever again. My book would now serve as those reflections of past, but with a much different ending than I ever imagined when I'd started interviewing Billy Jay Cader. It seems he'd escaped the electric chair, only to be hung, either on his own accord—or another's.

I looked out the window to help direct my thoughts away from the story I'd needed to anchor down onto paper. I'd run the unedited finished manuscript by a friend of mine in the publishing business. He'd shown interest and his small imprint publishing house, 3dogsBarking, was ready to edit my work. Of course, as soon as I was ready to let go of it. This seemed like it was a perfect time to take a break though. Between the writing of it and letting the completion jell within, I wanted to sit and contemplate the direction where I saw my life attempting to head. While I hadn't wanted to lose the freshness of everything that had happened in the last several months, my mind and soul were both calling out to me to sit back and let it all soak in. I'd wrestled my demons and tackled them to the ground. The words had both spilled out of me and poured unfiltered onto the pages from my unsettled memories at the time. I'd felt certain that although I'd never truly be finished—there, of course, would always be unanswered questions and details to flush out. No author's work is ever complete. But I also know that when published, this large and powerful piece of my heart would tell the story from both Jay's perspective with fragments of my own soul infused within. The outcome seemed to morph the intent I'd began with. Instead of a scientific approach of the "whys and how's" that had first piqued my interest, I would let the raw humanity and odd spark shared between us be the catalyst of the moment in time that we spoke of life as we sat in a cold and callous atmosphere. Death was hanging over his head while life was being born anew in mine. This wasn't only Jay's story alone, his life reached over and painted broad powerful strokes into mine.

His small shrinking window of life mixing with the large broad-viewed openness of mine had collided into something awakening. This book would become a shared painting for anyone with an interest, to see for themselves the feelings that can be blended from the darkness of one and the brightness of another.

I heard a faint knock on the front door and slowly meandered over to it. I leaned down to peer through the peephole and smiled to myself when I saw Georgie standing there, holding a basket covered in a checkered towel. I swung the door open and greeted her beautiful smiling face. "Good morning, Georgie!" I could smell the aroma of bacon and eggs as it seeped from under the covering.

"Good morning, Amy Jo." She appeared as if she could barely contain herself. "I hope you're hungry!"

"Come on in, that smells delicious!" I pulled the door completely open so she could come in with the covered basket. Georgie made her way to the kitchen counter and placed the basket on the surface. She shuffled a thick manila envelope out from under the basket and laid it down, along with some mail. "So, what is all of this?" I asked. "It's not my birthday—or at least I don't think it is…" My grin stretched across my face.

"No, no, I don't think so, Amy Jo. I just have felt so sorry for you lately and know you used to have this for breakfast regularly when your grandmother was still alive. It seemed like maybe the perfect thing to brighten your Saturday morning!"

"Did you walk out to the mailbox too?" I asked. "And what's in the thick brown envelope?" I reached to pick it up.

"I don't know, it was in your box with the others."

I picked it up and looked at both front and back. It had no return address. "I wonder what's in it. It's heavy and there's no name other than mine on it. That's odd." I tossed it back on the counter with the rest of the mail. "This smells so good, Georgie, and you're right—the house now smells like it's supposed to in the morning!

Thank you!" I reached over and pulled Georgie into my arms and squeezed her just like I did my grandmother. I moved my mouth close to her ear and whispered, "You are such a great friend, Georgie. I hope you know how much I love and care for you." I unclutched her so I wouldn't cause her to feel uneasy, hoping she understood my love was genuine and in a friendship way. I'd learned my lesson about any other motives.

She looked at me with a wink and I wasn't sure exactly how to take it. But she quickly uncovered the basket, letting the full aroma fill the room. She went right to the cupboard where the plates were always kept, and then opened the drawer, which held the serving spatula. It was as if she'd been a student of my grandmother's and worked at cooking and baking in her kitchen classroom for years.

We sat at the dining table to eat after serving up two plates. I hardly ever sat here after the plane went down. With both of my grandparents now gone, I rarely felt like sitting here alone. It was too quiet—too empty and haunting. But, with Georgie sitting here with me, it felt right again. Probably for the first time in five years. I sat where my grandfather sat. The finish on the oak tabletop was beautiful. Everywhere except this seat. This was where Grandfather tinkered with broken things, many times tearing the item of repair totally apart in order to diagnose the problem and what parts were needed. His place setting was also his workbench top, and it showed. Nicks and scratches—dents and mars. Grandmother used to be so upset when he'd drop something on the table or drag his screwdriver or whatnot across it. Grandfather would say, "Maggs, these blemishes you say I'm putting in this wood, merely gives the piece character! When you and I are long gone, Amy Jo will be able to make a fortune from selling our antique dining set because of all the mysteriousness I've spent time adding. Each bruise and disfigurement tell a story!"

How could Grandmother question a statement like that? Grandfather won that skirmish and now here I sat—amongst all of grandfather's marks of memories and stories. I felt thankful I was present and witnessed most of them. I'd never sell this table or their chairs for any amount of money. I cherished every single item in the house—this home. It was their home, but it was also my home. I could never think of doing what Malcolm suggested by renewing or replacing anything. The "character" in each item, like this table, is what kept their memories alive to me. While their bodies were interned in the Atlantic Ocean somewhere, their memories were buried deep inside every piece of furniture complete with dents and scratches, which filled this home, our home, the home my momma decided to run away from. And it would stay just the same as if they were still here with me. Every item where they left it and the porch light lit brightly day and night so anyone weary or in need of help could easily find the entryway.

39

Georgie and I cleaned our plates and we had to brew another pot of coffee.

"I feel like going somewhere or doing something today—are you in, Georgie? It's way too nice to spend the day indoors…" An idea popped into my head. "…are you up for a drive? Maybe a six or seven-hour drive and then spend the night there?"

"Where Amy Jo?"

"I've always wanted to see Dauphin Island, Alabama. My grandfather always talked about it. There's a fort or something there. He loved it. I wanna see it. I suddenly feel surrounded by his spirit, and I think it would be a great way to clear my head of all this Billy Jay stuff that's got it clogged. You in?" I asked.

Georgie held a look of surprise, but it was mixed with excitement of a spur-of-the-moment decision. "You know what?" Her cheeks spread with the grin that formed across her lips. "Let's do it! I'm in! Two best friends on a road trip!"

"We better get to packing! Daylights burning! See you in an hour and a half, packed and ready," I said. And with that, Georgie packed what was left back into her basket to leave for her parents, and she lit out the door like a fourth of July bottle rocket.

I quickly showered and packed and then returned to the kitchen to make sure everything was cleaned up and put in the dishwasher. I reached for my mail and went out to the living room to make sure there was nothing pressing that was delivered. I sat down on the couch and went right for the envelope that stood out amongst the others. I looked it over again, wondering what it contained and from who. I slid the letter opener under the flap and slid it across, cutting the seal. Leaning forward I looked inside and then poured the contents onto the coffee table. There were several photographs of girls. I peeked inside and pulled out a letter of about a couple a dozen or more pages that were folded and remained within, not tumbling to the tabletop as the photographs had. I reached in and pulled the pages out, then opened it up and began reading the first page—I glanced down on the back of the last page to see who signed it. "Holy shit!" I exclaimed. "This can't be!" I leaned back up quickly and picked up the pile of photographs. They appeared to be snapshots of young girls. As I thumbed through them, I counted. There were seven in total of girls, and then one, like an old self-portrait style black and white. It would be like one you'd expect to see of Jesse James or Clyde Barker, but it was Billy Jay, and he was holding a handgun. He was creepy looking, and my fingers began to shake and tremble. He was much younger than now. I stared at it, and it scared me. It brought a vision of him I'd rather not have seen.

I glanced at the pictures of the girls, and I laid them out side by side before reading the contents of the letter. I was almost too scared to, too afraid of what it would say. A sinking feeling inside my gut told me these were pictures of the girls he was about to confess his wrongdoing to me. Girls he'd hurt and or killed. I dropped the letter on the table and quickly got up to run to the restroom, my hand covering my mouth.

As soon as I rounded the corner and lifted the lid, I wretched. Over and over until my morning breakfast had all but left my body. My stomach rolled and cramped, I felt instantly chilled as I wiped liquid from my face, first with the back of my hand and arm until I could reach down in the cabinet and pull a washcloth and towel out to clean up with. Two things suddenly hit me. First, this meant Jay was alive and in hiding somewhere. The second, I pictured how excited Georgie was about the trip we were about to take. I knew I mustn't mention any of this to her just yet. I felt I couldn't quickly read such a letter, and that I must put it up somewhere nobody would see it. I'd spend the time it deserved when we got back. It would be difficult to have it hovering over my mind while we were gone, but it would be impossible not to cave and read it if I were to bring it with me. I quickly walked out to the living room and gathered the letter's contents up and looked around at some place to put it. My eyes scanned the room and when my vision passed the fireplace—my head stopped and looked at the wooden box on top of the mantel. That is where I will keep it. It blended in where it wasn't really something that drew attention. Everyone I knew, also knew it was sacred to me, that it held the last unopened correspondence from my momma. No one would ever open it up without my permission. I gathered the snapshots, attempting not to look at them and then refolded the note and put them back into the envelope. I walked over and picked up the box and opened it, retrieving my momma's letter, and putting the envelope from Jay on the bottom before replacing momma's letter on top. I stared at her letter again, studying her handwritten lettering of the words she'd written: To Amy Jo Whitenhour, in care of Jeffrey and Maggie Langstone. A tear began to quickly well up. Her handwriting was shaky. I wondered if it was from being drunk or stoned, or nervous from what she'd written inside to tell me. I also thought about the quandary Jay's letter put me in. Withholding evidence that showed he was still alive. I also, as a reporter, should be allowed to keep my informants anonymous. I closed the lid and placed the box where I'd retrieved it from. "I don't have time for this right now!" I said aloud to myself. "For the love of...."

A soft knock on the front door. Georgie was here and ready to go. I looked at the box one last time, my mind filled with concern and angst. "I can do this." I told myself out loud once more. My heart pounded as I walked over and opened the door, my bag packed and waiting beside it in the entry. I thought to myself as I pulled on the knob. *Keep it all to yourself Amy Jo. Make this weekend the good time it was supposed to be. This will all be waiting when I return.*

"Ready to go, Georgie?"

40

I drove in the quietness of the late morning sun. Georgie turned the radio on and dialed it to a country station. I was surprised by the choice she made but one of my grandfather's favorite Willie Nelson songs immediately began playing. I glanced over and Georgie's leg was bouncing to the rhythm of the banjo on "Bloody Mary Morning." The trip just felt right all the sudden. Windows open, breeze blowing our short hair and the faint sound of the tires rolling down the highway in the background. I smiled. The perfect song was blaring from Grandfather's truck radio as the miles disappeared in the distance along with any troubles one wants—or needs to leave behind them. The fresh open wounds beginning to heal from the power of being outside one's normal surroundings. My soul drifting in the open air, seemed the appropriate medicine for my mind. A curing of madness, a soothing to my tension, releasing the stress I carry in my right shoulder.

Georgie shouted just above the sound of the music, "Thank you, Amy Jo, I needed this, and I didn't even know it!"

I looked over and grinned with a feeling of relief of her being happy being with me, "If you only knew, Georgie! I needed this too. I'm so glad you came. I need time away with a good friend!" Looking to the south, or out my side of the truck, the gulf coast seemed to try keeping up with our pace of travel, not wanting to let us out of her sight too long. Her beautiful sandy shores would come in and out of our view as the road would occasionally slip north at brief moments before returning. It brought a thought to mind. Something my grandfather told me once when I begged him to stop and retrieve a turtle in the middle of the road. I was out the passenger door the minute we'd rolled to a stop and headed over to return the lost turtle back to safety on the side of the road he'd come from. I still hear his words in my head as he spoke before I was able to reach the turtle to pick him up. He asked me to wait, which felt like an impossible task to complete as an excited young child. "Why," I blurted out. "Someone may hit him while I'm waitin' on your slow legs!"

"Now, Amy Jo, there is a right way of helping nature and a wrong way. Let me show you the "proper" way."

I spoke back with sass in my tone, "Proper way? It's just a turtle, Grandfather! He doesn't know the danger he's walked into. I'll show him better!"

My grandfather quickly bestowed some wisdom of the animal worlds way of life and how it is sometimes is very different than ours. The two rarely understand the other's perception of the way it was viewed. He looked both ways for traffic first before he bent down and gently picked the turtle up by the edges of his shell and carefully put the turtle's belly into his palm. He only lifted him mere inches from the road. Again, watching for traffic both ways, he slowly moved the turtle across the road in the direction the turtle had been moving. He then settled him easily back down to ground a couple of feet past from the road's edge. He then turned to me and began explaining. "Sweetheart, that little turtle isn't just on an afternoon stroll. He has a destination in mind. He's driven, by nature's way, to get where he needs to be. Just like you and I." He grinned lovingly at me. "What would you do if you were alone and on your way to Grandmother's and my home, so you could see us—and some rather intimidating and larger form of life picked you up and turned you the opposite way of where we live?" He paused, waiting to hear my answer.

"I'd turn back around and go the direction I was headed—so I could get home where you and Grandmother were."

"But what if you'd almost passed a very dangerous part of your journey and then you were put back on the same side you'd come and pointed around to the direction you'd just been walking away from?"

I remember not even needing to think the question over before I answered. "Grandfather, that's easy, I'd turn back around and cross the danger again to get to where you were!"

He smiled. "Exactly! But you'd be facing danger once again, even though you'd made it past. You're driven to make it to your destination. That's the same thing the turtle would attempt. He has a driven purpose and if you change his course, you enable another risk for him to overcome along with the fact by redirecting him, he may need to spend the rest of his life getting back on track. The path he was destined to take. Do you understand what I'm trying to tell you?"

I knew instantly the point he was making. I remember immediately feeling a horror within as I thought about all those turtles I'd redirected on their life's journey, before I knew and understood the wisdom not to interfere with nature, if possible. Another quick notion entered my brain. I now wondered if my interview with Jay was an interference in his life's travels to where he had been called. How many other people changed his walk from a straight and narrow journey to one full of twists that led him into the path of danger—again? It hit me like a freight train—he'd quite possibly changed my destiny crossing paths at an intersection of both our troubled lives of the past. I'm no philosopher or human container of vast knowledge, but my thoughts now seemed to have left me treading water in the deep end of the lake. Thinking about this random memory would now tire me mentally on the drive, keeping the thought either in the background or foreground. There would be no shaking it from the sides of my brain in the usual way

I was inherently used to attempting. Would my thoughts in the book I hoped to publish to the world possibly have any ill effects on an unwitting soul?

    I looked over at Georgie whom I now felt had been studying my actions and possibly figuring out there was something I hadn't told her. A new problem in my life I'd kept from her. She was very observant and smart. Full of intuition. It was in her Spanish heritage and beliefs. She would more than likely pry the secret of Jay's letter, I'd not read yet, before we made our way to Dauphin Island, Alabama. Have I been changing her path's direction in all my neediness, or were we both like turtles crossing the road, not realizing all the dangers surrounding us in this crazy thing called life?

41

"Mitzi B, I've made up my mind. I'm taking a trip."

"Where mom? I mean, I think it's a great plan, but…" Mitzi was caught off guard, her mom said she would need what money she had banked, to start over. "Are you talking for the weekend or overnight?"

"I'm going to Springfield, Missouri. I'm going to see what I can find out on my own about Ethan's trip. Something changed after that trip and while we will never be what we were before, especially after talking with Cali, I have to know."

"Mom, that's a bad idea. Why do you need to know anything other than he is and was already very bad news?" Mitzi questioned as she shook her head back and forth.

"If you were me, Mitzi B, I know you'd feel the same. Your fruits are from my tree, and they don't fall far from the limbs they grew on. Besides, I have a new job to start next week!"

"What?" Mitzi B asked with joy in her voice. "Where and with who?"

"James T. Bollard. I can't believe it happened so easily! I saw an ad in the Tallahassee Gazette, and I called. I just had a phone interview. When he heard I'd previously worked for Ethan Kendrick, I barely got it out before he asked when I could start! He'd just lost his own paralegal and is snowed under with work for me to help with!"

Mitzi stood silently with her mouth hanging open before she

could muster up a congratulations. "Mom..." Mitzi paused. "I will go with you if Darrell says it's okay."

"What about Katie? Darrell can't work and take care of her too! He's new at the daddy thing. He's a man, for crying out loud!"

Mitzi laughed. "He's a very capable man, Mom! And he works for Ben. Ben who has a pregnant wife, Gina, who I know would love to have him and Katie stay with them for a couple of days..." Mitzi looked at Joyce as if she wasn't going to take no as a viable answer. "Gina already told me she would babysit anytime I needed her to. We're just talking a couple of days, right?"

"It could be dangerous, Mitzi B. I don't think so...."

"Then I know I'm coming along. I'm not letting you go alone! Besides, I'm a damn good investigator and it sounds like you need one! I'll be like James Rockford of 'The Rockford Files,' and you'll end up not having to pay me!" She laughed out loud.

"Oh, Mitzi B! I love your crazy random sense of humor! If Darrell says you can go...."

***

"So, anyway, my mom is going to Springfield to see what she can find out. I'm a much better detective than she is so I wanna go with her. She's in a weird state of mind and I don't want her to go traipsing over to a city she's never been to without going with her. Is that okay? It won't be more than a day each way to drive there and a day or two investigating what we can."

Darrell looked at Mitzi with concern. "I thought you said this Ethan was a dangerous guy? And you and your mom want to go play Cagney and Lacey in a town where you know absolutely nobody? I don't like that idea. I'm not ready to be a single daddy."

"You know I can take care of myself, baby. I could take you right here and now!" Mitzi laughed and jabbed him in the arm.

"I'm serious, Mitz. I don't like the idea. I'm not gonna play the 'no, you can't go, card,' but I definitely don't like the idea one bit."

Mitzi moved closer and put her arms around Darrell's waist. "I'm so glad I have you. I'm not going to risk anything because I don't want you to be a single daddy. We'll be cautious and careful. We just want to see what's going on with the local news and see the police there. That's all!"

"I'm not for it, but I understand you needing to help your mom. You'll keep me posted? And you won't be gone more than you need?" Darrell asked.

"Of course!" Mitzi leaned into his shoulder.

"When are you guys leaving?"

"As soon as I pack. I love you, Darrell." She held her hands out and took Katie in her arms, covering her with kisses.

Darrell leaned in kissing Mitz and their little girl. "I love you, Mitz. I need you back safe and sound. Promise me." His eyes drooped with a sadness that tugged at Mitzi's heartstrings.

Two hours later, Darrell and Katie watched the taillights pull out of the parking lot and onto Highway 98, headed west out of town. He looked at Katie and smiled a smile with weariness woven in. "It looks like it's just you and me for a few days, Katie." He leaned in and kissed her forehead. "Let's go visit Grandma Cat, what do you say?"

Katie's bright eyes stared back at her daddy. She smiled and began to coo as if the excitement of her daddy's soft-spoken words could not be contained from dribbling out of her wet, bubbly lips.

***

The stroller stopped at the first step to the Watkin's porch. Cat was sitting on the swing and smiled as Darrell lifted Katie and made his way up the steps. "I saw you two coming down the sidewalk! Best sight I've seen! My two favorites."

"Hello, Momma. This little one was wanting to see her Grammy Cat. Of course, I was needing to see my Momma too." He held out his sweet little girl and set her in Cat's lap. Katie cooed and smiled up at her grammy. Her little arms moving in awkward jerky displays of excitement at the new face to look at. Cat touched her tiny forehead and tummy, baby-talking to her granddaughter with high-pitched words and giggles. Darrell watched looking down at the love between them. His momma's eyes sparkled as if all in the world was right for her again. Maybe in the first time ever. He hadn't witnessed such a happy look on her face for a long, long time. It's amazing how the bright eyes and giggles of a baby girl could at least temporarily heal the pain within another person's heart and soul.

42

Georgie reached up and adjusted the radio volume. It was as if she was inside my mind. "I love this song!" I hollered out loud. And I needed my body woken up from the quiet. My eyes felt a little heavy.

John Waite's "Missing You" was turned up to a volume that instantly got my heart beating to the tempo. Georgie looked and smiled at me as she danced along to the tune in the truck's passenger seat. She glowed with an infectious joy across her face. I instantly began moving and gyrating in place from the driver's seat, glancing and sharing grins and giggles as we both sang in unison. We were both disappointed when the tune was over, but low and behold, "When Doves Cry," Prince's number one hit followed, and kept our lively spirits going.

Each mile or so, brought another favorite. It was like this year of 1984 was the best year ever, musically. We couldn't seem to stop our bodies from interpretating the rythms and bass we felt inside. There was never a bad song that played for over eighty or ninety miles.

"I'm starving and thirsty." I said as I glanced to see what Georgie thought about finding a place to stop for a breather.

"Me too! I thought you'd never mention it!"

"Georgie! This is your getaway trip too! If you want or need to stop for a break—you need to speak up." I saw a sign that listed fast food up ahead in Miramar Beach. The sandy beaches looked so inviting, we decided to grab some burgers and go eat on the nearest we could find and then walk in the surf for a bit after eating. We chose McDonald's and Henderson Beach State Park. It was gorgeous and the water was a brilliant clear green with shallow waves rolling in. Perfect for walking in without getting our shorts soaked.

After sitting on towels and eating our lunch, we walked out to the waves rolling in and began walking side by side. I suddenly felt the urge to tell her about my surprise I'd found in my mailbox.

"What? How can this be? I thought he died, and his body was in the ambulance the two brothers stole in their getaway?" Georgie asked.

"I think maybe I might be the only one that knows he may still be alive. Unless someone is playing a prank on me," I said.

"What about the letter? What did it say?" Georgie questioned.

I kicked at the water rushing up around my ankles, causing a splash that sprayed us both. "I haven't read it yet." I looked over at my friend's response.

"You haven't read it? Is it with you?"

"I left it at home. I wasn't sure I wanted to know what was written before we went on this short getaway. I didn't want to spoil it." I smiled.

"Oh my, I can't believe you didn't read it—or bring it. You must be going crazy. Should we turn around and head back to get it?" Georgie inquired.

I laughed. "Hell, no! That would be letting the letter spoil our getaway! It'll still be there when we get back!"

Georgie hesitated, not wanting to keep beating a dead horse, but her curiosity was too much. "What do you think it says? I don't see how you do this. You have your mother's letter unread and now this." She lifted her index finger to her temple and began twirling it in circles. "You are crazy, Amy Jo. I just don't understand. The not knowing kills me and it's not even my business. You would never make a good Spanish woman, never!" She exclaimed and then giggled.

I burst out laughing and she quickly followed.

Turning to look at her but, squinting into the sun shining brightly behind her silhouette, I responded, "I think it's his confession to me concerning his killing of some girls in his past. Young girls." I paused, almost feeling a little sick to my stomach again. "I'm pretty certain he was about to tell me that night when I passed out during our last visit. The one the warden realized what more than likely happened and put an end to any future interviews—and then he threw Jay into solitary confinement for two weeks as punishment for something. Something I'm assuming Jay must have told him." I questioned aloud. "Shortly after he got out is when they found him hanging in the cell block's laundry facility by a sheet and electrical cord." I splashed in the water again and grabbed Georgie to turn back around towards the truck. "The whole thing is bizarre. The timeframe being so quick. The fact that two inmates could steal an ambulance and escape a high-security prison like that. Something fishy is out there. It just hasn't washed up on shore yet. Maybe this letter I received, will give some clues to the whole thing." Georgie reached down and grabbed my hand, placing hers around mine.

"No matter what, Amy Jo, I'm here for you and 'I got you.' To help or just listen, whatever you want or need."

I looked up, finding it hard to see her face clearly with the sun shining brightly behind. "I know that now, Georgie. And you're right—I wish I would have brought that damned letter with me." I grinned. "It's going to make me wanna go all Nancy Drew on Lake Correctional Institute and Warden William Gerald Wilkerson. I smell a conspiracy, or something being buried under the people's noses. I think he has hopes they're too stupid to unbury it and bring out for all of us to see. I guess he doesn't know how much I love a scoop with a challenge."

We brushed the sand from our bare feet before climbing back into the truck. All sweaty from the humidity and heat. I couldn't wait to get moving so the air would blow over us. Grandfather never believed a man needed air-conditioning in a farm truck. "Ain't no need to get all cooled down between chores—just make a man never wanna get out from behind the wheel to do his danged work like he's suppose ta." I smiled as I heard it plain as him sitting where Georgie sat. My grandfather was quite a man. A very opinionated, but usually practical man who was almost always correct in his thoughts. His words, "Just money not needed to be spent. 'Sides that, another gall damned thing to have to get fixed when it breaks. That's where the dealers make their money—fixin' shit that sure 'nuff gonna break. It's planned and figured into their system. Engineered faults." He'd smile as if he knew he was smarter than those who looked down their noses at him. I remembered how he sparred with the salesman who sold him this truck, trying to sell him all other kinds of extras and extended warranties and such. "Why you tryin' to sell me extra warranty? You already know what day the damned things a gonna break on me." He guffawed and took his right hand swathing it downward through the air toward the salesman—a "get the hell outta' here gesture showing him he knew the drill.

My grandfather was a smart old cracker. He rarely bore such a feisty tone—unless he felt he was being taken advantage of like being sold fine dirt acreage in the middle of swamp land. He'd become hell on wheels when "those types" were offering tonic to sooth his ailments that weren't ailin', and by God, I loved him more than all the oranges in our fields at harvest time. He was generally as sweet or even sweeter than the best orange produce peeled in its prime.

***

That damned letter was back inside my brain again. I looked to my right and Georgie was watching all the scenery out through her window rushing past. The wind was blowing her loosely buttoned top, enticing my eyes to take in what was exposed. I didn't want to, but I was still drawn to her beauty, both physical and spiritual. The physical part now, forced me to shake my head back and forth, trying to get my mind straight. Back to that damn letter where it should be, instead of on Georgie's sweet caramel colored body that carried little sweat droplets down her neck and into the cleft between her breasts.

My foot pressed down on the accelerator without my being coherent about the action I'd performed until the roar of the motor reeled me back to my senses. I lifted my foot slightly to ease back to the speed limit, again, shaking my head back and forth yet again, feeling the wind on my face and the hairs battling to stay behind my ears.

"There's a sign, Amy Jo—only twenty-one more miles to Mobile! How far south to Dauphin Island from there?"

"I think it's only about an hour! We're almost there, lady!" My shoulders were holding some tension in them now. From the driving, the letter, or the sexual frustration I seemed to have again—I held no clue which was the culprit. Could be the combination. All I knew was that I was ready to hit the little room I'd reserved at a two-story beach house sitting on stilts. It had been turned into a small bed and breakfast and that, I thought, would remind me of home in the morning. *I just remembered though; I hadn't updated the reservation to two beds after Georgie agreed to go. Oops. I hoped there was a couch to sleep on—or did I? Had I subliminally forgotten to change room arrangements on purpose? It wasn't like me to be mischievous or deviant like that. It must be an honest mistake. Maybe they'll have another open room?* I suddenly felt the need to let her know of my delinquent overlook.

"Georgie? I hope you're not going to be angry or think I did this intentionally—."

"What Amy Jo?"

I kept my eyes on the road. "I just remembered I never updated the room at the bed and breakfast for two after you agreed to go at the last minute...."

She looked over at me. "Does this mean I can't stay in the room?"

I glanced over quickly. "No, no, nothing like that. There may...there...may be just one...bed...or maybe a couch too...I don't know. They may have an extra room too. We just won't know until we get there. If there's only one bed—you can have it and I'll make a pallet on the floor with blankets."

"The heck you will, Amy Jo! We're both adults, we can share the bed if we need to. I'm not scared of you!" She laughed as she turned her head away and kept staring from the side, as if she were playing.

The sight of her toying drew a large loud and boisterous laugh from me, before I turned, "I was afraid you might think I did it intentionally...."

"I've never known you to have a deviant bone in your body, Amy Jo. Why would I all the sudden think so now?" She smiled. "Because you kissed me? Oh, paaleeze!" She used both hands to do the palms up and then swoosh them forward as if pushing me away from her. We both laughed together again.

43

I opened the door to room 4 on the second floor of the most beautiful beach home which sat only thirty or forty feet from the surf. We could see the walls of Fort Gaines down the beach and around to the east point of the island. We both seemed to avoid checking out the sleeping accommodations, opting to head straight out to see the view from the upper deck just outside a pair of French doors from the kitchen.

"Gorgeous view!" Georgia said with elation.

We both caught each other peering back towards the bedroom when we thought the other wasn't watching and we both laughed when one caught the other.

We finally walked back in and saw that, yes, there was only one bed. And no, there were no available rooms to add or change to. Good news, it was a queen-sized bed so there was plenty of room for us two thin women to share. I'll say one thing about Georgie, she never really looked worried. I took it as she really did trust me, but I somehow still held hopes that she has some sort of feelings hidden inside that could possibly one day appear—more than just good friends. I know it's not looked at as a natural thing, but I somehow think I could easily fall in love with her and stay in love for a lifetime. After my childhood experience with my dad—there is only one male person I could ever foresee me showing that kind of interest in. And that would be a personal battle inside the first time we would attempt intimacy, if I could ever overcome that fear. The only other man I'd be interested to see if anything clicks—would be Cable Lee Johnson. My savior of eleventh grade. The boy who claimed to have gotten into my panties to his male friends so they would leave me alone and stop calling me TeeBee, short for Little Amy Tommy-Boy. Yes, Cable Johnson—the son of a bridge builder who built a bridge for me allowing my access to places I'd never been able to get to before.

I don't know why his name popped into my head, but it's in there now, and suddenly—my heart feels jittery—but a good jittery—the way it felt after kissing Georgie. *Am I really a messed-up piece of work, who just won't admit it?* I suddenly opened the door of my psyche that held the tensions taut on the drive here. I was instantly exhausted and needed to sit down. I picked the left side of the bed, the side I normally slept in at home, and sat on the foot of the bed.

Georgie walked over and sat down on the right side. I looked at her, she at me. We both smiled, each looking worn out. I wanted to kiss her so badly, I was afraid it was tattooed across my forehead.

"Georgie." I paused trying to get my head straight on what I wanted to say. It seemed jumbled from the drive. "I need about an hour's rest before we head out and explore, is that okay? Don't let me sleep the evening away!" Georgie sighed. I wasn't sure if it was from relief or just what.

"Amy Jo—I have to admit when you started by saying my name—I thought maybe it was...."

She never finished her sentence and I never pressed. I didn't want to make her feel uncomfortable in any way. I quietly told myself if she were to finish her sentence it would have gone something like this, *when you started by saying my name—I was hoping you were going to give things another chance between us....* Of course, that's more unlikely than not what she was going to say, but I laid back onto the bed and fell asleep daydreaming it was.

__44__

The people in Apalachicola, Florida and the surrounding area all the way up to Orlando, more than likely don't feel like they are any different than anyone else in the state or country. Truth is, they probably aren't.

Two women from Orlando seem lost in their past and have either internal or external troubles they don't know how to handle, feelings each has the need to face and wrestle with and the desire to conquer. They're on a trip together trying to navigate their way through the twists in their paths, each looking for that something inside that makes them feel more alive and in control. They've invited their paths to weave together in some sort of pattern that is not yet known or perceived. They'll eventually figure it out. It is what life gives us. Questions to be asked and searched, answers eventually unearthed within the time doled out from an entity we don't understand but hold in faith unseen.

Two women from Apalachicola, are on an adventure also. They have no idea that in the miles between them there are yet undiscovered pasts, even though they are mother and daughter—they are tied together in ways unimaginable. While these two women travelling to another city, in another state, in search of answers that will no doubt bring pain, they live in the same world as any other soul traveling the highways and byways. Everyone has a ghost or a skeleton or two in tow within. We shove them down deep sometimes, refusing to seek the knowledge about them or reveal them to those close to us in fear it will impact our relationship in ways that bring devastation or distance. Will these two find the answer that will unshackle the younger one's mother, so she can find happiness in her life? A gift she felt she'd already found. Isn't it the truth that all of us humans are somehow tied together? Our desires like the heart pumping, and each person like a vein traveling through the twisted body trying to make its return way back inside that beating heart. Some of us are the veins, making our way slowly and meticulously back to the heart, while others are the arteries, rushing quickly to leave the heart behind, running from what they'd called home. With any luck, the body will sustain no mortal wounds throughout its life, which would allow the blood to escape the paths leading us to or from the heart that may eventually be the connection between the two.

We live this life not knowing our future, but only our past. Try as may, we try to base this future under the constraints of only things remembered. If we'd just let it all go and trust our Maker to lead us down journeys that are best laid in a plan, we can't see but designed for us with the utmost forethought and care, life may very well turn out for best. But then, there's that whole thing of free choice we're given. Free to decide the paths we want to follow. Travel those we feel in our heart were meant for us, or instead follow the paths less traveled, and journey through the untamed and wild. It's what gives us the flutter in our hearts at times. Palpitations of either overwhelming joy or all-consuming fear.

One thing is true to all. Our lives will march on until the day we are called to discover what's instore for our next journey. And so, the story goes, as we wait until the future becomes our past. There's nothing we can do about the fact, other than accept it and soldier on. The questions will no doubt be answered if our bodies hold out and misfortunes are avoided. We should live life for today, for tomorrow is never promised, but we should also live today with love and compassion in our hearts—because we also cannot foretell the end that will certainly come, and judgment of our choices will be reaped.

To be continued with Book 5
SNAPSHOT INTO A KILLER'S MIND by
Amy Jo Whitenhour

THE RECLAMATION

Note from the author.

This book was written with a different feel and character POV. The way this saga ended, left things that will be neatly tied up in near future offerings. This next book **SNAPSHOT INTO A KILLER'S MIND** will be an interesting read and will also give some foretelling chapters from Book 5 at its end that will help usher in-**THE CALL HOME**.

I certainly hope you have enjoyed this tale up to this point and are looking forward to continuing as much as I am looking forward to sharing the character's future. I have no immediate plans of ending the series soon as these characters are very much a part of me now. My plans as of now are to continue Ms. Amy Jo Whitenhour and Georgie Anne Rovaria into future editions as either anchor characters or possibly another series that runs parallel with The Mason Jar. Feel free to contact me at **3dogsbarkingmediallc@gmail.com** or if you are on FB look me up at **author eli pope** or my group page **The Mason Jar Room** to give your opinion or contribute to discussions.

Eli Pope

About the Author

Eli Pope lives with his family and two dogs in the heart of the Ozarks. He is currently working on several writing projects that includes upcoming additions to The Mason Jar Series and writing short macabre horror stories for a brand-new podcast titled **Fear from the Heartland** hosted by narrator/producer and good friend Paul J McSorley. New live casts air each Wednesday @5 pm central and previous shows can also be found by searching **YouTube** for **Chilling Tales for Dark Nights**, the mother of it all!

His love of writing is his escape from the everyday grind of working full-time in the real world of paying the bills and providing for his family.

This is his passion along with painting and creating art of all mediums.

Pope is a proud member of the *Springfield Writers Guild, major writing contributor to Fear from the Heartland, and proud recipient of silver and gold awards from Literary Titan for his Mason Jar Series.*

(Author's Note) Thank you for taking time to read 'The Reclamation'. I hope you enjoyed it.

Please leave a reader review with amazon.com, goodreads.com, barnesandnoble.com and other online retailers. I would greatly appreciate it.

Eli

COMING SOON by ELI POPE

BOOK 5 - THE MASON JAR SERIES
SNAPSHOT INTO A KILLER'S MIND

the true story of billy jay cader

NOW AVAILABLE

THE MASON JAR SERIES

BOOK 1
THE JUDGEMENT DAY
BOOK 2
THE SPARK OF WRATH
BOOK 3
THE GLASS HOUSE

also
THE WANING CRESCENT
By Steven G Bassett

Visit *elipope.com* to keep up with upcoming books and projects. Occasionally, Eli makes available to purchase paintings and artistic creations. He lists them on his website.

3 dogsBarking Media LLC strives to bring you quality entertainment. Please let us know if part of our product is not up to your level of satisfaction as a loyal customer.

Contact us at:
3dogsbarkingmediallc@gmail.com

Made in the USA
Columbia, SC
02 August 2024